Enthusiastic reviews for Lior Samson's novels –

Gasline (The Homeland Connection)

"Samson turns up the heat with a high-energy plot and . . . a perfect mix of techno thrill and human conflict. . . . *Gasline* takes the reader on a rip-roaring ride. Excellent!"

- Avraham Azrieli, author

Bashert (The Homeland Connection)

"Perfect! . . . a page turner that spins a good story."

- Peter Gordon, publisher

"Samson writes with a crisp elegance, like John Le Carré, and weaves his plot magically, sustaining suspense throughout the novel. The ending is a satisfying and surprising climax."

– James A. Anderson, author

"An ambitious novel, . . . moving with the speed of light between interconnected events, three continents, and a group of unique and memorable characters. I recommend it." - *Avraham Azrieli, author*

"Samson keeps the pages turning in this retro-techno-thriller."

- Brett James, author, film producer

The Dome (The Homeland Connection)

"Suspenseful and timely, . . . I cannot say enough good things about this novel." *- Alan Caruba, critic, BookViews*

"An excellent read, and very highly recommended."

- Midwest Book Review

"Crisp, sardonic, sometimes amusing, and highly entertaining. [Samson is] a real story teller." *– James A. Anderson, author*

"Showcases his talent for melding thought-provoking intrigue with non-stop action." *- Peter Gordon, publisher*

Web Games (The Homeland Connection)

"This extraordinary author has the ability to anticipate events in ways that enhance his novels, and *Web Games*, his latest, is no exception. . . . You will not put it down."

- Alan Caruba, critic, BookViews

"An outstanding tech thriller—better than Tom Clancy. . . . This ranks up there as one of the best [thrillers] I've read in 2011."

- James A. Anderson, author

"For readers who want their brain to be well-fed while enjoying the thrill-ride of action suspense. . . . I couldn't put this book down."

- Dawn Jones, teacher

"The story swiftly pulls the reader into a stream of events, . . . [and] the characters instantly come to life, as if you've known them for years."

- Jos P. van *Leeuwen, university professor*

Chipset (The Homeland Connection)

"Lior Samson hits another one out of the park. . . . Few thriller writers can match Samson's ability to deliver a gripping story."

- James A. Anderson, author

"Few novelists can match Lior Samson's ability to deliver a multi-dimensional thriller that will satisfy discriminating readers who crave realistic stories populated by flesh-and-blood characters."

- Avraham Azrieli, author

The Rosen Singularity

"The plotting is ingenious and the characters come through strongly. It succeeds marvelously on the thriller level, but it also delivers a substantial intellectual and emotional kick."

- Rebecca Goldstein, MacArthur Fellow, author

"Vibrant and distinctive characters, and thoughtful, yet engaging narratives and conversations, . . . an exciting, pulse-pounding story."

- Laurie Jenkins, book blogger

GASLINE

Also by Lior Samson, from Gesher Press

Bashert (The Homeland Connection)

The Dome (The Homeland Connection)

Web Games (The Homeland Connection)

Chipset (The Homeland Connection)

The Rosen Singularity

Avalanche Warning

Requisite Variety: Collected Short Fiction

Available from Amazon.com and other booksellers.

The HOMELAND CONNECTION

GASLINE

a novel by Lior Samson

GESHER PRESS

Gesher Press is an imprint of Ampersand Press
Rowley, Massachusetts

Gesher Press | Ampersand Press
Rowley, MA 01969
Author site: www.liorsamson.com

Printed in the United States of America.
5 4 3 2 1

ISBN 978-0-9885275-5-3

Cover photo: Warren Patterson, "West Virginia Landscape"
Cover and book design: Larry Constantine
Text set in Gentium, Gentium Book, and Calligraph421 BT; title, chapter titles, and running heads in Baccus Expanded

For Robert Granum (1929-2013), who made Twain come alive and inspired the beginnings of a lifelong journey. Thanks, Bob.

GASLINE

PART ONE
Chapter One

Blue-white sparks, out of step with the pulsing moonlight, caught Kat's eye as she sped toward an early rendezvous with her inspection crew. Flashing like a strobe through the trees, a buttermilk moon, gibbous, nearly set, turned the row of pines between the road and the pipeline into shaggy fence posts, the even spacing and uniform height betraying their unnatural origins. They had been mere seedlings when Kat had first worked on this section of the line.

Black coffee sloshed in her Car Talk commuter mug as she wrangled the pickup one-handed along the narrow road. She rumbled past a break in the trees where a scrawny seedling had never been replaced. There it was again, the glint, like the ghostly cold beam of an LED flashlight.

Kat slowed the 4-by-4 and started scanning the hillside below. Here, the buried thirty-inch natural gas transmission line emerged, took a right-angle bend, and ran on the surface parallel to County Road 94 before crossing the deep wedge that was Sadler Creek Canyon. The moonlight and predawn sky glow turned the fat pipe into a bright yellow slash across the hill and out over the dark emptiness of the canyon. The pipeline, supported by its own suspension bridge, soared into empty space and disappeared into deep shadows on the far side. It hung cradled in a web of cable stays that Kat, as an enthusiastic young engineer, had helped install on a summer internship. Sixteen years later, she was still with the same company, long since renamed and reorganized. Spanergy

Holdings had grown through a succession of mergers that made it the third largest interstate natural gas company in the East, but Kat, despite picking up an advanced degree, had progressed no further than riding herd on a maintenance and inspection crew.

Whatever resentment she might have about being passed over, Kat was proud of her work. She had fought the hierarchy to have her name lettered on the doors of her truck. "K. Gaudet," it read. Underneath, in parentheses and quotation marks, "Go-day," a hint that she did not appreciate people mispronouncing her name.

Now, with the turnoff for the old construction access road already three miles behind her, Kat glanced at her watch and decided to pull over. She slowed further, looking for a spot where the rough gravel shoulder was wide enough for her truck. She did not want to keep her crew waiting. They had a complicated inspection to start today that would require excavation and a blowdown to vent the natural gas in a section of pipeline before they could send a camera-equipped robot in for the tedious job of visually inspecting the pipe. No one expected to find anything, but that line was forty years old and came from a supplier whose seam-welding inspection records had since been found to be less than perfect.

The single-lane road was deserted at this hour, but Kat did not want to risk the company truck on the bet that it would stay that way much longer. Locals in this part of Appalachia had their own definition of speed limits and traffic laws. Sober and alert, they were masters at breakneck negotiation of the narrow mountain roads, but they were not always sober, not always alert.

The uphill side of the road offered only a couple of feet between pavement and rock, and the downhill side was little better. Kat raised herself in the seat for better visibility as she maneuvered the truck into a perch on the outside of a curve where it would be visible from both directions. Just in case, she switched on the flasher bar, spraying the night with pulsing amber light.

She grabbed her big Maglite from its holder and slipped it into a loop on her belt, shoved her white hard hat over her black curls, and reached for her tool bag behind the seat. She left it there. Two hands might be needed for the scramble down the steep embankment to reach the line some fifty feet below. She hopped down from the cab and stood, listening for a moment. Beside the big commercial pickup truck, she looked like a high-school wrestler, with her short, stocky frame and broad shoulders. She took a lot of teasing from the men of her crew, but they also knew she could arm wrestle any of them to a draw and was ready to demonstrate.

She climbed over the safety rail, retrieved her flashlight, and started down. Forty feet below, as she neared the pipeline, a cantaloupe-sized rock slipped from underfoot and sent her sliding on her backside. The rock tumbled and bounced, striking the steel pipe, breaking the quiet of the hills by a deep gong followed by the crash of branches below. Kat grabbed at a scrub pine to try and keep from following the rock into the canyon. The branch snapped, whipping into her face, scratching her cheek. She reopened her eyes just in time to see the pipe rushing at her.

Desperately trying to regain her footing, she kept herself from sliding through the two-foot gap underneath by body-checking into the pipe with her right shoulder. The Maglite flew from her hand, sailed over the top of the pipeline, and tumbled into trees and shrub below. Kat peered over the top of the pipe and watched the bright spot of white blink in and out as it rolled farther, then finally stopped on a ledge well below.

As she leaned against the pipeline to catch her breath and survey the bodily damages, she felt something. Kat was a tactile professional who trusted her own senses almost as much as instruments and gauges. She tapped on pipes to assess the integrity of the metal, she put her hand to the sides of turbines to diagnose vibrations, and she listened to the whispered flow of natural gas rushing through miles of pipe.

Having left her instruments in the truck, she put her ear to the pipe, listening to the sounds carried by the thick steel tube. The faint whine of a turbine at the compressor station four miles upstream was a half-step sharp and rising—too fast. Under the tone of the compressor another sound started: the almost inaudible whirring of a gear-drive motor. Kat was unsure, but it might be a large ball valve being rotated closed. Where? Why? It couldn't be upstream of the compressor station; she would not be able to hear that. Downstream made no sense, not with current demand levels. Then the pipe suspended over the canyon started to creak and groan, like ice in a river under strain.

Something was seriously wrong. Whatever it was, there was nothing to be done here. She had to get through to the control room, and her radio was back in the truck. She started the hard climb up the steep slope and was nearly to the top when she heard a sharp crack and the clang of metal on metal behind her. She looked back, but could see nothing.

She scrambled up the bank and reached through the open passenger window to turn on the roof-mounted spotlight. Twisting it, she played the beam slowly along the section of pipe just below. As the ellipse of light reached the suspension-bridge structure supporting the aerial portion of the pipe, she noticed one of the stays dangling free. Somehow, the stay—really a tie rod—had broken or come loose and had banged against the pipe itself. This was serious, but hardly an emergency, given the built-in redundancy of the suspension design.

Kat decided to head directly for Spanergy's Control Center in Charleston, where she could use the monitoring computers to help figure out what was going on with the pumps and valves. First, she needed to let her inspection crew know that she would be a little late. She would also alert maintenance to the need for repairs at Sadler Creek.

Kat spun her wheels getting back onto the pavement and reached for her radio handset as she accelerated.

"Dispatch, this is Katherine Gaudet. Good morning."

"Spanergy Dispatch, Corcoran here. Morning, What can I do you for, Kit-Kat?"

She hated being called Kit-Kat but had learned to let it ride. "Let the Control Center in Charleston know I am on my way down there to review the situation on the trunk line crossing Sadler Creek. It's SG-70 on the charts. And notify my crew waiting at Dainesville Crossing that Mark Stoddard is in charge this morning. I'll catch up as soon as I'm finished in Charleston."

"What's up? I hain't heard a thing from Control or nothin' else."

"Just some things I want to check out, Hank."

"Is this more of that intuition stuff you been famous for?"

"And rightly so, Hank. Just remember that pig I rescued from the Charleston feed. I told everyone exactly where they would find it."

"Won't none of us forget that, Kit-Kat. You some kind of a dowser?"

"No, just damn smart."

"And damn lucky."

"So far. Oh yes, send a bridge crew out this way, okay? Gotta go. My turnoff for the Interstate is coming up. Later."

"Later, Kit-Kat."

Kat merged onto the two-lane state highway and slowed as the entrance to the Interstate neared. The flash, brilliant orange, flared in her rearview mirror, lighting her face; it was not the rising sun. Figuring she'd driven about a mile, she tromped the accelerator to the floor and counted off five seconds. Explosive thunder struck just as she skidded on two wheels around the curve into the road cut of the Interstate onramp. The shockwave lifted the back corner of the pickup. The truck did a complete twisting roll before slamming down upright, half on, half off the pavement. Kat spun the wheel into the skid, hit the accelerator again, and fishtailed back onto the highway. Behind her the fireball mushroomed high into the early morning sky.

Chapter Two

Len Bergen slipped the yellow highlighter back into the snap pocket of his western shirt, swung his cowboy boots off the desk, and closed the manual he had been pretending to read. Standing over him was a short woman in blue jeans and a blue-striped Spanergy work shirt. He noted her cherubic face was marred by fresh scratches and sooty smudges. “Hey, what are you doing in here?”

“Looking for someone in charge. That you?”

“I’m on duty. Smitty is in charge, but he’s out getting coffee to keep awake. He has to stay on to report for the handoff to the day shift at eight. He should’ve been back by now. What the hell happened to you?”

“I was up at Sadler Creek.”

“And? You been arm wrestling a black bear over a campfire? Looks like the bear won.”

“No, I said Sadler Creek. It’s on the radio, TV. WVAH Fox News already has a chopper up there. Don’t you read the board?” She waved toward the twin fifty-inch display screens that showed the status of every valve, turbine, and section in the nine-thousand miles of pipeline in Spanergy’s trunk-and-grid natural gas network. Several smaller monitors arrayed along the elongated desk showed bar charts and scrolling details of set levels, flow rates, and data from a variety of sensors in the company’s Supervisory Control and Data Acquisition network.

“SCADA network looks fine to me. Whole damn system is

just purring." Len made a show of studying both of the big screens before leaning in close to the monitors in front of him. "I'd say that bear must have done you some damage to your head. Everything here is nominal, same as it's been all shift. See?" He gestured like a band leader signaling for instruments up. "And who exactly are you?" He turned back and read the name stitched on her shirt. "What do you do, Mizz Gawdette?"

"It's pronounced Go-day. It's French, French-Canadian. Katherine Gaudet. I'm a Safety Engineer, I lead a field inspection team. I'd shake hands, but I'm rather dirty and smell like smoke. Blowback from the fire."

"I still do not know what you are talking about."

"How is that even possible?. Even the receptionist knew what I was talking about. The pipeline explosion at Sadler Creek Canyon? Don't you look out the window or listen to the news?"

"No windows in this room. TV over there is broken. My job is to watch these screens here and take action as needed. Graveyard shift, when I can get it. Or whenever they assign."

"So you spend your time reading comic books." She picked up the manual Len had discarded. "*Siemens S-700 Programming.* Fascinating read, I bet. And what about this one? *Farsi for Dummies.*"

"That's Smitty's. He has this thing for languages—Mandarin Chinese, Ruby on Rails, Java, C#, Hindi—always studying. He also writes haiku poems and reads—"

The three phones along the desk all started ringing just as a man stomped through the door wearing a wrinkled summer-weight gray worsted suit that looked like it had been rescued on short notice from the bottom of his closet. A spotted necktie dangled untied over his paunch. "What in Christ's name is happening here, Bergen?"

"Nothing. Not a damn thing that I know of, but I think I am

about to find out. And a good, good morning to you, too, Mr. Greely."

"Don't get cute with me, Bergen. You are in a shitload of hot water. Didn't you see the pressure-drop alarms?"

"No, sir. The board's been clean as a new car showroom for my whole shift."

"Then what's that?"

Len swiveled to face a constellation of blinking red. "That wasn't there, sir. Not five minutes ago the board was all green, I swear. Well, except for the usual yellows from the trunks we've been running on high pressure, you know. She can tell you."

Greely turned toward Kat and gave her a look of disdain. "And who the hell are you? What are you doing in my Control Room."

"I'm Kat Gaudet, Safety Engineer with Spanergy Infrastructure. I was on my way to join up with my inspection team for an early start when I saw a light near where the SG-70 line crosses Sadler Creek Canyon. You know it? Anyway, I pulled over for a quick visual check. I left to come here after hearing some strange sounds in the pipe. The explosion damn near blew me off the road. I started to go back to the site for a look-see, but the heat and smoke were too much. I called it in to 9-1-1 and our Emergency Response Team, then waited for the ERT to show up. So, now here I am."

"Well, here you ain't. We got serious work to do here, lady. This is a serious damn emergency now, and soon it will be a serious damn PR disaster. So make room for my men to get this under control."

"Your *men* will need all the help they can get. As long as those valves are still open, we're frying the hills of West Virginia and sending carbon credits up in flames."

Len pointed. "The valves are closed now. At least that's

what the board says. I just sent the override command codes to shut down the Hanlon Compression Station and also to close the next two downstream valves so there's no chance of backflow."

Kat smirked. "About time."

"Hey, lady, those alerts just now were the first indication that anything was amiss. You saw. I acted immediately."

"Yeah, cowboy, immediately after someone else had to call your attention to it."

Greely held up his hands. "Cut it out, you two. Before you can say 'screwed again', we are going to have the NTSB swarming over us like flies on molasses pie, so let's start pulling log files and running diagnostics to see if we can figure out what in blazes happened and what to do next, including how to cover our blessed behinds. Meanwhile, you, lady, better report to your supervisor. As you said, we are going to need everyone we can get, 'specially out there in the field."

"But I was on the scene. I want to try and correlate whatever's in the log files with what I heard."

"You want to coh-ree-late? With what you heard, huh? Like voices in the wind telling you something's wrong in Sadler Creek Canyon." He held his hands in the air, fingers spread, and shook them.

Kat's eyes narrowed as her back straightened and went rigid. "I felt the pipe and listened to it. Just before the explosion, the turbine on the upstream compressor started winding up, and I think a downstream valve cycled."

"You got all that from listening to the pipe?"

"Yeah."

Greely snapped his fingers. "Now I know where I heard of you. It was at a compliance conference. They talked about you. Called you 'The Gas Whisperer.' Yeah, I remember. I couldn't believe we had someone like you on our team. Gas whisperer my fat butt." His shoulders bounced with suppressed laughter.

Kat's face reddened. "At Dalhousie, we took a hands-on approach to design and engineering."

"Doll house what?"

"Dalhousie University, Halifax, Nova Scotia."

"Nova Scotia. Hain't that Canada? I knew there was something real 'northern' about you. Don't get much more northern than Canada, now do we? Down here, we use pressure gauges and flow meters and x-rays and that shit. We don't do the laying on of the hands shit—'cept in church."

Kat fumed. She knew better than to start an argument, but couldn't resist getting one last tap in. "I've got my West Virginia engineer's license, if you want to see it."

"Now, that I would like to see: a girl—a Canuck girl—with an engineering license. Don't that beat all. Like a dancing pig with pink ribbons. But not right now, lady." A synthesized version of Mo Bailey's "Pipeline Blues" started playing in Greely's pocket. He pulled out his cellphone and put it to his ear. "Greely here. Yeah, I know the damn phones been ringing. Yes, of course. Ten minutes. I'm on my way." He slapped the phone against his other hand. "You two, both, get back to your jobs. I'm being summoned to HQ. Gotta help the suits prep for a press conference. Should be about as much fun as walking butt naked through that fireball out at Sadler Creek. That damn thing is still burning, set half the damn mountain on fire." He started tying his tie as he turned and pushed out the door.

Kat watched him through the glass partition as he yelled something at the receptionist, then at the guard, before heading toward the executive parking area. She turned her attention back to the screens. "So, let's start scanning those log files."

"I thought you were told to get back to work."

"That's what I'm doing. And you're going to help me."

"I,"—he let the word hang in the air—"am going to help you? Yeah. Right." He retrieved the highlighter from his pocket and waved it at her. "Do you know anything about SCADA networks? RTUs? That's—"

"Remote Terminal Units. Yeah, I know. I have a Masters in Industrial Engineering. We studied SCADA networks, Distributed Control Systems, did PLC programming, the whole enchilada."

"So, if you know all about DCS, what are you doing driving a pickup for peanuts?"

"Maybe I like getting up in the dark before dawn, working outdoors, digging dirt and shoveling shit with the guys. And you? What's your excuse for staring at these slow-motion cartoons, hanging out with computers and network nerds for eight hours a day, and going too long without a shower."

"Really? It's only six-and-a-half hours. We get breaks. And do you want me to show you mine?" His eyebrows bounced. "Engineering license, that is."

Her eyes narrowed again as she swung her head slowly side-to-side. She reached past, pressed the Escape key on the keyboard behind him, then shouldered him out of the way to take the empty seat beside his. "What's the admin password to get access to the log files?"

"Uh, user ID BERGENDORF, password ELVISCO, all caps. Wait, forget it." He pulled at the seatback of her chair, but she swiveled back, finished typing, and tapped Enter. She scrolled down, clicked on a link, then typed in the date and a time range.

"See, girls can do this stuff, too. Wanna see me pull a moonshiner's turn into a downtown parking spot?"

"You do have an attitude, lady."

"Gotta have attitude or the guys on the crews will eat you

for lunch."

It was Len's turn to smirk. "Eat you for lunch? Now that's something I could—"

She cut him off with a derisive snort. "In your dreams, cowboy."

As she typed and Len tried to think of a comeback, Smitty Jackson arrived with a tray of coffee in one hand and a bag of Krispy Kreme donuts in the other. J. Smithers Jackson had better credentials than Len, but he was a tall black man with a short temper—and a gift for rubbing managers the wrong way. These had not proved conducive to climbing the corporate ladder, especially not at a southern company started by rednecks and still stained with a greasy residue of the old wellhead culture from its wildcat days of drilling for gas. Smitty and Len Bergen shared a similar sense of victimhood, a conviction that they had been passed over by a company that looked down on blacks and didn't trust Jews, all the while claiming to be equal opportunity to the core.

Smitty gingerly slid the tray of coffee onto the end of the long desk and waved the bag of donuts at Len. "What you do now, Bergen? I leave for a few minutes, and you set the damn hills ablaze."

"I didn't do a damn thing, Smitty. Nothing. Kat here is checking the log files to verify that the boards were clean the whole time."

"And why is this Kat woman diggin' into our data?"

"Because she—"

Kat interrupted. "I was at the site when the pipeline ruptured. I'm just giving Cowboy Bergen here a hand. I'm cross-correlating log entries with what I had on the event."

"That so?"

"Yeah, she is. Doing that. You find anything, Kat?"

"I didn't. Or rather, I didn't yet. I—"

She was interrupted by a squat guard waddling into the control room, his Reid Security Services shirt stretched to the limit over his bulk.

Smitty waved him in. "Hey, Caleb, come join the party. Ain't had this many folks in here at once since they installed the new system."

"Sorry, Smitty, but I got a radio call to escort you and Len—and the lady, I guess—from the premises."

"What the hell's that about, Caleb? Somebody gotta keep eyes on the board."

"I don't rightly know, just what they told me. I'm s'posed to go witcha to the parkin' lot and see yuns leave. Her, too, I guess. Like I said."

"That don't make no sense, Caleb, and you know it. Let me call Greely on his cell and find out what the hell's goin' on."

"I was told—"

"You was told? You wanna also be told it's your ass in a sling if another line blows, Caleb? Or do you wanna gimme two shakes to clear this with Mr. Greely."

"I s'pose . . ."

"Yeah, good call, Caleb. Now lemme talk to Greely." Smitty slipped a beat-up black Motorola Razr from his hip pocket, walked to the other end of the long desk, and turned away. A minute later, he exploded, shouting into the phone as he held it at arm's length in front of himself. "That's bullshit, and you know it. Fuck that! And fuck you, Greely." He snapped the phone shut and turned back to Len. "They suspended us, as of now. Pending. Pending my ass. They don't have diddly shit, don't know nothin' yet, but they already makin' the moves. Makin' it look like it was our fault. Fuck it."

Len looked unsure whether to say anything. "What about the SCADA network? Who's going to watch the board?"

"They already got their hotshot techies down in South

Carolina switchin' control to the backup center." He slammed his hand down on the desk hard enough to make the closest keyboard bounce. "Ow! Damn, now I broke my damn hand."

Kat was still typing away at the keyboard in front of her when the screens all blanked at the same time and displayed an emergency shutdown message. Caleb stepped toward her. "Whatya do now, lady?"

"Nothing."

"No, Caleb, she didn't do nothin'. It's them storm-trooper bastards down in South Carolina takin' over like . . ." Smitty might have continued, but Caleb put a hand on his shoulder.

"Look, I gotta escort yuns outta here, Smitty. Orders."

"I know, Caleb, Just lemme grab my coffee here and my book."

"You ain't s'pose to take nothin' witchya. No comp'ny stuff."

Smitty held up his copy of *Farsi for Dummies*. "Does this look like gas company literature? See there's a library card inside. Come on, use your damn head, Caleb. And here, have a donut." Caleb hesitated but then reached over to pull a glazed donut from the bag.

Outside, Caleb wolfed down the donut as he followed them around to the side lot. Kat reached for the door handle of her pickup, but Caleb stretched across in front of her and put a chubby hand on the door. "Can't let you do that, ma'am. That's comp'ny property. You're suspended."

"Now how the hell am I supposed to get home, smart guy? I'm authorized— says right in my job description—to drive this mother 'between my place of residence and my place of work.' And see that? See that name on the cab? That's me, Kat Gaudet." She started to tug at the door, but Caleb just leaned harder. "Look, you big dumb shit, I said I was going to drive home. Now get the hell out of my way. If you think you can push me around just because I'm a woman and you weigh more than my truck, you got another think a-coming. So, step aside, fat boy."

Caleb switched hands to keep holding the door while reaching toward the handgun at his hip.

Len stepped between Kat and Caleb. "Whoa, now, you two. Easy. Calm down. I can give the lady a ride home. No need to turn this into something stupid."

Caleb looked at Len. "You calling me stupid?"

"No way. You're too smart to push this any further." He turned to face Kat. "And you're too smart to get hurt over a stupid truck. Come on. My car's the green Honda right over there. I'll drive you home."

Kat looked like she was giving serious thought to taking on Caleb but finally shrugged. "Okay, cowboy. Nothing more to see here. Let's go."

Sitting as far away as the front seats of the CRV would allow, Kat mumbled to herself and pretended to find the familiar countryside captivating. With only a mile to go, Len finally broke the silence with a single, quiet expletive. "Fuck it."

"What?"

"You heard me. Smitty's right. They're gonna pin this on us. At least on me and Smitty. It's always like this. We're the last to be hired and the first to go."

"Nobody's been fired yet."

"Yeah, but that don't mean it won't happen. And after all we put into that damn company, we get the shaft.

"You got some kinda persecution complex?"

"No, we're just the persecuted. Smitty's an uppity black, I'm an accursed kike in the born-again backwaters, and you . . . you are a little lady with a big brain and a mouth to match."

"The man giveth even as he taketh away. Thanks but no

thanks for the backhanded compliment."

"Oh, you're not welcome. The way I see it, you being in the control room did not exactly make our situation look any better."

"So now it's my fault?"

"Well, think about it. We might as well been like those dumb airline pilots with stewardesses on their laps in the cockpit."

"I wasn't in your lap, cowboy, and I was actually trying to help, if you can remember that far back."

"Some help. There wasn't enough time, and I'm not sure you would've . . . could've found anything, anyway. You got nothing."

"I saw enough. Not enough to figure it out but enough to know that nobody's going to make a case from those log files. Oh, that's my turnoff ahead, just past where the power lines cross over."

Len slowed for the turn. "So, what did you see?"

"The logs confirmed that you had steady over-pressure alerts showing on two compressors at the Hanlon Station and from sensors along the SG-70 line. That line was operating at 102% of max. That is not going to look good with the NTSB, but, given that the pipe hydrostatic tested at 200% when we installed it, that is not likely as the cause of the rupture. Seems as if the file entries confirm your story that everything was good through your entire shift. According to the logs, you didn't finally get red pressure-drop alerts from Hanlon and one of the SG-70 sensors until after I arrived at the Center, nearly forty minutes from what I estimate was the time of the explosion. That's when you finally shut down the runaway compressor and closed the valves."

She tapped on her window. "You can pull up beside the motorcycle." She pointed to a yellow and chrome BMW F800 at the side of the driveway.

"That's a serious machine. Yours? Or your guy's?"

"All mine." She reached for the door handle. "Wait. Got a minute? Let me finish the executive overview. The numbers looked legit: small fluctuations around mean pressure just as expected."

Len scratched his chin. "Maybe an RTU failure at Hanlon? Or the devices themselves misreported."

"Then why would they work properly after the explosion? And the log files show that the IEDs were functioning all along. They're called Intelligent Electronic Devices for a reason. They're not just dumb sensors; they monitor and report their own performance."

"You do like to lecture, don't you, lady."

She continued unfazed. "The first sign of anything wrong was when the two IEDs downstream of the explosion finally reported pressure drops and then stopped signaling about the same time—long after the explosion."

"This makes it sound like the SCADA network was messed up or the whole damn control system was haywire. But at least we have the proof to support our story."

"That, cowboy, is a laugh. No one is going to believe the whole system malfunctioned. They are going to look for a cause, a simple cause, one that the public can make sense of and will believe. And just like when a plane crashes, the favorite story is always human error." She opened the door. "Damn shame we just met, cowboy, because I don't think you and your partner have much of a future in the gas business. You were probably right in thinking paranoid; my guess is you are both going down."

Chapter Three

Cameras with long lenses and microphones with fluffy wind filters pointed across the open space in front of the gleaming glass of the Spanergy state headquarters in Charleston. A spokesman for the company stepped forward wearing a charcoal pinstripe suit over a white dress shirt open at the collar, as if he couldn't make up his mind whether to project an in-control corporate image or be one of the people. In the heat of a steamy afternoon, he projected neither.

"My name is Willard Ransom, I'm head of Public Relations for Spanergy West Virginia. We just received word from the State Fire Marshal that the fires started by the gas leak and explosion at Sadler Creek Canyon early this morning are now all contained or extinguished.

"Spanergy is fully cooperating with the Fire Marshall's office as well as the National Transportation Safety Board, which has responsibility for interstate pipeline safety under the Department of Transportation. A team of NTSB investigators is expected to arrive tomorrow and begin their investigation into the causes of the explosion. In the meantime, we have already begun our own inquiry into this incident. Pending the outcome of these two investigations, I can only say that Spanergy West Virginia and its parent company, Spanergy Holdings, always put the safety of our customers and our own employees at the top of our priorities. Every inch of the nearly ten-thousand miles of pipeline in our network conforms to all applicable standards." He glanced down at an index card peeking from his palm. "Our operations are in compliance with all applicable state and federal regulations, and the Spanergy family of companies is recognized for industry-leading, state-of-the-art technology for controlling and monitoring natural gas transmission and distribution and in applying the latest in methods for conducting continuous safety inspections." He looked up. "At this time I will take questions."

"Can you tell us if this is another Sissonville incident?"

"Thanks, Bill. As you know, because you covered the story for the paper, the rupture at Sissonville in 2012 was not one of our pipelines and occurred in underground pipe that was nearly fifty years old. The longitudinal weld, the weld along the length of the pipe that split, proved to be badly corroded. Our line passing over Sadler Creek Canyon is only fifteen years old and had been thoroughly inspected and given a clean bill by a smart pig sent through that very section only last April.

"I see hands popping up so, please, before we provoke any animal rights group into sending letters of concern, let me explain that a 'smart pig' is a self-propelled, self-contained robot that moves through the pipeline to perform maintenance and inspection. Pigging the lines allows us to maintain flow and safety without interrupting service to our many customers here in West Virginia and our neighbors to the north and east. Needless to say, we are not using trained piglets or any other animals in our operations. Next question."

"Were there any casualties in today's explosion?"

"We were told by the Fire Marshall's office that, to the best of their knowledge at this moment, no one was seriously hurt in the explosion this morning. We were informed that two firefighters have been treated for minor injuries and were released. In addition, one of our own brave field technicians was at the scene at the time of the explosion but was unhurt."

A woman from the local Fox affiliate jumped in with the next question. "Sir, Bill O'Malley, on his cable program, Fact-Zone, said earlier today that all of our energy infrastructure was vulnerable to terrorist attack, that this could be, quote, just the first warning shot across the bow from Islamist Jihadis bent on crippling America, unquote. What's your response?"

"Mr. O'Malley is entitled to his opinion, which he never hesitates to express, I might add." He paused for a polite flutter of laughter. "However, we have no information whatsoever to conclude anything other than that this was an accident, an unfortunate event, yes, but an accident. Once we allow the investigations to complete, we will no doubt know the full cause of this accident, but I am confident that the findings will show no fault or negligence on the part of Spanergy or any of its affiliates or subsidiaries."

"Can you tell us when full service will be restored?"

Ransom looked at his watch. "About ten minutes ago. As soon as the ruptured section of pipeline was isolated, we were rerouting natural gas supplies and negotiating temporary deals with other suppliers. With the exception of a handful of customers in two towns, the interruption of service was minimal.

"Thank you all. No further questions."

═══

Tank Parsons picked up his small folding suit bag and a large aluminum road case from the United baggage claim at Yeager Airport near Charleston. The rest of his team would join him in the morning. Two of them had been delayed back in Washington while they dug further into background material. Another investigator, an outside consultant who lived higher on the hog than any government employee could manage, was flying down from an energy-sector security conference in Calgary in order to catch the red-eye special from Denver to

DC. The three of them would arrive in Charleston mid-morning the next day. Tank and the NTSB employees would be staying at a downscale motel near the Interstate; their consultant would be at the Marriot downtown.

Tank picked up his government-rate rental car and headed south on Interstate 77 toward Downtown Charleston, then followed the Interstate right back out to the jug-handle exit to the east. He was already familiar with the interchange and the area; the El Patron Mexican Bar and Grill in the adjacent strip mall had been his regular after-work watering hole when he was a junior investigator on the Sissonville incident.

In the barebones motel room that was acceptably clean but smelled of dog and citrus-scented disinfectant, Tank sat on the edge of the bed with his laptop and started pulling up files about Spanergy. The seat on the regional jet out of Dulles International had been barely adequate for Tank's six-two frame, ruling out any in-flight work on his laptop. Now, he dutifully read through the history of the company, its recent growth, and the mixed record of previous actions and citations from state and federal regulators. He was most interested in the pipeline itself: who were the contractors, who manufactured the steel and turned it into pipe, what grade of steel was used and what anti-corrosion coating was employed.

Tankut Samuel Parsons, Tank to everyone who worked with him, Sami to his ex-wife, was a materials engineer who had joined the NTSB after working in metallurgy for a decade. His name was only a footnote in an appendix of the official report on the Sissonville incident, but he had risen rapidly since in an agency where methodical intelligence mattered. Arriving during an administration that was particularly open to promoting talented minorities, Tankut Parsons, with his African-American father and Turkish mother, was doubly endowed.

Sissonville had made Tank distrustful of inspections and tests. At the time of the rupture, Columbia Gas Line SM-80 had been operating at 93% of Maximum Allowable Operating Pressure. It was an open secret in the industry that many interstate trunk lines were now routinely operated at 98% of MAOP and even exceeded MAOP for short periods. This practice increased throughput—and revenues—substantially, not only because gas at higher pressure was that much more dense, but because the pumps moved it faster through the lines.

The public was always curious about how escaping gas ignited, and news stories about explosions would often mention the possibility of a stray spark, but Tank and his team knew the back story. In any rupture from a high pressure pipeline, friction between the break and the stream escaping at supersonic speed invariably ignited the gas. Guaranteed fireball. With even the briefest of delays to promote better mixing with air, the explosion could be devastating and would be followed by an incinerating fireball fed by the flammable gas still pouring out. A thirty-inch line could blow some three-hundred thousand cubic feet of gas per minute, turning a burst pipe into a gargantuan flamethrower.

Tank took his laptop with him to El Patron, where he picked a table in a back corner and became one of the crowd of stranded second-tier business people sipping Dos Equis, munching nachos, and responding to emails. He finished his reading, checked the industry news feeds, and then sent a note to Dean Phelps, his supervisor in Washington, with a CC to his teammates. After a Grande Patron burrito special and two more beers, he headed back to the motel.

Before turning in, he switched on the TV in time to catch the late local newscast.

" . . . and sources within the company will neither confirm

nor deny that two technicians working in the control center at the time of the explosion have been suspended without pay pending a full investigation. Calls to the two men, identified as Jebediah Jackson and Leonard Bergen, both of Charleston, have not been returned.

"Police are now looking into a possible fatality in connection with the explosion after the badly burned body of a hiker was found not far from the site of the explosion. Remnants of what appear to have been a campsite were also uncovered in the area. The identity of the dead man has not yet been determined. Police are asking for anyone with information to call the hotline number now on your screen."

Tank zapped the TV off and lay back on the bed without turning off the lights.

═

The last United flight out of Dulles International arrived in Charleston just before midnight. The handful of passengers onboard included a pretty blonde reporter and a cameraman from one of the DC-area television stations, a family of four with sleepy kids returning from a vacation in the Nation's Capital, a bearded young man wearing cargo pants and carrying a backpack as his only luggage, and two men in non-descript business attire who recognized each other but skillfully avoided any acknowledgement of the fact.

Chapter Four

The grass around the Interstate onramp was already criss-crossed with muddy ruts, and an assortment of vehicles parked at odd angles crowded the area. A roadblock prevented access to the county road, but, after Tank flashed his credentials to the state trooper at the barricade, his NTSB team was allowed through. They drove as close to the site of the explosion as they could, then ended up having to walk the last half mile.

Fire crews were still working the perimeter. Black skeletons of charred trees dotted the hillside, and tendrils of smoke seeped from the ground in places. Two officers from a forensic team were looking over a site on a ledge marked off by police tape.

Tank and two inspectors carefully picked their way down the slope to where the pipe emerged from underground and ended with its irregular edge hanging in midair.

"Morning, Sheriff." Tank held up his ID to a tall man with a pronounced beer-belly and an air of impatient authority. "Tank Parsons, NTSB. This is Grant Stanhope and Evan Rialto. I sent our consultant, Jess Tisdale, in from the other road. That's him over there checking out what's left of the pipeline from the other side."

"Jacobs, I'm Chris Jacobs." They shook hands all around. Sheriff Jacobs nodded toward the ledge below. "I'll ask you men to keep clear of the area where the forensics team is working. And let me know if you find anything you think we should know about. If my men can assist you, just ask."

"Thanks. Will do."

Grant edged over to the drop into the canyon and pointed. "Looks like the biggest section is clear down at the bottom of the canyon."

Tank raised the binoculars hanging from a lanyard around his neck. "From here, it doesn't look like the seam ruptured. We'll need to get down there to take photos, then try to get a crane or a drag line to haul it out for testing. We might have to section it first. Let's see what we can learn up here before we tackle that."

Tank trusted his team to start on their own the methodical process of gathering evidence for the investigation. Grant and Evan were career investigators, and Jess had headed the department before retiring to become a consultant. Tank had notched up a series of solid investigations over the last couple of years to help advance his career, but the others had far more field experience under their belts.

As the others started taking photos and placing markers at the location of possibly significant debris, Tank headed for the blackened curve of pipe protruding from the ground. Under the force of the blast, the suspended section had sheared off, leaving behind the coupler and the pipe elbow, both of which had proved stronger than the aerial pipe itself. The rupture had been relatively clean, but not so clean as to be suspicious. From the shape of the break, it looked to Tank as if ignition had started at the far end of the suspended aerial section, the explosion twisting the pipe up to separate it at this end before the entire length hurtled skyward and arched down into the canyon. The resting position of the piece at the bottom, where the canyon widened out, fit with that scenario. The blast probably had occurred aboveground simply because that was where the pipe would give most easily.

Tank looked up as Grant and Evan approached. "Find anything?"

Both shook their heads. "Nothing startling." Grant gestured toward the canyon. "From the flaring visible on the piece down there and the edge of the intact stub across the way, it seems pretty clear that this was an internal explosion, not something from a bomb. You can't see it from here, but Jess just reported over his radio that from the other side he can see the longitudinal weld on the piece down below. It looks intact, didn't rupture."

This was surprising to none of them. Barring corrosion or a hidden flaw, the longitudinal weld would have been stronger than the metal being bonded. Tank lifted his hardhat, ran a hand through his hair, and then replaced the hat. "So, we can probable strike the easy scenarios, which leaves us with some tough questions. Anyone have some guesses as to how a pipe that, according to the records, tested out at twenty-two hundred pounds after the line was installed, that showed no sign of corrosion when pigged last April, and which was visually inspected from the outside not two months ago, how that pipe could fail at only eleven hundred and change yesterday?" He got only raised eyebrows and head shakes for an answer.

"Okay." He tapped a note into his smartphone. "You keep working here. I'm going to head back into town to see about getting an empty hanger at the airport to do initial testing and forensics. I'll also interview the eyewitness and the technicians who were on duty monitoring the SCADA network when this happened."

Grant's brow was creased with concentration. "Yeah, especially that eyewitness. Don't you find it maybe a little funny that this field technician just happened to be out here in the boonies at that hour and just happened to escape in the nick of time when the gas exploded?"

"You guys know me. I'm suspicious of everybody and everything. That's how I do my life, that's my job. But we're still engineers. Until and unless we find evidence of sabotage or tampering, it's just coincidence."

"I don't believe in coincidence, Tank, any more than I believe in luck. Stuff always happens because of something or someone."

"Maybe so. Keep working here; I'll go see what I can learn from the technicians."

There was a commotion at the ledge below and the crackle of quick conversation on radio handsets. "What's up, Sheriff?"

"They found a couple of flashlights. One was plastic—not much more than metal parts in a charred, melted mass. The other was one of those heavy-duty tactical lights like we carry."

═

Tank, who was methodical and observant to a fault regarding the details of an accident investigation, had not noticed that he was being followed as he drove out to the cluster of red brick buildings that housed the Spanergy Infrastructure Group. He entered through the wide gate in the chain-link fence around the facility. He had called ahead to make sure that the safety engineer who had been at the explosion would be available. The building he was directed to was an enormous garage, overhead doors open all along one side, with a variety of vehicles lined up in rows inside and out. A woman stood, arms crossed, next to the cab of the nearest truck. She was more attractive than the company mug shot he had been shown earlier.

"Hello. Are you Katherine Gaudet? Did I pronounce that correctly? Good. I'm T. Samuel Parsons with the NTSB." He held his identification wallet open and tried to smile disarmingly. "I'd like to ask you some questions, Ms. Gaudet, regarding the incident at Sadler Creek. Do you have a couple of minutes?"

"Sure, since they told me to wait for you. What do you want to know? I already filed a report. And you can call me Kat."

"Okay. Everyone calls me Tank." He took her hand and gave her a soft, closed-mouth smile that put dimples in his exotically handsome face. Against the light mocha of his skin, his brown eyes shone almost black.

Kat met his eyes and matched his grip as they shook hands. "Okay, Tank it is." She looked up at him with a puzzled expression.

"What is it?"

"No, never mind."

"No, go ahead, please."

"Well, I was just curious. My mother was always on my case for just blurting out questions. Canadians are not supposed to be abrupt. Anyway, I was going to ask, how did you get that handle?" She gave him an approving up-and-down glance. "It doesn't seem to fit. Were you in the army or something?"

"I was in the army—signal corps—but the nickname is short for Tankut. Turkish. From my mother's side. I guess I don't need to ask about your nickname. Anyway, I already read your report. What it doesn't say is what you were doing out there so early in the morning. The spot is rather remote, isn't it?"

"You been there? It's what they say is far enough out in the hills they have to import sunshine. But, for me, it's a shortcut from home to the Interstate. I was headed north that morning, on my way to rendezvous with the rest of my inspection crew for a dig-and-blowdown. That's—"

"I know—excavation of a section of pipeline, isolation, and venting of the residual gas. I do this stuff for a living, too, Ms. . . . Kat."

"Right, of course. Anyway, taking the county road saves a

few miles if I'm heading north."

"So, you were in sort of a hurry, were you? But you stopped."

"Yeah, I saw a flashlight beam—anyway I thought it was a flashlight—near the pipeline. Like you said, it's pretty remote. So, I'm thinking, like, what is someone doing with a flashlight out in the middle of nowhere, where the only thing around is a thirty-inch main carrying natural gas? I figured I'd better check it out."

"And did you find anything?"

"It's in the report. The flashlight, if it was that, disappeared. But I thought I might as well check the pipeline as long as I was there. I think the compressor at the Hanlon Station was cranking up while a down-stream valve was closing. Hardly standard operating procedure."

"And how did you know this was happening? Were there indicators, or did you have a wireless link into the SCADA network?"

Kat's face reddened. "I put an ear to the pipe. Steel pipe can carry sound for miles. I listened."

"And you got all that from listening to the pipeline?"

"Yeah." She gave him a look that invited him to make something of it.

"Then you left the area, though, just in time."

"And what is that supposed to mean, 'just in time'? I left then to get to the Control Center after I called in. I got lucky."

"Lucky."

"Yeah, that happens sometimes, you know. I once was just a block away when a backhoe operator misinterpreted the dig-safe markings that I had just verified. If I had hung around to watch him dig, I might have ended up on the burn ward, too. I'm not the kind to hang around. I do the job and move on to the next one."

"So, you've been lucky more than once. A charmed life, apparently."

"Meaning? Look, Mr. Parsons—"

"Tank."

"Yeah. Look, I had nothing to do with the pipeline explosion except to guess that something was wrong."

"We retrieved the records from the control center and downloaded from the remote data loggers over the network. Needless to say, we will examine them all in detail, but the initial review this morning does not support you."

"So you already checked them, too? Then you know that something's rotten in Charleston."

"What exactly do you mean?"

"If you really studied them, you'd know the SCADA network logs are clean until some forty minutes after the blast. That doesn't make sense because low-pressure alerts should have popped up right after the explosion. Something failed someplace. You're the investigator, you figure it out."

"I intend to. Your report also said you were in the Control Room shortly after the incident. According to the security guard, you were doing something at one of the computer terminals when he came in."

"You think I did something with the records?"

"Did you?"

"Yes, I looked at them. I wanted to try and figure out what had happened at Sadler Creek."

"That's not your job, is it? You're part of a maintenance crew."

"Infrastructure Integrity, like it says on the side of my truck right below my name. I'm a Safety Engineer. My job is to keep the lines safe and operating. It may not be in my job description, but it is my job to know what happened and what might happen next." She ignored the skeptical look Tank shot her way. “If you don’t have any more questions, I have work to do.”

“If I do have more questions, I’ll be back in touch. Here’s my card in case you think of anything that I should know.” She took the card and slipped it in a pocket without bothering to look at it. “Nice to meet you, Kat.” He held out his hand, but when she didn’t take it right away, he shoved it in his pants pocket.

Kat watched him stride out of the building. “Too bad so many of these good looking guys are such jerks.”

“What did you say?” It was Veronica Perly holding out a clipboard for Kat.

“Nothing, just bitching. What’s this, Veronica?”

“You need to sign this before going out again: paperwork for your suspension which wasn’t a suspension because it was a mistake. So, who was the cute guy? Well, cute if you go for that Omar Sharif type, I mean.”

Kat scribbled a quick signature at the bottom of the job sheet. “Not my type. That’s what I was saying.”

“Ha! So you say, Kat, but I saw you eyeing each other.” Veronica spun on her heel and headed back to her glass enclosed office.

Chapter Five

Tank tapped a note into his smartphone and scrolled down. Next on his list was the supervisor who had been on duty in the control room during the incident. Tank called ahead on his cellphone and Smitty Jackson agreed to meet at his apartment. With the help of his GPS, Tank located the apartment building, one of a cluster of faux Southwest-style structures arrayed like covered wagons in a circle behind a shopping center west of town.

Smitty Jackson seemed surprised when he opened the apartment door. "Yeah, well, hi. Come on in."

"Were you expecting someone else?"

"Well, no. Wasn't expectin' nobody else. I guess you look different than you sounded over the phone."

Tank knew exactly what Smitty was referring to, but he was not about to make a comment about having a "white voice." Both men spoke with the baritone resonance that went with their height, but Smitty's country accent and casual grammar didn't fit with his education.

The two black men eyed each other for several seconds before Smitty gestured toward a chair. "Make yourself at home. I'll try to help as well as I can. I'm as curious as you 'bout what happened with that pipeline."

After an exchange of pleasantries that included comparing college experiences, Tank used up the better part of an hour with an interview that covered well-trampled ground. Knowing it was required, he persisted.

"Did you look at the log files yourself?"

"No, as I told you, there was no time. Shortly after I got back from the Krispy Kreme, our resident gorilla got the word to usher us out. I mean, Caleb is an okay guy—not real bright, mind you—but if you saw him you'd understand the gorilla part. Anyway, I only caught a glimpse of the logs while that Gaudet girl was checkin' through them."

"A glimpse. Did you notice anything while you got that glimpse?"

"Yeah, come to think of it, I did. She was scrollin' through pretty quickly, like she was lookin' for somethin' particular. Probably trying to get down to the time of the incident. I noticed somethin' as it whipped past—reco'nized it."

"Recognized it?"

"Yeah, it was the same as we got two days earlier, when we were doin' a temporary backflow to feed another line. Makes a very distinctive pattern of alerts as valves are closed and opened and the pumps are reversed. First, I thought she was on the wrong day. I figured, like, this SCADA business was not her thing, really. She mighta had the wrong file. But I looked at the top of the screen, and it was the log for our shift, all right, right date."

"What did you make of it?"

"Didn't rightly make nothin' of it. Still don't. Seems peculiar, though, 'cause we weren't doin' any backflow yesterday."

"So, you think I should look into it, do you?"

"I think you know your job, that's what I think. The data loggers record every damn thing in the whole system. The files should tell you exactly what happened with that explosion. If they don't, that's mighty peculiar, wouldn't you say? Mighty peculiar."

"Okay, I'll look into it. Thanks."

"No problem. And say hello to your buddy sittin' out there in the parkin' lot."

"My buddy?"

"Yeah, the one that's been sittin', readin' the paper in that Town Car across the way."

In the parking lot, Tank circled around to place himself in the blind spot of the Lincoln before walking straight toward it. He quick-stepped the last few feet and used his hands to rattle the trunk lid with a flat-handed drum roll. The driver jumped and was opening the car door as Tank came around to the side. The man was as tall as Tank, with a tailored sports jacket and a blue shirt opened enough at the top to show off a well-tanned chest. His right hand was slipped behind his back, pushing the jacket aside. Tank recognized the gesture. "Are you on duty?"

"What?"

"On duty. You must be part of the investigation. Police?"

"Uh, yeah. You?"

"NTSB. You know your guy has made you, don't you?"

The man grinned but said nothing.

"So, you don't care."

"We don't care. But I do suggest you move on and drop the matter."

"The matter? The investigation?"

The man laughed. "No, this. The surveillance. Just forget about it, okay?"

"Sure thing. Although I don't think this guy knows anything, and I certainly don't think he had anything to do with it. He mostly wasn't looking where he should've been at the right time."

"You don't say. Okay. Carry on."

"You, too, Officer."

═══

The investigator from the NTSB was no sooner out the door when Smitty decided, on impulse, to see if he could still link to the Control Center. He fished a small device resembling a USB thumb drive from one of the cubbyholes in his roll-top desk and plugged it into the back of his laptop computer. The red-and-gray Protexient dongle was his master key, one of the perks of having become a supervisor. It gave him remote access to the company's computer systems through a Virtual Private Network that enabled him to work at home as if he were actually at the office.

Using the VPN link, he connected to the Spanergy system. He was pleasantly surprised to find that his account and login credentials were still valid. No one had yet thought to block them after he was suspended. Once logged in, he figured he might as well take advantage of the oversight to do some digging on his own.

Smitty spent the next hour following one lead after another. By the time he logged out, his hands were shaking.

He pushed his chair back from the roll-top desk and reached for the phone to speed-dial a number.

"Hey, Len. It's Smitty. I found somethin', got somethin' for you."

"Yeah? What did you find?"

"I think it would be better if I show you. You gonna be home for the next hour or so?"

"Can we do this tomorrow? I've been fending off reporters all afternoon."

"Sure, I suppose. What time? Where will you be?"

"Right here. Where else? Where would I go? I've been laid off, too, remember."

"I remember. Just bein' polite. I'll drive over tomorrow. See you, maybe 'round ten?"

"Whatever. You know where to find me."

═

Unable to stay away from the computers, Smitty returned to digging into the Spanergy files, broadening his search, looking into not only the data, but also the code base that ran on the system. Suddenly, something leapt out at him in the header of some code he had opened almost at random: a time stamp with the original file name and path to a project folder left in the code by a C++ compiler. In the path, a text string appeared repeatedly: L-O-N-G. It could be anything, but it was what the string was paired with that sent Smitty over to the shelf where he kept his language books. He flipped through several of them before he found the confirmation he was looking for.

Chapter Six

Smitty spent a restless night of frequent awakenings to imagined noises interspersed with fitful dreams of fire-breathing dragons with long fangs scorching the nearby hills. He finally dragged himself out of bed just before nine in the morning. The tight-hat, fuzzy-headed feeling was familiar to him. He knew it would take him another week before his body would get used to sleeping through the night instead of working through it.

With dreams not yet faded into grayed memory, Smitty sat down with his fountain pen and a sheet of hand-laid paper. With careful, canted strokes, he wrote:

Whirlwind under earth,
Foul breath of long dead swamps;
Above: dragon wind.

He titled the haiku with a string of numbers, folded and creased the paper, then tore off the lower half to be saved for another morning's inspiration. The new haiku he placed atop the neat stack in the center drawer of his desk.

As he sat and sipped reheated coffee, he logged in once again at Spanergy, this time remembering to save off copies of files and screenshots as he revisited what he had found the day before. Watching the desktop clock ticking off toward ten o'clock, he hurried through the last of the files, downloading copies of everything he found on the off chance that it might be meaningful or useful later. After finally logging off and shutting down his laptop, he reached around to unplug the dongle. With all the files already on his computer, he wouldn't need it to show Len what he had uncovered. He tossed it back into a cubbyhole, rolled the top of the desk closed, and grabbed the keys to his car.

As he neared his car in the parking lot behind the apartment building, Smitty saw that his way was blocked by a black El Dorado stopped at an angle in the exit. He waited for the driver to back up or come forward, but the car didn't move. When Smitty reached in and tapped his horn, the Caddy rolled forward, stopping right at his rear bumper. The driver, a tall woman in a gray pantsuit with eyes to match, got out and approached. She was holding up a badge.

"FBI. Are you Jebediah Jackson?"

"I am. And who are you, ma'am?"

"Special Agent Barbara Delacroix, FBI Cyber Crime Unit. This is my partner, Special Agent Arkady Pohl." She nodded toward the stout figure extracting himself from the El Dorado. "We'd like to ask you some questions."

"And what if I don't like questions?"

"We can come back with a federal warrant, if you prefer being taken into custody."

"I'd prefer being back at work. I'd prefer to be tailgatin' with friends with a brew in one hand and a burger in the other. But I don't think I am likely to get my prefers right now. So, what questions do you wanna ask."

"May we come in?"

"Is that another one of them questions that ain't a question 'cause if I say no, you gonna be back with a warrant?"

"It's your choice."

"Then I guess you might as well come up to my apartment and ask your questions." As he led the way, Smitty pulled out his phone and sent a quick text message to Len.

Agent Delacroix caught up with him. "What was that about?"

"Oh, just lettin' a friend know that I'd be late. We were gonna meet for coffee. Here, let's take the back stairs, it's shorter. I'm on the third floor. Hope you don't mind climbin' stairs. No elevator."

Smitty started having second thoughts as soon as he ushered the agents into his apartment. "Maybe you should get that warrant. This whole thing, the Sadler Creek incident, maybe I shouldn't be talkin' with you. Maybe you should be talkin' with somebody at the company, like official. I don't know as there's anythin' much I can tell you anyway."

The two agents both fixed their eyes on him as if waiting for the answer to a question. Delacroix leaned forward from her seat on the sofa. "You do realize that unauthorized access to secure computer facilities is a federal crime."

"I s'pose that's the case, but I wouldn't make any unauthorized access to any computer."

"What about the computers at Spanergy? Have you made any attempts to gain access since you were suspended?"

"You seem to be on top of everything, so you already know the answer, don't you?" There was no response from across the room. "Okay, so you know I logged in using my credentials, my perfectly proper credentials. As a supervisor in Network Control, I have remote access, fully authorized. I'm allowed to monitor the network in real-time or review history whenever. Nothin' unauthorized about that."

"Except you have been suspended."

"True, so as I been told. But nobody told me I can't access the computers. If this was what you called unauthorized, why was I allowed in? You answer me that."

"We don't set policies of private companies, we just investigate violations of the law."

"Well, I think you oughta get on with that, then, since there wasn't any violations of the law goin' on here abouts." He leaned back in his chair and crossed his arms.

The agents looked at each other, but Delacroix continued as the spokesperson for the pair. "That remains to be seen, Mr. Jackson. But, can you tell us why you attempted to gain access to confidential information on the company computers?"

"Didn't attempt. I did. I reviewed the records connected to the Sadler Creek incident. Tryin' to figure out what happened. That's my job, even if I've been suspended from it. I wasn't suspended when it happened."

"Is that all?"

"No, not all. To be perfectly honest, I was lookin' to protect my ass. Pardon the language, ma'am."

"Do have reason to believe you need to protect yourself?"

Smitty guffawed. "You got eyes, ma'am. I'm a black man in a white man's job. I was in charge of the SCADA network when this thing went down. I got suspended within an hour of the blowout. And you ask whether I have reason to wanna protect myself?"

"If you had nothing to do with it, you should have nothing to fear."

"And that's bullshit. It happened on my watch. That's enough to get me fired, just that. Look, ma'am, I work for a redneck boss in a backwater state that some folks mistakenly think is part of the Commonwealth of Virginia. I'm doin' a technical job for which I am over-qualified. Even before this mess, I was in trouble because I don't pick my words or my subjects too careful. I been tellin' those bozos for years about vulnerabilities in the control system and SCADA networks and they do nothin'. Too expensive, too complicated, too this and too that. They don't like hearin' this, and they particularly do not like hearin' this from no too-smart black man."

"Just what vulnerabilities are you talking about?"

"The network, the whole SCADA network is riddled with security holes."

"Like what?"

"You know about this stuff? SCADA and stuff."

"We're with the Cyber Crime Unit, Mr. Jackson."

"Okay, so you know what RTUs and IEDs are. Well, you can walk up to some spots on the pipeline and open a box and tap right into the network. You need to know what you are doin' and have the right tools—torx drivers, wire strippers, connectors, stuff—but all that you can get from Home Depot or Radio Shack. If you know the command structure—and that stuff's in PDF manuals on the Internet—you can make a real damn mess of things. Some places you just need the right kind of radio."

"A real mess?"

"Yeah, like send a few million cubic feet headed the wrong way or stopping the supply to Pittsburgh or whatever."

"Like blowing up a thirty-inch pipeline?"

"Maybe."

"You wouldn't happen to know how to do that, would you, Mr. Jackson?"

"Can't rightly say I do. Never thought about it."

"Never?"

"Not until now, anyway. You got any more questions, ma'am?"

She looked to her partner who shook his head. "No, I guess not at this point. We'll be in touch if we think of anything else."

Chapter Seven

Yet another day had passed, and Smitty, still burdened by what he had found and still struggling with recovering from the graveyard shift, was late again. After the FBI interviewers left, he had made the mistake of taking a nap, which lasted until early evening and left him wide awake into the night. He had finally managed to fall asleep around four in the morning, then dragged himself out of bed again with only a few hours of rest. After swigging down two black coffees, he logged into the Spanergy system one last time to look for other instances of the interesting file names. He hastily sent Len an email with apologies and promises, then slipped his laptop into a backpack.

Fighting off a strong sense of déjà vu, he started his car to leave for Len's place. This time there was no FBI crew blocking the exit, but before heading out of town Smitty drove once around the block just to see if anyone was following him.

═

Halfway to Len's, a blue Ford Focus, tires squealing, pulled out of a side road just ahead of Smitty, then slowed suddenly as if preparing to make a quick turn. Smitty hit the brakes to keep from rear-ending the car, which kept slowing further, forcing Smitty to ride the car's bumper. The man in the passenger seat kept looking back over his shoulder. Then, just before reaching Whitechurch Road, the car sped away, slowing again just enough to negotiate the hairpin turn ahead.

As Smitty neared the turn, he heard a dull click as his car

doors unlocked, then another as they locked again. He wondered if the stupid on-board computers were acting up. He hated the level of automation on the newer cars, with dozens of electronic control units taking over hundreds of functions, the ECUs making decisions on their own and often operating erratically. He made a mental note to have the computer diagnostics and sensor checks performed when next he took the car in for service.

He stepped on the brakes to slow for the approach into the tight turn. The brakes grumbled loudly, but the car didn't slow. The harder he pressed, the louder the rumbling noise, but there was no other effect.

"Christ!" He downshifted quickly, but nothing happened. He reached for the handbrake and tugged, but the grumbling only continued. In desperation, he turned the wheel to make for the inside edge of the road, hoping to flatten the curve enough not to skid out or flip the car. The power-steering unit chattered as he fought to turn with the car accelerating even as he pushed with both feet on the brake pedal.

He reached the curve just as the county sheriff approached from the other direction. On the outside of the turn, Smitty's car struck the buried end of the guard rail with enough speed to climb over and plunge down into the ravine beyond. Smitty let go of the wheel and put his arms up in front of his face just before the car struck a boulder and the airbags deployed.

The acrid odor of the airbag charge mingled with the smell of raw gasoline. Smitty shook his head to clear it, then tried the door. It was jammed. He struggled with his seat belt, got the buckle open, and slid over into the other seat. The passenger side door was also jammed. As he butted his shoulder against the door, he heard a sharp pop, like a ladyfinger firecracker detonating under the dash.

Above, Sheriff Jacobs skidded to a stop on the shoulder just beyond the curve and climbed out. "Jimmy, you call it in, get an ambulance out here while I go and check out the driver." He stepped into the road and flagged down the vehicle that was following them, a Forestry Division truck loaded with firefighters returning from Sadler Creek. Scrambling sideways down the sandy slope, he approached the crashed car as flames erupted from under the crumpled hood. "Nate," he yelled, "get your crew down here."

Nate Peterson waved to his young volunteer firefighters. "Okay, boys and girls, let's put that out before we have another forest fire on our hands."

With the flames growing, the sheriff tugged at the passenger door. "Together on three," he shouted to the driver. The door didn't give. "Get back to the other side and cover your head." He picked up a football-sized rock and smashed the window, then battered the broken glass clear from around the frame with his nightstick. "Come on." He reached in through smoke and flame, felt an arm, grabbed another, and heaved with all his strength. He fell backward with the driver, clothes in flames, on top of him. He beat at the fire as he rolled with the man over the rough ground.

The car exploded just as Nate reached the gully where the two men had ended up. "You all right, Sheriff?" He reached down to help him up.

"Better than this poor bastard, Nate. Give me a hand getting him up the hill. Is that ambulance on its way?"

"We got a chopper coming. Said fifteen minutes."

Nate and his fire crew had the car dowsed in foam by the time the med-flight helicopter landed on the road. Sheriff Jacobs shook Nate's hand. "Good work."

"That part was easy." Nate flicked at an invisible fly. "Would have burnt itself out in a few more minutes anyway. The gas tank must've been near-empty. That's why it blew."

The sheriff gave Nate a look as if he were expecting more. "And the driver?"

Nate shook his head. "Hard to tell. The paramedics didn't say anything. They're taking him direct over to Huntington."

"Why not the Med Center in Charleston?"

"The Burn Intensive Care Unit at Cabell Huntington Hospital—only one in the state."

"Right, I 'member somethin' in the *Mail-Gazette* about the new unit opening. That bad, eh?"

"Didn't look good. You better get those burns of yours looked after, too. And let one of my guys put a dressing on those scrapes."

"I'll be fine. I'll check in when I get back to town. Right now I need to keep tabs on the scene here."

Sheriff Jacobs was about to leave the scene of the accident when a Town Car pulled up, dusty from recent travel on dirt roads. The driver, tall and swarthy, stepped out and flipped open a badge holder as he approached.

The sheriff squinted and pulled the brim of his hat lower against the high sun. "Tell me, Special Agent Gray, why is the FBI interested here? Place is crawling with G-men. First yesterday with that gal and her silent sidekick and now you showin' up at the scene like the cavalry, but not quite in the nick o' time."

"I picked up your call on my scanner. I was nearby, so here I am, seeing if you need any help."

"That's mighty big of you and your mighty big Bureau, but I think we're doing just fine here. Not sure what the hell you'd do to help anyway. There's been a pipeline explosion, an accident. And now we have a driver who probably fell asleep at the wheel, another accident. I haven't heard about a crime being committed, much less one that would bring in the feds."

Gray put his sun-wrinkled face within inches of the sheriff's and looked him in the eyes. "I'm here for consultation, offering my services in the investigation."

"Well I'll be sure and call you if the need arises." The sheriff took a step back.

"You do that, Sheriff. You do that." He started to leave, then turned back. "Any idea who the victim was?"

"Not yet, we're checking the plates. Anything on the registration, Jimmy?"

Jimmy called over from the sheriff's car. "Yeah, just got it. The car was registered to one Jebediah Smithers Jackson. Say, ain't that the colored guy from the gas company?"

"Yeah, think so. Wonder where he was goin' in such a damn tear-ass hurry."

Agent Gray touched a finger to the brim of an imaginary hat. "Looks like you're busy, Sheriff. I'll leave you to it. Keep me in mind. I told the same thing to the police in town." At his car, he paused with the door open and did a slow pan of the whole scene before leaving.

═

The tires complained as the blue Ford snaked down the road. The passenger steadied himself against the arm rest. "Slow down, Aaron. Attention we do not need."

"I want to return the rental car early. We need to switch cars and get out of state." The driver sounded mildly impatient.

"You think our tracks are covered well enough?"

"Maybe, maybe not, but I hope so. We're not going to wait around to find out."

"I would feel a lot better if we had retrieved the laptop before the posse arrived."

"Well, you fried it when you blew the car, Ari."

"The sheriff was approaching. What else could I do at that

point? You think we've been made?"

"We go on that assumption. So, we call home and arrange for someone to exfiltrate us."

"At least the operation's over."

"Hardly. Our part is over. Now it's someone else's mess. And it may be getting messier by the minute."

"We still don't know what this was about, do we? I mean, that guy from the Control Center—ever wonder why we had to take him out?"

"Because we were told to. That's how it works on a wet team. We are merely the instruments. You'll learn. You'll get used to it. Who knows what he did? Maybe he just knew too much or was onto something. We can just assume he was some kind of a threat. Otherwise, why would we get this assignment? And why would they send us on short notice? I hate it when I have to improvise. I don't like surprises, and it's these kind of ops that always have the surprises. Anyway, we need to switch cars and get back to DC before there are any more surprises."

Chapter Eight

Detective Duane Carleton threaded his way through the usual early morning comings and goings in the Charleston police station. He gave a knuckle tap to the doorjamb of the Captain's office and poked his shaved head in. "So, we got the results back on that flashlight. It's a special private label commercial product, rebranded and sold in bulk to companies. That particular model was made for Midlantic Corporation."

Captain Dayton, who already sported a five-o'clock shadow, looked up with his customary surly expression. "Is that supposed to ring a bell?"

"Maybe. Midlantic was acquired by Spanergy in 2001 and folded into Spanergy Infrastructure Group."

The surly look vanished for a moment from the Captain's face. "Where our eyewitness happens to work. Any prints?"

"Yes, including one good match with her prints on file with the state from when she was picked up for a drunk-and-disorderly and spent the night in lockup."

"Okay, so this puts her at the scene. But we already knew that. Big wup."

"Well, it's a little more than putting her at the scene. The flashlight was found near the body recovered from a ledge in Sadler Creek Canyon. Also near the body was a backpack containing tools, including a pair of wire cutters like the ones electricians use, plus a coil of wire, which turns out to be Ethernet cable. Maybe they were working together? Maybe he just didn't get out?"

"Maybe you oughta become one of those thriller writers. You got the imagination for it. But let's stick to police work, Duane, leastwise until you write your first bestseller novel. Any progress on ID-ing the body."

"Not yet, we're checking dental records and searching for matches on that partly melted driver's license. Forensics is pretty sure it's a Massachusetts license. We're going on that assumption."

"What else do we know about the vic?"

"Male, between the ages of 20 and 26, five-foot-four. The surviving corner of the driver's license includes part of his ID photo. Makes it look like he might have been Asian or maybe Latino. We'll know once we match records."

"What about the girl?"

"The eyewitness? We're bringing her in for questioning."

═

"I already told the whole story before." Kat looked up from her seat on a metal chair that was too high, leaving her feet dangling off the ground. "My flashlight slipped from my hand and rolled down into the canyon. Now, I wasn't about to climb down there in the dark with no flashlight, was I? That's it. We're done. You got something new, then you tell me. I've got nothing I haven't already said."

"We'd just like you to tell us again. Make sure we got it right."

"Don't pull that bullshit on me, Duane Carleton. I know that stuff. I dated your cousin, remember? He was on the force then. I know all these games. You are just trying to trip me up. You got anything on me, then charge me. Then I lawyer up. Then I walk out of here."

Captain Dayton chose that moment to come into the tiny interrogation room.

"You watching behind the funny mirror, Dayton?" She gave

him a wink.

"Did you really date Abner Carleton?"

"No way! You serious? Me date that cretin? No, I dated Bernie. Well, for a summer after college, I did."

"Didn't last long, did it?"

"About as long as Bernie's police career." Both men laughed with her. "We here to gossip about dating in the valley or what?"

"We're done talking. For now. You can go."

"Thanks a heap, Dayton. Tell your goon squad to knock more politely next time. Better yet, tell your goon squad to leave me alone."

"I'll tell them to keep an eye on you. And maybe you better look into getting that lawyer. There's a man dead and maybe a million in damages out there."

"And I had nothing to do with any of it except to call it in. Check the damn 9-1-1 recordings and the call log at Spanergy Dispatch."

"We did. But you gotta admit, it looks suspicious that you just happened to be there just before the pipeline goes boom."

"Yeah, right, it's very suspicious. Somebody whose job is checking pipelines stops to check a pipeline. Whoa, very, very suspicious. Stick it in your ear, Dayton. You, too, Carleton." She pushed past both of them and marched out of the police station.

From the exit of the parking garage, she squealed her tires defiantly as she pulled out, but the tears started before she was a block away. She blinked them away and checked her mirror to see if any police were following her, but there were no flashing blue lights, no blue-and-whites on her tail. She didn't notice the Lincoln Town Car pulling out from a parking space and slipping in two cars behind her.

Chapter Nine

"Len Bergen here." There was silence on the other end. "Hello? Bergen here."

"Uh, Len, this is Thadeus Greely."

"Oh, hi, Mr. Greely. What's up?"

"I'm afraid something has happened. Smitty . . ."

"What about Smitty? He was supposed to have—"

"He's in the hospital over in Huntington. Burnt real bad."

"What happened?"

"He hada accident yesterday, sailed right off the damn road near the old quarry. I just found out and thought you might wanna know."

"My god. I was just talking with him yesterday. We were going to . . ." Len's heart was racing. "What happened?"

"They don't rightly know, not as yet. Looked like he just drove off the road, ended up at the bottom of the ravine. Maybe fell asleep. Sheriff is looking into it, but he called it a single-car accident. You know how Sheriff Jacobs talks when he's bein' official and all. Not a soul around. The sheriff happened to be a-comin' back from Sadler Creek and saw the car fly off the road."

Len dropped his voice. "Thanks for telling me, Mr. Greely. I really mean that. Smitty is . . ."

"Yeah, he was good, a black man but he was smart, worked hard, always could trust him. Not like some."

Len bit his tongue and waited.

"Well, things is busy here, what between bein' short-handed and all, plus the extra work of repair and that."

"Yeah, must be tough. When are they going to let me back."

"Oh, I don't know. I'm only a manager. You think they tell me anythin'? Look, you take care. I'm sorry about Smitty."

"Yeah, me too."

Len hung up, then Googled the hospital and checked on visiting hours. It would take him better than an hour to get over to Huntington. That would work.

He stopped and picked up some flowers before heading west out of town on I-64. In Huntington he took the exit for Hal Greer Boulevard and turned in at the hospital with its sweeping glass facade reflecting the cloud-dotted sky. At the new BICU on the 4th floor, Len asked to see Jebediah Jackson.

The nurse at the desk, a pudgy blonde with too many barrettes in her hair, gave him a half smile as she shook her head. "I'm sorry, but he can't have visitors at this point."

"What? Why is that?"

"Are you family?"

"He's got no family. Not 'round here."

"Then I'm afraid I can't tell you about his medical condition or treatment."

"You dang well better tell me." Len tapped forcefully on the counter. "I'm his best friend. And I work with him."

"I'm sorry. I can't—"

"Is there a problem nurse?" A white-coated woman with straight black hair cropped in a bob just below her ears and a uni-brow above her coal-dark eyes stepped to the counter beside Len. He couldn't tell whether she was Vietnamese or Korean or what, but her name badge said Dr. Johnson.

"Look, Doctor, I'm Leonard Bergen. Smitty . . . Mr. Jackson and I . . . we're friends."

"You're Len, then? The patient mentioned you before we put him under."

"Mentioned me?"

"Yes. He said something about wanting us to tell Len to check the files. Does that make sense?"

"Yes, it does. Was his laptop with him when he was brought in?"

"No, he was flown in by helicopter. I was on duty. There was nothing with him."

"Can I just talk with him? Obviously, he knows me. He'd want to talk with me."

"That may be, but he's not going to talk with anyone for a while. He's in a medically induced coma while we began treatment and prepare for a series of skin grafts."

"Ah, so that's his condition." Len faced the nurse behind the counter and flashed her a look of triumph which earned him a scowl in return. He turned back toward the doctor. "Thanks, Doc. Can you say when he'll be out of this coma thing?"

"It would be hard to say at this point. Maybe a week. You can try coming back then."

"Sure. I can commute from Charleston. Got nothing better to do. Thanks again, Doc." He thrust his flowers at the nurse. "Here, tell Smitty these are from Len. When he wakes up." He turned toward the elevators before the nurse could respond.

═

Len was back on the Interstate, annoyed and driving too fast in the passing lane, when his cellphone rang. He fumbled with the touch screen. "Bergen here."

"Gaudet. Can we talk?"

"Sure, shoot."

"Not over the phone. You remember where my place is?"

"Yeah, of course."

"Then pick me up after work in an hour. If I don't come out when you honk . . . Oh, never mind. Just be there."

"Count on it." For no discernible reason, he started grinning after he disconnected.

═

Len reached across and opened the door for Kat. She got in and buckled her seatbelt without a word. "You look annoyed," he said. "You did say to honk. You okay?"

She gave a quick shake of her head. "Just drive."

Len reversed and backed to the end of the driveway. "Which way?"

"Head out, not back toward town. And take the first left." As he accelerated down the road, she pivoted in her seat to face out the back.

Len dutifully drove past the last of the houses, then made the turn onto the dirt road she indicated a couple miles farther. "Now what?"

"Just drive." She continued staring out the back window. "I think we're okay, but see where the road turns away from the creek? Just hang a hard right and drive right over the creek and up the bank. Don't slow down or your wheels will slip on the rocks. You can't see it at first, but there's an old fire road on the other side."

Len turned off the road, skidded over the rocky creek bed, and powered his way up onto the fire road.

"Okay, pull up and wait."

"Can you tell me what we are doing?"

"Talking."

"Out here."

"Yeah, where I know it's just the two of us. I want to keep it that way, so keep your eyes peeled."

"You are one scary lady, you know that? The word that comes to mind is paranoid schizophrenic."

"That's two words.

"All right. Just what do you want to talk about while you're nervously watching the road across the creek."

"Spanergy, Sadler Creek, accidents that may not be accidental. You know about your boss?"

"You mean Smitty? Yeah, I was just over to see him at the hospital in Huntington."

"How is he?"

"Badly burned, it seems. They got him knocked out. What a damn shame. You know, he was on his way to my place when the accident happened. Wait a minute. Are you suggesting that he didn't have an accident?"

She ignored his question. "The police hauled me in for questioning today. They found my lost flashlight out at Sadler Creek, near the body of that hiker or whatever. They got some dang conspiracy theory going or something. They found some tools in the dude's backpack. I don't know what they think he could've done out there with some wire and wire cutters. So far, I don't think they found any evidence of tampering or explosives. It's not like you could drill into that pipe or anything." She made a twisted-mouth face. "Actually, you could drill into it with a good carbide bit if you wanted to badly enough and didn't care much about blowing yourself up.

"Anyway, from the talk around the garage, those NTSB boys are looking into everything, even checking for bullet holes. Nothing so far. But the police still seem to think I had something to do with it somehow. And now this Smitty is in the hospital. I also overheard something at the police station as I was storming out of there. They had brought in an outside forensics guy, an explosives expert, to go over Smitty's car with a fine-tooth comb."

"What did they find? Anything?"

"They found something, all right; I just don't know what it is. Something about the diagnostics connector. Couldn't hear that part of the conversation too well, but it doesn't sound like an accident to me. I just don't know why anyone would want the man dead."

"Maybe because he knew something."

"Like what?"

"Like whatever he called me about yesterday and was going to tell me this morning. I should have let him come over after he first called. I should have, but I was tired, and I thought it could wait. Stupid of me."

She reached over and laid her hand on top of his. "What exactly did he say to you when he called?"

"He said he had something for me. Wouldn't tell me over the phone. I think it was something about Sadler Creek, but he didn't say."

"How could he have found something? He was on suspension?"

"I don't know. I remember that sometimes he worked from home to do reports and things. Maybe he had remote access. He'd have to use a dongle to access through the VPN, but maybe he had one."

"You know, I'd love to get another look at those logs myself. Maybe I could spot what he found."

"Maybe. He might have had the VPN dongle with him when he headed for my place, but he could have left it at home." He caught Kat's inquiring look. "Hold on, lady. I don't think I like the way you're thinking."

"And what way is that?"

"Like breaking-and-entering thinking."

"Who said anything about a B-and-E? Look, we're the gas company, and the gas company has to check appliances and look for leaks, you know."

Chapter Ten

After picking up the company truck back at her house, Kat and Len took the long way around to the other end of town. It was already nearly dark when they pulled in at Smitty's apartment complex behind the shopping center. Kat parked her truck at the rear of the last building where it would be partially obscured but still visible from the building super's apartment on the first floor. She pressed the intercom button and waited for a reply.

"Yeah?"

"Gas company. We got a call to check a connection in apartment D31."

"Whatcha doing this time o'day?"

"Gotta check these things when they get reported. Can't have a building blow up on us now, can we? Can you let us into D31?"

"Blow up? My building?"

"No, nothing to worry about as long as you let us check that apartment."

"Okay, okay. I'll meet you over there in a jif."

The supervisor was a gray-haired black man who anxiously let them into building D, then hemmed and hawed about not having master keys but nevertheless opened the apartment door for them. He nervously followed them into the living room.

Kat's tool belt jangled as she turned. "Oh, I wouldn't advise you to hang around, sir. We're paid to take the risks and trained to handle these things."

"What about him? He don't look like no gas company guy."

"Him? Hell, he's the boss man. Show the man your ID, Mr. Bergen." She waited as Len flashed his Spanergy ID and the man nodded gravely. "So, can we get to work? Or would you rather wait around for a spark or something."

"No, no way. I'm a-goin', I'm a-goin'." He skittered out the door, and Len closed it behind the man.

"You are funny, you know that? One clever little lady."

"I'll accept clever and the lady part, but the last guy who called me little is missing his front teeth."

Len dropped into a slight crouch and struck a boxer's pose with his left fist in front of his mouth. "Not the face, lady. Please, not the face." Kat swung at his solar plexus and pulled the punch but still connected. "Oof! Not below the belt, either."

"Just where do you wear your belt, my flyweight friend? But, hey, let's stop messing around and get to work on what we came here for."

Len didn't answer but went straight for the roll-top desk on the far side of the living room. "Um, there's a dangling Ethernet cable here but"—he rolled the top of the desk back—"no laptop. Smitty must have brought it with him. I wonder if he left the dongle."

Len opened the center drawer. "And look at this, here there be dragons."

"What do you mean?"

"It's a poem, haiku." He read the poem on the top piece of paper. "The title is just a number: 61398."

"What do you make of it?"

"Not much. The Japanese sensibility just never did much for me. Smitty was really into it. There's a whole slew here." He shuffled through the stack. "Like, here's one titled 'Choir'."

He read:

Girls in lavender
Rapping songs of salvation:
Early-onset dementia.

Len chuckled. "Smitty's a man of contradictions. He ridicules religion but goes to church regularly." He returned the stack of poems to the drawer and closed it, then crouched down to better see into the recesses of the old-fashioned desk. "Hey, I think I got it." He reached into a cubbyhole and fished out a red-and-gray Protexient device. "This is it. We're in. So let's get out before we're found out." He used his sleeve to wipe at the handle of the roll-top.

"Aren't you forgetting something?"

"Like what?"

"Don't we need a screen name and password?"

"Don't you remember? Smitty and I work together. We know each other's passwords. He was SUPER and his password was CLARKK3NT, spelled with a number three. So, your place or mine to do our software sleuthing?"

"Yours, it's closer."

They spotted the flashing blue lights through the windows as they hurried down the front stairwell. Two uniformed officers were approaching the entrance below.

"Methinks the back stairwell might be less crowded right now, my lady."

"Methinks you think well. On the stairs we would not want to draw stares."

"Groan. You are quick. So show me just how quick."

She led the way as they took the steps two at a time back up to the top floor, ran the length of the hall, and trotted down the back way. They circled around behind the buildings to her truck.

Kat smiled as she maneuvered the pickup over a curb and out through the supermarket parking lot. “That was invigorating.”

“Not the word I would pick. My heart is pounding like a mad drummer in a punk band.”

“You know, you are funny when you’re scared. I’ll have to remember that.”

“I see. When you want to be amused, you just frighten me.”

She gave him a knowing smile. “We did time that rather close. If we had arrived an hour later, there would have been police tape across the door.”

“Yeah, and if we left two minutes later, we would have left wearing handcuffs. So let’s make hay while the sun shines and get into the Spanergy computer systems while we still can. Maybe it’s already too late.”

“Maybe. The sun’s already setting. Too late for hay.”

Len glanced out the back window. “At the next corner pull over.”

“What?”

“Pull over. I think we’re being tailed.” She angled over to the curb, shifted into neutral, and pulled the hand brake. He leaned toward her. “Now kiss me.”

“What the—” The rest of her words were muffled by his mouth on hers.

He finally came up for breath. “Okay, all clear. They went by. I’m not sure. Maybe I was mistaken.”

“You . . .” She pushed him away, not knowing what to think. “You did that.”

“Yeah, that was the idea. I wanted to see if I got a reaction from the driver of that car I thought was following us.”

“You got a reaction all right—from me. I should punch your lights out. That doesn’t make sense. Trying to get a reaction from that driver?”

"I saw it in a movie once. The spy kisses the woman until the car goes past."

"A movie? How lame."

"Thanks for not punching my lights out."

"Yeah, sure." She checked her outside mirror for traffic and tried not to smile. "We are rather easy to follow in this rig, plus, all the company trucks have AVL—automatic vehicle locators. What say we head back to my house, which wouldn't be out of the ordinary. After you leave, I'll hop on my bike and meet you at your place. I'm pretty sure me and my BMW can ditch just about any tail I might pick up. It's a dual-sport that's as happy off-road as on the highway."

Chapter Eleven

Kat watched Len drive away, then went inside to change clothes. The moon was already rising as she left the house. Grabbing the handlebar of her motorcycle, she squeezed the clutch and walked it to the end of the driveway. She let two cars pass before starting the engine. With a quick twist of the throttle, she roared up the road, slowed for the first left, then raced down the dirt road. At the same spot she and Len had returned from earlier, she crossed the creek, gunned the bike up the bank, and headed up the fire road.

In her headlights, the trees and brush formed a bright surreal tunnel that rushed by like the dizzying scenery in some faster-than-light video-game simulation. She slowed to a stop and turned off her lights, letting her eyes gradually adapt to the darkness. Under the full moon, the straight tracks of the fire road were easy to see. Far behind her, headlights flashed through the trees.

"Okay, whoever you are, just try and keep up." She accelerated slowly, letting herself get used to the cold moonlight and blue-black shadows on the straight road until she was roaring through the countryside, concentrating, hyper-alert. "Damn, this is fun!"

West Virginia was cheap living for Len, who had grown up in New Jersey and gone to school in California before being offered a job with Spanergy. Here he could afford to own a small house on a salary that would not even cover the rent on a one-bedroom apartment in lower Manhattan.

Len was pacing in front of the bay window in his living room when Kat finally pulled up in the driveway. She maneuvered her bike around to the side of the garage where it would be less visible from the road, then rang his doorbell. She was wearing a tight-fitting motocross-style outfit: black with pink and orange trim. It made her seem tough and inviting at the same time. She tucked her matching helmet under her arm as he opened the door.

"I lost them."

"Really? You were followed?"

"Maybe not. But if you can use that excuse, so can I. The moon is full and the back roads and tracks were clear. Felt good."

"So, come in. Can I get you anything?"

"Yeah, a glass of water and a VPN tunnel into Spanergy."

"You got it. My computer is over there. I'll get the water."

When he returned to the living room, she was already seated at his desk and typing away on his laptop. "What are you doing with my computer?"

"Logging in at Spanergy. Oops! Must have mistyped the password. What was it again? I thought it was CLARKKENT."

"Yes, but spelled with a 3 instead of an E."

"It still doesn't work. Let me try once—"

"No, wait! If we fail three times in a row, it locks out not only the account but also the VPN link. Another so-called security feature. So, let's use my credentials. No, better yet the administrator account. You remember? It's—"

"I know, BERGENDORF and ELVISCO."

"Good memory."

"And we're in." She started scrolling through options.

"Hey, slow down."

"I'm too fast for you, huh?"

"I want to follow what you're doing. I'm the industrial control guy, so let me do this."

She spread her elbows playfully to keep him from the keyboard.

"Hey, whose computer is it?" he protested.

"It's mine now, cowboy. You been schooled."

"You think?"

"I know. See there's the section I was looking at when your boss walked in."

"Hold it. Go back. Let's run through that part just a little slower and think about what Smitty might have seen that would have drawn his attention. The numbers and event codes are all green, scattered yellow, and . . . Go back! No, not that far." He pointed at the screen. "There, stop. You know how to take a screenshot?"

She scowled up at him as she held down the FN and Alt keys while she tapped on Prnt Scrn without looking. "See, blindfolded."

"Cute. Now save it in a local Word file. And download a copy of the entire log. You use the drop-down menu in the corner there."

"I already figured that out, cowboy."

"Well, whoop-de-do. Now, can you pull up the log file for two days earlier? Yeah, that's right."

"What are we looking for?"

"Something that looks like the screen shot you took. Just scroll through really slowly."

"Why do that? I can search for one of the alert sequences."

"No, just scroll."

She stopped scrolling, called up a search function, and typed a string. "See? There we are, the easy way."

"Okay, so you are smart. We've established that. Now go down three lines. One more. There. See?"

"So? The same sort of thing happened on two different days. I have whole weeks that go that way."

"Don't you get it? This is not the same *sort* of thing. Flip back to the screen shot; now back to the earlier log. See what I mean? Those are the exact same values coming from the RTUs and the IEDs. That is just impossible."

"You sure?"

"Take another screen shot and put it on another page in the Word file. Okay, now page back and forth between them."

"You're right, they are the same, not almost, but exactly the same series of numbers in the exact same sequence. And what are these red lines?"

"Those are when we were switching over from a backflow after reversing the gas on a line to feed to another gas company. It results in temporary alerts with a particular pattern. We were doing that during my shift on Monday; we didn't do it on Wednesday."

"So you're saying the log was faked."

"Yeah, copied from that earlier file."

"That would cover up whatever might be actually happening on the pipeline."

Len paced as he kept shaking his head. "It's not just the files; it was that way on the board, too. What we saw then was all green and yellow, nominal values, nothing happening. Somehow we missed that backflow sequence." He slapped at his leg. "Of course! What are the times for those red alerts? No, not on the earlier log, on the log for the morning of the rupture. There, look at the time. That was just, like, ten minutes before the explosion, about the time Smitty left for coffee. He was asking me if I wanted anything, and I was trying to decide. Neither of us were paying much attention. Those few warnings could have slipped by. It's only a small part of the events from two days earlier, just the tail end."

"What does it mean?"

"It's not good. For one thing, Smitty conveniently distracts me from the board just when there was something that might have drawn our attention. For another, he is conveniently gone much longer than expected, for the whole time of the incident at Sadler Creek. Then, he walks in, all casual like, after you show up."

"Aren't you running the same number on him that was run on us? It might all be coincidence."

"It can't *all* be coincidence. Something is going on, and the guy I worked with the last six years is lying in a coma in the hospital. Somebody pulled something, and somebody is still pulling stuff."

"Shouldn't we tell somebody, somebody else?"

"Who? The police? We really don't know all that much, and what we do know is pretty technical."

"The FBI?"

"We don't know if this is criminal. And why the FBI?"

"Interstate commerce. That line runs to Pennsylvania."

"Right! That's why we need to go to the Department of Transportation, the NTSB. This is stuff the NTSB should know about, if they don't already. They are the ones trying to figure out what happened out at Sadler Creek. Move over. I want to grab a couple more things." Len sat down in front of his laptop and started typing. A message popped up indicating that his session had timed out. He tried to log in again, but got an incorrect-credentials message. A second try also failed. He tried once more using his own ID and password, but the VPN tunnel closed and he was staring at a screen that said the connection was lost. They had been locked out.

PART TWO
Chapter Twelve

The visitor from the State Police Forensic Lab held up the plastic evidence bag by the corner and wiggled it. "I really don't know quite what to make of it. Not a lot we really know."

"Well, tell me what you do know." Captain Dayton spread his hands in supplication.

"Well, there are traces of an electrical squib, residue from a small explosive charge—incendiary—fused bits of electronic parts, and the remains of the plug that connected it into the under-dash socket for the diagnostic port of the victim's car. There's really no way we can be sure what it was doing or why it was there, but it is conclusively not a standard part."

"Then speculate. Give it your best shot."

"It seems to be . . . have been a small, special purpose computer attached to a radio receiver."

"Like a model radio control receiver?"

"Maybe. We've been doing some digging. Seems that just this past summer some security experts used a laptop attached by a cable to the diagnostics port of a car to hack into the onboard computer and take control of the car. Among other things, they were able to make the brakes fail at the mere tap of a key."

Captain Dayton tapped the report on his desk. "The driver said something about the brakes to the medic on his way to the hospital."

"That could make sense. A wireless link would even allow someone to take command remotely. We're sending this off to the FBI for more help, and we've got an automotive expert re-examining the vehicle."

"So you think someone tried to kill this guy?"

"Looks like it."

"Who?"

"Bad guys. Smart guys. Captain, this stuff is very sophisticated, very advanced. If the sheriff and the fire team hadn't come along, the guy would be dead and there might not have been even this bit of evidence of what happened. A driver speeds and misses a turn, car burns, tragic accident—end of story."

Dayton fiddled with his ear. "So, there's the explosion at Sadler Creek, and this so-called accident comes a short spell afterwards, and this guy is connected with the explosion. I hope he pulls through so we can question him. I got a heap of questions, that's for sure, a heap of questions."

═

Severson had worked out a route when he first arrived in Charleston, one that would look like a casual walk around the downtown area but gave him opportunities to check for surveillance without being seen as checking. It was standard tradecraft. He bought a *Washington Post* at the row of dispensers down the block from the hotel, then checked the headlines while glancing intermittently at CNN on a big-screen television in a Mosely's Electronics store. That gave him a chance to check the far side of the street reflected in the window.

The man in the dust-gray suit was there. Still. Now he was stopped outside a coffee shop. Severson ducked around the corner just as the man looked up. The next play was Severson's call. He could lose the man, string the guy along with a wild goose chase, or confront him. Based on his tactics, the guy was probably a pro, just not very good at pulling off a tail without being made. Most likely FBI.

Severson entered the electronics store from the side street and knelt down in the first aisle pretending to examine digital camera cases on the bottom row of hooks. The man came trotting after, pushed into the store, and looked around anxiously. Just as he rounded the end-cap display of SD cards on sale, Severson stood and faced him with a smile. “Fancy meeting you here, Arkady.” He took two steps forward, putting himself less than a foot away. “I must say, you look a bit stressed.” He leaned forward and studied the man’s face.

Arkady Pohl fought to slow his breathing. “So, who are you this time, Severson.”

“Me. I’m just Gil Severson, same as always.”

“A true-name op, is it? No cover name? I thought the CIA couldn’t work here at home.”

“Who says I’m working? What’s wrong with a little vacation in wonderful West Virginia? Besides, we can work on American soil as long as we are pursuing foreign elements. There’s more of us posted Stateside than in the rest of the planet put together. You know that.”

“Foreign elements? What in hell are you talking about? There’s an off-shore piece to this story?”

“What story? I’m here for a few days off. And you?”

“You are so full of crap, Severson, always have been. You know what story: the pipeline story.”

“You’re here because of that? That explosion? Are you saying there might have been something criminal about that? I thought it was an accident, plain and simple.”

“Damn you, Severson. You and the whole Company. You’re always playing spy games, even with your own. We’re on the same goddamn team.”

“Are we? You know, you should keep your voice down. The clerk at the counter looks like he might be listening. Wouldn’t want him to hear all about your investigation."

Arkady gritted his teeth and cursed under his breath.

"You always were so excitable, Arkady. Maybe you should consider changing careers. The stress of being in intelligence work is getting to you. You've put on weight. You were out of breath when you came through that door. Your complexion is pasty. You need to spend less time sitting at a desk. You know, you're headed for a coronary."

"Fuck you, Severson."

"I was just kidding, just kidding. Don't take everything so seriously. I was just pushing your buttons. It's really great to see you." He reached out and pulled the shorter man into a hug. "Let's find a coffee shop and sit down. You can catch me up on this case of yours. Come on. I think I saw a nice place, local chain, across the street. Or we can go in search of a Starbucks, if that's more your thing." He had a hand on Arkady's back and started steering him toward the exit.

Arkady, his expression a mask of confusion, turned to face Severson, who smiled back warmly. "I've always liked and respected you, Arkady, but you're too quick to let things get to you. Let's just relax over coffee, and you can fill me in. You really think the explosion was not just an accident?"

═

Agent Delacroix watched from the drug store as her partner exited the electronics shop and was steered across the street by a familiar figure: good old Gilbert Severson. There were advantages to be reaped from the low regard that some of the Langley crowd had for the Bureau. And Arkady could play the crude, slow-witted Slavic part better than anyone. She had little doubt that he would pick up some useful intelligence about what the Company was up to.

Still, they would have to keep a close eye on Severson. She knew Gil was good, but the stage was becoming crowded with players. In addition to the FBI, the County Sheriff, and the local police, she now had to factor in not only the NTSB crew, but also the CIA. And there was a wild-card player in the bunch: the mysterious agent Gray mentioned by the Sheriff. Whoever he was, he was not FBI as he claimed, not unless she and Arkady were being deliberately left out of the loop. Not only that, but Severson was not one to be out in the field as a singleton. Maybe the mysterious stranger was his partner. She'd have to kick the matter up the line and see if the Bureau's CIA liaison could get an admission from someone at Langley. So much for an integrated approach to national security. If they all weren't careful, they'd soon be stumbling all over each other like Keystone Cops.

Chapter Thirteen

The side door banged shut, echoing in the cavernous space of the hanger. Tank looked up from the Masonite folding table in the far corner that was serving as his temporary office. "Ah, visitors." He waved them over. "It is good to see you again, Kat." He smiled warmly at her. "What's the occasion? And I see you brought a friend."

She planted herself squarely in front of Tank and scanned the papers spread on the table. "You busy?"

"Oh, no. I just got 6,000 pounds worth of pipe to examine end-to-end. We already know the point of initial failure—nothing special about it, so now we have to compare with the rest of the pipe—every inch of the forty-eight feet of it. Then we have to cut out and ship a section to a facility where they can do a pressure test to failure, so we know what actual pressure that thing can hold before it ruptures. And then we'll have to compare that rupture to the one that happened out at Sadler Creek. Then I have to make sense of it all and write up a convincing report that explains why the whole thing ended up at the bottom of a burned-out ravine. I do all this with reporters and the DOT and Congress looking over my shoulder." He paused for breath.

"All that is nothing compared to the pressure coming indirectly from Spanergy. They don't dare interfere with an ongoing investigation, but they want the report completed the day before yesterday and they want it to say the right thing, to exonerate them of any wrongdoing or negligence. Plus, right now I am doing all this alone because my guys are all out at Sadler Creek supervising a Spanergy guy getting paid overtime to use an atomic-hydrogen torch to cut off a section of a pipe elbow we need to study more closely. No, I'm not busy."

Len opened his hands and thrust them forward. "Maybe we can help."

"You're Bergen, Leonard Bergen, isn't that right?" Len nodded. "You're on my list to talk with, but I got distracted after they brought these mothers in here." He pointed toward the two sections of pipe resting on blocks and stretching across the hanger. "Let's see. You went to Cal Tech. Your father was Saul Bergendorf, taught at Pratt, right?"

"You seem to know a lot about me."

"Only what I could get from the files. Whose idea was it to drop the 'dorf' from your last name? That's not in the files."

"My idea."

"May I ask why? Just curious. Names intrigue me."

"Simpler. Easier for people to spell. More modern."

"Less ethnic?"

Len shrugged. Kat, who was shifting from foot-to-foot with impatience and discomfort spoke up. "Are you boys going to chat about ethnic identity or are we going to get to the reason for us being here."

"And that would be?"

"As he said, we thought we might be able to help."

"Help away."

She glanced at Len, then mugged a poor-baby look for Tank. "You been kinda buried in this pipe and the site out at Sadler Creek. We thought you might not have looked into some other angles."

"Angles?"

Len answered. "Like the system log files."

"We looked into them."

"And what did you see when you looked?"

"Not much."

"That figures." Len spoke as if addressing the floor.

"Oh, really?"

Len and Tank glared at each other. Kat took a step forward. "Now, boys. Let's just get on with business. Len and I have been studying the data recorder files, and we found something really peculiar."

"Like what?"

"Like a block of events on Wednesday morning that duplicates entries from Monday."

Tank, suddenly interested, leaned forward. "They were altered? Like a cover-up?"

"No, not after the fact," Len said. "They were wrong at the time of the explosion."

"How can you know that?"

"Because I was there at the time of explosion." Kat emphasized the point with her index finger. "And Len remembers the board. I can corroborate Len's account, at least for the time I was there in the Control Room. The displays at the time fit with what the log files show, not what happened at Sadler Creek."

Tank looked unimpressed. "Yeah, we got that, too, but we don't know why."

"Neither do we, but we know the how—sort of. Both the data logger and the displays were duplicating events from Monday rather than the data actually coming from Sadler Creek."

Tank put a fist to his chin and squinted in concentration. He took his hand away and punched the air. "Stuxnet."

She cocked her head. "Say what?"

"Man-in-the-middle attack."

Kat had her mouth open, but Len was nodding. "Yes," he said, "that could be it. Like what the Israelis pulled against

Iran back in 2010."

Kat turned toward Len. "Remind me about that, and tell me what in hell it has to do with Sadler Creek."

"The Israelis joined forces with our Department of Homeland Security. Together, with a little help from some German friends, they created a malicious piece of software, a worm that would seek out and cripple or destroy equipment in the uranium enrichment plant at Natanz in Iran. The program ultimately embedded a piece of itself in the PLCs controlling the process, where it started systematically destroying high-speed centrifuges. While it alternately red-lined the motors and slammed on the brakes, it tricked the operators into thinking everything was fine by playing back normal data recorded at a previous time. Like the bank robbers playing back a videotape loop from security cameras to fool the bank guards. It's called a man-in-the-middle attack."

"Yes, I see! Just like in the Spanergy system."

Tank was pursing his lips. "It's a possibility. But unless we can find the bogus payload code, it's only a good guess."

"What it would mean is that the explosion was deliberate, caused by computer code injected into the Spanergy control system."

Tank looked from Len to Kat and back. "I'm going to ask you to keep a lid on this until I can get a cyber-threat expert in on this case. Not a word to anyone. And don't do any more digging into company files. Please. If we are right, this is criminal hacking, and all that stuff is evidence."

Chapter Fourteen

Len was getting ready for bed when the motion-sensor floodlight above the garage lit up, spilling thin shafts of warm light through the bedroom window. He pushed the curtains aside. A Spanergy pickup truck had pulled into his driveway, and a woman dressed in blue sweatpants and a dark gray hoodie was walking toward his front door. Len hurriedly pulled his pants back on and tucked in his shirt.

Kat was waiting at the front door when he opened it. "What brings you here in the middle of the night. Did somebody report a gas leak in the neighborhood?"

"Wanna come with me out Hanlon way?"

"What for?"

"A little up close and personal inspection. An idea I got—from you."

"Why in the middle of the night?"

"Isn't it obvious. We don't want to have to explain ourselves."

"The more I get to know you, the more you scare me."

"Then don't go. I can do this myself. I thought . . . I thought you wanted to find out what this is all about."

"Well, I do. But what do you think we're going to find out there?"

"Don't know for sure. That's why I'm going. Grab a jacket and let's move."

Len tugged on his cowboy boots and reached for a windbreaker hanging from a peg by the door. "What about the

AVL? I thought the pickup was tracked wherever it went?"

"It's okay: a temporary fix I picked up from a trucker. We're good for tonight."

==

Clouds obscured the moon as Kat maneuvered her pickup off the state highway and onto a gravel road. "I have only been here a couple of times before. The compressor station is smack dab in the middle of this farmer's field, chain link all around. We gotta do a little fence climbing. You up to that?"

"Anything you can do."

"We'll see about that, cowboy. We're almost there."

It was impossible to miss the compressor station. High-pressure sodium floods on poles at each corner cast pink-yellow light over the small concrete-block building and the surrounding garden of fat pipes growing from the ground. Kat slipped a backpack over one shoulder, slid a folding aluminum ladder from the back of her truck and slung it over her other shoulder, and started walking out across the tall grass on the fallow field. As they neared the station, an electric buzz and the insistent whine of turbines drowned out the chirp of crickets. At the station, Kat opened up the ladder and leaned it against the fence. "Up and over, cowboy. Careful when you drop on the other side. You sprain an ankle, and they'll find you here in the morning, 'cause I am not about to throw you over my shoulder and haul you out."

"Don't worry."

"Not worrying, just warning. Here, put on these work gloves so as you don't hurt your hands on the wire at the top."

"Ladies first." He took a low, sweeping bow and gestured like a courtier. By the time he straightened back up, Kat was already nearing the top of the ladder. As she gingerly negotiated the ragged top edge, he was thinking that it was a good thing that the fence wasn't topped by razor wire. Kat lowered herself partway while hanging onto the fence top, then took a backwards leap and landed as quietly as a kitten jumping off a sofa.

When Len followed, he landed with a sharp double thump and almost lost his balance. "It's the boots," he said. "Better for riding horses than jumping fences, I guess."

"You ride?"

"No, not really. I just like the style. Picked it up during a summer in Texas."

"Working on gas lines?"

"No, pumping gas—the other kind. My uncle in Austin got me work at one of his gas stations between my freshman and sophomore years. I had to wear company coveralls on the job. Guess I rebelled when I was off work. Girls down there were into guys with the Western look. Goes with the Texas two-step and Texas hold 'em."

"Bet I can best you at both."

"I'll take that bet. But right now, shouldn't we do whatever it is we're here for?"

"We're here because of what you said about that Stuxnet thing with Iraq."

"Iran."

"Yeah. Anyway, I got to thinking how a SCADA network like this is different from a factory control system."

"Yeah?"

"Well, what we have here is a distributed system, with widely dispersed assets. It's not centralized like on some factory floor. We got sensors and controllers scattered over hundreds of miles all over the state."

"And out of state, too."

"Yes. And how does that data get to the Control Center in Charleston and how do the commands get back to keep the pipeline network under control?"

"Different ways."

"Exactly. Between the temp-and-pressure monitors downstream and this compressor station, some of it's wired and some of it's a wireless link. From here back to Charleston, it's telco, a leased line from Frontier. And then there are ad hoc elements: sensors, data loggers, and the like used for maintenance."

"Where is this going?"

"It's going in there, right where we're going." She pointed toward the building adjacent to the jungle of pipes.

"And how are we going to get in? It's gotta be locked."

"Which is why field crew carry RFID badges. I would have to requisition a key for the padlock on the gate—which is why we climbed over—but this I always have with me." She held up the badge hanging from a lanyard around her neck. When she placed it against a black square next to the door, a deadbolt released with an audible thunk. Kat pulled on the heavy door, opening it enough to slip in. "Follow me, and close the door behind you." She clicked on a flashlight, swept the beam around the room, and spotlighted a box the size of a toaster oven. "That's it."

Len's face lit up. "A local data logger. I should've thought of that. We could even have queried it remotely while we still had VPN access."

"No, we couldn't. Remotely all we would have seen is the same story the NTSB got when they retrieved all the data over the network from the Control Center. Surprise, surprise—they all looked just like the bogus logs at the Center. This baby is field equipment, installed temporarily during maintenance work earlier this year and never retrieved. You know how it is. We get busy and it's a ways out here, we lose track of things. Anyway, it's local and you would have to know it's here and address it specifically."

"Pretty clever to think of it. How did you know it was here?"

"I'm the one who left it and never got back."

"Okay, so, what are we going to do now?" He squatted down to get a closer look at the small box.

"What field technicians do, desk jockey. We plug a portable terminal into the buss and read out whatever we need." She slipped off her backpack and took out a ruggedized tablet computer. She ran a cable from the computer and plugged it into a slot on the back of the data logger. It took a few minutes to get the logger to respond to commands from the tablet and to find the right part of the records.

Len watched as entries scrolled by on the tablet screen. "It's in a different format than we use back at the center. Looks like just the raw data: codes and readings just as they come from the devices. We'll have to take this back and work out a conversion into something we can make sense of. Wait a minute. Can you stop the download?"

"Sure."

"Okay, back up a couple of screens' worth. There, those are some codes that don't need translating. The E at the front says it's an error. There's suddenly a tsunami of error codes. And look at the time stamp on those entries: right about the time of the explosion. There was nothing like this in the log files at the Center."

"We got it, then. This is proof that the system at the Center had been hacked into to keep the real stuff from displaying or entering the permanent records there."

"Right. Let's get out of here and take this home to analyze fully. And we need to get it to that NTSB guy."

"You mean Tank?"

"Right, Tank. Weird nickname for a skinny guy."

"He's not skinny. It's from his name. Arabic or something. I forget." She turned off her flashlight as she opened the door. The ladder was gone.

"Looks like somebody knows we're here."

"And doesn't want us to leave. I shouldn't have left my tools in the truck. If I had my cutters, I could just cut through the fence—wouldn't be subtle, but it would get us out."

"I think we can still climb out. Here, let me give you a boast." He held his hands, fingers interlaced, to make a step for her. "Now, up on my shoulder. That's it. Can you reach the top?"

She stretched. "Yeah, just barely. This is going to be one tough chin-up, but I think . . ." She pulled herself up enough to swing a leg over. "Argh, that hurts."

"You all right?"

"I left some flesh on the fence, but I'll make it." She worked herself into an awkward position with one sneaker on the edge and her body arched to keep it from resting on the protruding wires at the top. "I don't like the thought of straddling this, and I don't like the thought of jumping from this height either."

Len stood watching her and feeling awkward and helpless. "Can you, like, vault over?"

"I didn't ask for suggestions from the peanut gallery, cowboy." She worked her second foot up so she was balanced, momentarily, in a bridge, but then started to wobble. She slipped and was suddenly hanging by her hands on the outside of the fence. She let go, dropped the few feet to the ground, and ended up falling backwards.

"You all right?"

"I'll probably have bruises in the morning, but I think I'm in one piece. Let me run back and get some tools from the truck."

"If it's still there."

"Well, let's hope. It's a hell of a long hike back to Charleston." She started to walk through the tall grass toward the road.

"Wait up."

She turned and saw Len climbing by jamming the pointed toes of his cowboy boots into the links of the fence like a lumberjack ascending a tree with spikes. He reached the top, threw one leg over, and twisted his foot to jam the toe into the fence from the other side. He steadied himself and did the same with the other foot. Then he climbed down the outside by the same technique.

"See, these boots are good for more than just doing the Texas two-step." He lifted one foot and turned it in the harsh light. "Course, they're pretty much ruined now."

He caught up with Kat and the two of them trudged across the field toward the road where they had left the truck. It was still there, and the ladder was lying in the pickup bed.

Len scanned up and down the road but it was deserted. "Somebody is watching us and wants us to know but not who it is or what it's all about."

Chapter Fifteen

Flashes of light flickering on the walls and the crackling sound of a cutting torch greeted Kat and Len when they arrived at the hanger in the morning. In the center of the space, a man wearing a welder's mask was busy cutting a six foot section from the nearest pipe while a crew with a portable crane supported the piece he was working on. Tank was trying to talk on the phone above the noise. He held up a hand to signal Kat and Len to wait, so they stood at a discreet distance until he finished. He did not look happy when he hung up.

"Problems?" Kat asked as she approached.

"Usual shit. What can I do for you this time?"

"Ask not what you can do for us, ask what we can do for you."

"All right, Kat, I'll bite. What can you do for me this morning."

"Give you proof that the Spanergy SCADA system had been hacked to fake the records and spoof the displays."

"Now, how did you get that? Or shouldn't I ask?"

Len folded his arms. "Maybe you shouldn't, but you can get the proof yourself by heading out to the Hanlon compressor station and downloading from a local data logger left there. The local log file doesn't match the master file at the Control Center or the ones you retrieved remotely. It's peppered with error codes, and it shows exactly how the pipe was ruptured."

"Really?"

"Yes, really. We . . . acquired the data and just spent the

night analyzing it. You can do your own analysis, but you are going to reach the same conclusion about what happened."

"Which is?"

"Shortly before the explosion, the compressors at Hanlon were directed under computer control to switch into a cascade configuration so one compressor was feeding into the next, both of them feeding the SG-70 line. Next, the two compressors were given the command to ramp up to maximum. While they were spinning up, the first valve downstream of Sadler Creek, which normally either passes through or diverts flow into the SG-70A shunt, was rotated into the fully closed position. With the compressors at max and doubled up and the end of the pipe closed, the pressure quickly climbed until the pipe failed."

Kat took over with the explanation. "My guess is you have already determined that the weakest point was at the junction with the elbow that led back underground. The pipe probably ruptured initially at some small point, the gas ignited, and the whole thing blew. Instead of shutting down immediately under program control, the compressors continued to blow gas down the line until Len sent a manual command to them some forty minutes and fifteen million cubic feet later. The only thing limiting the fireball was that the Mercer station another forty miles upstream of Hanlon was not similarly ramped up, so there was an effective vacuum forming between there and the Hanlon compressors."

Tank looked incredulous. "Are you two now suggesting this was sabotage?"

"Bingo." Len gave him a thumbs up. "It's a scenario that's been known—and dreaded—in the industry for years. Real simple: under program control you close one valve, crank up a compressor behind it, and boom—holocaust. Not only that, but this kind of sabotage has actually happened before."

"Really?"

"Really. In fact, we were the ones who set the precedent way back in 1982 when we blew up a Soviet gas pipeline in Siberia with what was then called a 'logic bomb', a few lines of incorrect code deliberately planted in exported technology. That was out on the tundra, but you could do something like that almost anyplace along our entire network of pipelines. It's fairly quick, too, with so many of the lines operating at or near 100% MAOP. Sadler Creek is in the boonies, in the open, but it could also be pulled off in some cities or many places along the East Coast urban corridor. An underground explosion could create one hell of a crater. Remember the pipeline explosion in California a few years back?"

Tank nodded. "Yes, San Bruno. That was also a thirty-inch line."

"Yeah. Left a huge crater. Killed eight people. Burned out thirty, forty homes. In a city, you could take out several square blocks and start a fire that would need an army of firefighters to bring it under control."

Tank looked from Len to Kat and back. "I wasn't on the San Bruno investigation, but I did study the report. The conclusion was that the rupture resulted from a bad weld, an accident waiting to happen. But you're now saying that Sadler Creek was deliberate, an intrusion into the control system. How do you think an intrusion into the network would be accomplished?"

"As Kat will confirm, in some places you could walk up to equipment and deliver the instructions manually, in others you could tap into the SCADA network remotely and issue the commands. The information on how to do this is widely available. If you have some idea what you are looking for, you can download technical manuals for everything you need right off the Internet. There is even an online search facility called

Shodan that locates IP addresses of directly accessible SCADA systems, unprotected nodes, wide open equipment.

"In our case, it appears to have been a far more sophisticated operation, with the malicious software somehow remotely injected into the control logic itself combined with a man-in-the-middle ruse to keep the operators from seeing what was happening and intervening in time to stop it."

"So, hackers."

"No, not hackers," Len corrected him, "at least not ordinary hackers. I think this was sophisticated, military-grade hacking, like with the attack on Iran."

Tank stared at the ground thoughtfully. "I sure as hell hope you're wrong."

Chapter Sixteen

"That's right. I want a cyber-security team working on this case, ASAP." Tank paced like a caged bear as he talked on the phone with Dean Phelps, his boss at NTSB headquarters. Phelps was never an easy mark for a special request, and Tank was already mentally marshaling his arguments. "It seems fairly clear now that the Spanergy computer system was hacked. The physical point of failure is only the smallest part of the story."

There was the sound of a muffled side conversation heard through a covered phone. "Okay," Phelps said into the phone, "seems that there already is a team working the cyber-security angle. Not ours, but they're in Charleston now."

"What the hell you talking about? A team already here? Who?"

"The FBI Cyber Crime Unit has two people in West Virginia. Haven't you talked with them yet?"

"I can't talk with people I don't know exist. Who are they?"

"Let's see, er, Special Agents Delacroix and Pohl. That's Barbara Delacroix and Arkady Pohl. They should be checked in at the Sleep Inn near the airport. Want me to get the number?"

"Don't bother. I can get it. And thanks, Dean. Thanks for keeping me in the loop, letting me know that the FBI has been working the incident, too."

"Look, Tank, don't get in a huff over this. Today is the first I heard of it myself."

"Yeah, right."

"Don't put this on me. The Bureau should have informed us; they didn't. So, what else is new? Even after 9/11, the left hand doesn't know what the right hand does, even when they are talking sign language. Hell, even the President doesn't know what the NSA is up to, if you believe the President."

═

Tank was waiting in the parking area beside the hanger when the two FBI agents arrived. He put on an official smile to cover his irritation. "Come on in to my office, such as it is. I thought we could talk without interruption here, as long as you don't mind the noise. We're readying a section of the pipeline for shipment to a test facility. Oh, sorry, I'm not big on protocol." He held out his hand. "I'm T. Samuel Parsons, head of the NTSB team here. You can call me Tank. Thanks for coming."

"No problem. This is Arkady Pohl and I'm Barbara Delacroix. You can call me Agent Delacroix. Glad to be here. After all, we're all working on the same case."

"Yeah, except you knew who was on the team, and I didn't, not until an hour ago."

"What's there to know? We're with the Bureau's Cyber Crime Unit that looks into computer and network intrusions."

"And pipeline explosions?"

"We got a call on this from somebody at Spanergy about possible unauthorized network access. We always take these things seriously, but we're particularly vigilant when it involves a critical infrastructure facility."

"Well and good, but what do you know about SCADA networks?"

"Some. I know what the acronym stands for, but we're usually dealing with illicit access to files, funneling funds electronically, possible industrial espionage, that sort of digital duplicity."

"You mean like what the Chinese have been caught pulling in many sectors? I've read they have even been found to be trawling for information on control systems at natural gas and power companies."

"Well, we're involved on the domestic side. So what have you got.

Tank shifted his gaze between them. "I'm looking at malicious software injected into an industrial control system."

"That is a little out of the main areas the two of us work in."

"Me, too." Tank closed his eyes while considering his words. "I was hoping to get some help from you people."

"Actually, maybe we can help," Delacroix answered. "I know of some people who would be really good on this case, good at digital forensics, particularly tied with SCADA attacks. There's a team under DHS and Department of Energy out at Idaho National Labs. They're good and know it, if you know what I mean. Getting access to them could be a challenge.

"I understand you already have one consultant working with you on the Sadler Creek investigation. If we can go outside, the possibilities multiply. Ralph Langner in Germany is very good, a kind of rock star in industrial security but also a good collaborator. He helped finger the Israeli connection on Stuxnet. Of course, Eugene Kaspersky at the Kaspersky Lab up in Boston is arguably an even bigger security rock star, but he's likely too busy running his global enterprise to do much consulting himself. Besides, he's Russian, and we probably should limit this to US citizens. Oh yeah, there's another person I shouldn't leave out, a cyber-security consultant who specializes in SCADA and industrial security. The guy worked with the Bureau—at least helped—on the Bluedog affair a few years back."

"Bluedog? That's a new one on me."

"Well, it got hushed up pretty fast and pretty well. You may remember hearing about the power plant out in Utah that was taken out. Well, that's the guy I'm thinking of. Name is Karl Lustig. He and an Israeli team not only tracked down the perps but also helped prevent destruction of even more power plants on the grid. There was also another guy on that case. Can't remember his name, but he was with that anti-virus company. What was that company, Arkady?"

"Uh, Scenaria."

"That's right, but the Scenaria guy was also working the other side, spreading malware. I understand he now works on black-ops with some agency or other."

Tank pulled out his smartphone and entered a quick note. "That's what happens with way too many of these black-hat hackers. They break into a system, get caught, and get punished by being offered high-paying jobs or consulting contracts with Homeland Security."

"Well, they're not all the same. This Lustig character is clean, far as I know. There are others, too, but he's considered one of the best in the world and would be my choice as go-to guy on this stuff. You want me to see if we can pull him in?"

"It will have to be on your nickel; our budget is already almost tapped out for the fiscal year."

"The sequester mess hurt the Bureau, too. But maybe we can get creative. This case involves infrastructure, so we might pull somebody in through the NCIJTF. There's money around, but a lot of it's tucked away in 'black projects' at No Such Agency and The Company."

"What's NCIJTF? I deal with pipeline failures. I have enough trouble keeping track of the initials and acronyms in my own field."

"National Cyber Investigation Joint Task Force. One of their focuses is infrastructure. I'll kick something down field with the Bureau."

"Well, better kick it far and fast, because this is serious business. It's beginning to look like the blast was deliberate sabotage triggered through the SCADA network."

"Fill us in."

"My investigation is sensitive and still ongoing."

"So is ours, on both counts. But there can be no question about need-to-know in this case. If you need to cover your ass, we can get paperwork for you, but—"

"No, I don't need CYA paper. I just need discretion."

"Which you got."

"I figure as much, but my job requires asking. NTSB only releases information through channels and on job completion. A lot of money can ride on the outcome of an investigation."

"A lot can ride on the gas transmission network remaining intact."

"Right. Okay, so sit down and let me outline what I have."

Chapter Seventeen

The El Patron was unusually noisy despite being only half filled, and Tank almost didn't hear his cellphone. He put down his beer and picked up the phone. "Tank Parsons here."

"Agent Delacroix here. I have some good news and maybe some not-so-good news."

"I'm all ears."

"Good news is I got authorization to pull in Lustig to work with DOT and DOJ jointly. But, it turns out he's in Israel and won't be able to make it here for a couple of days."

"Wait, he's Israeli? I thought we were going to limit this to Americans."

"He is American, but married to an Israeli woman, I think."

"Is any of this a problem?"

"No, apparently not with anyone in the security community that I talked with. He seems to be very highly regarded in the highest circles."

"So, we don't get him until next week?"

"Right, but he agreed to a conference call. However, the Bureau doesn't have a field office here in West Virginia, so we'll have to make do with a Skype call. Not completely secure anymore, but pretty good. The NSA can listen in and maybe decrypt in real-time, but nobody else can crack the system—yet. At least that's what I understand."

"Okay, where do we do this? I hardly think either of our hotels is an ideal facility. Jess Tisdale, the consultant on our team, has a better venue in town at the Marriott, but it would hardly be more secure."

"You're temporarily based out at the airport. That would be pretty secure."

"Good idea. Our temp HQ there would hardly do, though—the hanger doesn't even have Wi-Fi—but let's see if we can get the TSA to give us Internet access and spring for an office or a conference room in the terminal building for a couple of hours. When?"

"ASAP. Haifa is seven hours ahead of us. I say we meet at the airport at six sharp tomorrow morning. Consider it confirmed if you don't hear from me."

═══

The terminal building of the Charleston Airport was just coming awake as Tank, Barbara, and Arkady crowded around the desk in the closet-sized office. Both men were surprised by the image that appeared on Barbara's laptop screen. The man was hardly the young cyber-security specialist they had been expecting. His hair was white and his face was ringed by a fringe of salt-and-pepper beard in a distinctive but hardly fashionable style. Barbara greeted him warmly and asked how things had gone after his hip replacement.

"My hip's fine, but my knees are beginning to complain." he said. "Thanks for asking. Speaking of thanks, I never did get the chance when you were at the Miami Beach field office to express mine to you. Thank you for intervening when the IDF cavalry came riding to my rescue. Or not intervening, to be more correct."

"Glad to help someone from the Office." It was a coded message to Karl. Among insiders, Israel's elite intelligence unit, Mossad, was referred to as the Office.

"We appreciate Assistants." It was another code word. *Sayanim*, Hebrew for assistants, was the word used within Mossad to refer to Jewish civilians recruited to informally assist its operations around the world. Barbara's husband, Abe Feingold, was a *sayan* who had greased the skids for Karl at a critical time when he had been in hiding in Florida.

Tank held up a stapled stack of papers. "I take it you've read through the files we sent. I hope you had no problems with the public key encryption."

"No, I deal with that stuff a lot in my work. At any rate, I can be there in person the day after tomorrow to help solve this problem."

"Any advice in the meantime?"

"Go public."

"What? Are you crazy?" Barbara's expression changed from warm to annoyed. "Impossible. We have an ongoing criminal investigation here as well as the NTSB work. Nothing's definitive. Plus, we'd have public panic on our hands. People would go nuts at the thought that somebody could blow up natural gas pipelines by remote control. The whole natural gas industry would be raining down rocks on us."

"I don't mean go to the press, but you need to get the code in the hands of the industrial security community. Get somebody from, say, Scenaria Security Systems to take samples of the malicious code off your system. They are a leader in SCADA security. I know the top management there. They'll play ball. Have them start studying it and also selectively releasing parts of it to the larger security community. At no cost to your agencies, you will have hundreds of people working for you—the best and brightest researchers at Symantec, Kaspersky, Langner, elsewhere—all toiling away to deconstruct what you have, how it works, and how it got there."

"What if there are leaks?"

"Then there are leaks. But it will take some time to analyze the code and there will be a further delay after that. Besides, there are going to be leaks sooner or later, anyway. If this really is black-hat hackers, there will be rumors, bragging, disclaimers circulating any day now on the online forums and discussion groups where hackers hang out. That may even have started already; I'll look into it.

"What you need to focus on is getting on top of this thing technically as quickly as possible so you know just what you are dealing with and how to combat it. To the extent that you can keep people quiet, do so. You shouldn't have to worry too much about the upper levels at Spanergy. They know that their livelihood and very existence depend on keeping this quiet while also solving the problem instantly if not sooner. So figure they are on your side. Lower level employees are more of a risk, so information about this must be tightly controlled and kept out of the hands of anyone who might harbor a grudge or have an issue with the company."

"Then we may have a problem. One of the people who made the case for the malicious software is a Spanergy control system operator who has been placed on suspension."

"Then he needs to be taken back into the fold or put into a cell."

Chapter Eighteen

Tank stood waiting just inside the big overhead door as Kat pulled back into the Spanergy garage at the end of the workday. He flashed her a too-brief smile as she drove past, then tapped his foot impatiently while she ran through a checklist and clocked out. "Sorry 'bout that," she said. "Just part of the job. What's up? More questions? New developments?"

Tank studied an oil stain on the concrete before looking up. "I came to warn you. I shouldn't be doing this, but I . . . I guess it's because I like you."

"I'm glad you do, Tank, but what do you mean about warning me?"

"Your co-worker is about to be picked up by the FBI for malicious destruction of digital assets."

"What? You mean Len?"

"Yeah. The log files have been tampered with. It's pretty obvious who did it, at least to the FBI."

"Well, then the FBI is wrong. Doesn't make sense. Why would he do that? And what's this got to do with me?"

"You're his accomplice. You've been working together; everybody knows that. At the very least, you could be charged as an accessory."

"Did you warn Len?"

Tank twisted his head as if the thought had never occurred to him. "No, I came right here. Coming here could even be called obstruction of justice, and the FBI does not take kindly to that."

"Well, I don't know what you expected me to do with the information. It's not like I'm going to take off for Mexico or something and leave Len to take the rap."

"I thought . . ."

"Or you didn't think."

"I just wanted to . . . to try and protect you."

"Well, now, that's real sweet, Tank, but I didn't ask to be protected. And I certainly didn't ask to be protected by leaving Len swinging in the wind. If the FBI wants me, they'll have no trouble finding me."

═

Len gripped his half-open front door and struggled to keep his voice down. "What the hell are you talking about? Destroying evidence. Come on, you two must be reasonably smart or you wouldn't be dealing with cybercrime. Why in blue blazes would I do that?"

"You need to calm down, Mr. Bergen. You'll only make this worse." Agent Delacroix straddled the threshold, one foot against the front door, with her partner in his usual spot one step behind her, craning to look over her shoulder.

Len's heart hammered in his ears as he repositioned his own foot on the inside of the door. "Look, I was the one who brought the evidence of tampering to the attention of the NTSB. Those log files are what can clear Smitty and me; they show we did our job. Somebody was pulling off a damn clever masquerade with the monitors, but it sure wasn't us."

"Do you deny that you and Miss Gaudet illegally accessed files in the Spanergy computers? You already admitted as much. And may I remind you that lying to a federal agent is a crime?"

"You may remind me all you want, but I didn't do anything to lie about. And you can leave Kat out of this. You should be able to verify that it was my credentials used to get VPN access to the files, but it was not illegal. I had legitimate access to those files as part of my job with Spanergy."

"Using a stolen access token. Do you deny taking the VPN dongle assigned to Jebediah Jackson?"

Len maintained a grim expression as he hurriedly weighed his alternatives for what to say and how to say it. "Smitty let me use the dongle. You can ask him."

"You know that would be impossible at this point. You went to see him. We checked with the hospital, so we know you couldn't have talked with him."

Figuring that he had nothing to lose at this point, Len continued with his line. "It was before. He called me, left the dongle for me."

"That story better hold up when Mr. Jackson comes out of the coma."

"Not to worry. It will." Len's heart was racing, but he smiled casually. "Am I under arrest or not?"

"We're not here to arrest you, not yet. We just want some answers."

"And you got them. Go look somewhere else. Something damn funny is going on, but I didn't have anything to do with it. Smitty didn't, either. As I told the NTSB guy, Smitty was the one who put me onto the problem with the files. Before his accident."

"Maybe—"

Agent Pohl was cut off by a hand signal and a cough from Delacroix. "Maybe so, Mr. Bergen. We'll look into it. And we'll verify your story with Ms. Gaudet. Anything else you want to tell us?"

"Anything else you want to ask me?" The two of them locked eyes, each looking for a clue or a hidden message. "If not, I'll be going. I was on my way out when you showed up." He reached across in front of Delacroix to shut the door.

She squinted at him, studying him in indecision, but she stepped back. “This is an ongoing investigation with national security implications. You are advised not to discuss any aspects of this matter with anyone else other than your lawyer. And you might want to get one if you haven’t already done so. We’ll be in touch,” she said. "Count on it.”

“Oh, I’ll be looking forward to that, Special Agent Delacroix. Nothing makes my day like a visit from law enforcement.” He watched as they returned to their car and backed out of his driveway. He waited several minutes before leaving for town. As soon as he confirmed he was being followed, he drove straight for the Kanawha County Sheriff’s Office and parked in a lot a block up on Virginia Street. He walked briskly up to the gray stone building and marched in as if he had important business.

“Sheriff Jacobs around?”

“No, he’s out at Hanlon investigatin’ reports of a possible break-in. Can I help you?”

“No, just tell him Len Bergen from Spanergy dropped by. I’ll talk with him later.” He gave a quick look over his shoulder. “I’ll drop by next week sometime.”

Len checked his mirrors several times before backing out of his parking space. He turned into the car wash next door, but immediately exited. With no cars approaching, he took a short jog the wrong way on Virginia, entered another parking lot, and drove straight through. He hoped no one had noticed his maneuvers. Finally, he headed out of town taking the long way around toward Kat’s place.

Chapter Nineteen

In recent years, Harry Krebber had lost hair and gained weight. The stress of taking over as CEO of a troubled corporation had added several inches to his waist and extra lines to his face; a messy divorce had multiplied the toll. His office at the Reston, Virginia, headquarters of Scenaria Security Systems had suffered along with him. The massive mahogany table and matching desk, legacies of his flamboyant and free-spending predecessor, Richard Talpa, were now in need of polishing and were scattered with folders in a disorganized form of organization that was a holdover from Harry's years as a hands-on network manager. Talpa was now rumored to be a highly paid consultant to the NSA but had effectively disappeared after helping to send his company into a tailspin.

The folder in front of Harry, with its forest-green Scenaria logo, had a bright orange "Confidential" label, a date, and a generic title: Threat Analysis Summary. "I'll have to go over this again for all the details, but nice work, DB. Fast work."

The challenges of taking over as Chief Technical Officer had had a quite different effect on Douglas Botteneau. The once awkward and overweight DB had shed pounds and gained poise. He was still a card-carrying gamer geek at heart, but he had learned to handle himself with investors and customers and to ride herd on the other geeks in Scenaria's Threat Analysis Group. Even more importantly, he had learned how to delegate, leaving responsibility for the Software Engineering Group and Technical Systems Group to his first-line managers.

"The analysis was easier than expected," DB said. "We got a lucky break on decryption and didn't even have to share out sections of the code to the security community; we kept it in-house and under wraps. Part of the reason we could analyze it so fast was that a lot of it turned out to be our stuff anyway, Talpa's doing, if you know what I mean: modules and code fragments we already knew about. There were also four zero-day threats exploited by the injector: clever stuff we had never seen before. The injector code was able to walk casually into Windows and Office as if the doors were wide open."

"You're telling me they blew four pristine exploits on one piece of malware? Shades of the Stuxnet. Last time we saw that sort of use of resources was in that 2010 nuclear plant attack."

"More than just shades. The man-in-the-middle code that fooled the pipeline operators is virtually a carbon copy of the software used against Iran. It saved off normal data blocks from one day, then plugged them back in and fed them to the operators later to cover the actual attack."

"Which was?"

DB looked incredulous. "Didn't they tell you about it when they pulled us in?"

"No, they didn't want to bias our approach; they wanted us to figure it out independently. So what did you find?"

"Well, we were biased somewhat by the source. Everyone knows the NTSB has been investigating that pipeline explosion in West Virginia. It helped knowing that, because it made it easier to make sense of the PLC logic running on the control computers and to identify the hooks into the SCADA network. Anyway, we are still working on tracing what seemed to have been a rather circuitous route into the system. The injection could have come from a Web exploit or social engineering to get some front-office bozo to open an email attachment. From there it could have traveled by way of either an infected USB stick or possibly a cellphone plugged into a computer to charge or swap contact lists. The software finally wormed its way into engineering work stations at Spanergy that were used to write and maintain code for the control system, dot-dot-dot. Eventually, the payload was delivered to the control computers themselves, the PLCs. Details are in the full report, but I didn't think you would want all that now."

"Thanks."

"The level of expert information needed to pull all this off almost suggests an inside job, someone in the industry, if not from Spanergy then from one of their suppliers of the hardware and software. Either that or some extremely sophisticated industrial espionage. The target was specifically Spanergy. As the summary says, there are also blocks of code lifted from Bluedog.Win64.sys, the destructive worm that we originally called cat.9.kernal and that your predecessor had a hand in. It was real easy to get a match from our deep archives, but it also makes me wonder who else is archiving that stuff."

Harry scowled in confusion. "But that worm, Bluedog, was designed to attack electric power plants. You're claiming this code blew up a pipeline."

"Yup. The actual payload code was a lot simpler than what Bluedog used against power plants and Stuxnet used against that uranium enrichment facility at Natanz. This was a one shot op. In this case, it only had to fool the operators briefly, long enough to crank up the pressure to the failure point in a section of pipe."

"I assume you already have a signature that we can deploy to detect and block this malware?"

"It's ready to push out to our industrial customers on the next auto-update cycle."

"Unfortunately, that won't actually help that much. Our

penetration in the gas transmission sector is not terribly good, maybe ten percent of the market."

"Right, and we really need to reach the entire sector. This is a potential national emergency."

"It's also a potential national panic; all information about it needs to be managed."

"Okay, Harry, how's this? Since we have the signature, we could share it with our competitors without fully disclosing what the malware does."

"And they will be asking themselves why the hell we would do that. They have research teams, too; they'll start digging and figure it out as fast as we did. No, I am going to have to take this back to the NTSB and the FBI. It's their call. We can go ahead and quietly push it to our customer base, but let's do it right away instead of waiting for the next update cycle. In the meantime, develop a removal tool to be ready to offer to anyone who finds it. And keep me posted."

"You got it. Where will I find you?"

"Look, I'm beat, and it's late. You seem to have this under control, so I am going to head home. Call me anyway if something comes up."

═

Just past midnight, DB called from The Vault, the isolation facility where his Threat Analysis team carried out research on malicious software. "We went ahead as you suggested and deployed the signature to our entire customer base, just in case. Guess what."

"What?"

"There were no hits. It looks like this malware was a singleton. The infection was precisely targeted. As far as we can tell, the Spanergy Control Center in West Virginia was the victim of a surgical strike tailored for their system."

"But we only know about our segment of the market."

"Well, yes, except there's this guy in Threat Analysis. He was a pen-test whiz, a real star player in constructing penetration tests before he joined us last year. He—what shall we say—did a little research on his own using a pen-testing technique to gather a sample of sites served by our competitors. If a system was open to any of the four zero-day exploits used by the Spanergy worm, his software would sneak in and poke around looking for the new signature. After crawling thousands of installations, it found nothing. Zip."

"Shit. If word gets out that we pulled that research stunt, we are doomed. We're still clawing our way out of the aftermath of the cat.9.kernal debacle."

"Not to worry. This kid virtually lives in The Vault, virtually worships me, and is a complete chauvinist when it comes to Scenaria. We saved his ass and hired him for far more money than he could ever spend on his monkish lifestyle."

"Maybe, so, DB, but these nerdy types who act independently are precisely the ones that worry me the most. I've learned that the hard way." There was a long pause before Harry continued. "What I don't get is why anyone would go through the trouble of devising a sophisticated, targeted attack like this, potentially blowing the cover on four zero-day exploits, for so little effect. I mean, it was just a few feet of pipe and a handful of hill-country trees, from what I understand. You got any guesses, DB? Why would anyone do that?"

"Proof of concept, maybe?"

Chapter Twenty

The hotel's modest breakfast area had already emptied out when Delacroix's cellphone interrupted her morning coffee. The voice on the other end sounded stressed. "Good morning. This is Parsons. I just got a call from Scenaria."

"And?"

"This man Krebber wants me to fly back to DC and meet him. His office is not far from Dulles. He says what they have should only be discussed in person. I'm here in the hanger, so I'm already at the airport. I checked, and there's a United flight at 10:12. I thought you would want to be part of this. Can you make it?"

"We can meet you at the ticket counter in fifteen minutes. You can tell Krebber we should all be at his office about noon." She slipped the phone back in the pocket of her pantsuit. "We need to go, Arkady."

"I heard." He took another bite of a soggy cinnamon roll and washed it down with the last of his coffee. "What about Bergen and Gaudet?"

"They'll have to wait on hold. I don't think either of them is going anyplace. I think we put the fear of God and Big Brother in Leonard Bergen."

"What about that stunt he tried to pull last night, trying to throw us off the trail?"

"So what? We picked him up again near his house, easy. These geeky types are smart but not street smart. If need be, we can ask the local police to keep an eye on them, but I don't think it'll be necessary at this point. Let's just get to the airport. We don't want to miss our flight."

═══

Harry had cleared off the big conference table in his office for the meeting. With the clutter stuffed away into file drawers and credenzas, the room could almost pass again for the office of the head of a major US corporation. After introductions all around, Harry turned the meeting over to DB who did a run through of the analysis and findings from the Threat Analysis Team.

Delacroix frowned just enough to put faint apostrophes between her eyebrows. "I thought we agreed to follow the consultant's suggestion and spread pieces of the code around for analysis?"

"We didn't need to. Our people cracked it like that." DB tried to snap his fingers but failed. "We already deployed a signature of the worm out to our Industrial Shield customers."

"We didn't say you could do that."

Harry swiveled in his chair to face her. "And you didn't say we couldn't. It's standard operating procedure here—and in the industry. As soon as we identify a threat, we devise a way to detect it and neutralize it. We deploy these to our customers as quickly as we can. This is our business. It's no different with any other anti-virus vendor."

"All right, then, I suppose." Delacroix was clearly none too pleased. "So, now we need to look at next steps. This thing is extremely dangerous, and it's still loose."

"We agree that it's dangerous, but it may not be loose in the wild. The code contains a poison pill, a set of self-destruct instructions that causes it to erase itself and all its tracks if it doesn't find what it's looking for. There was similar code in Stuxnet, but this is more refined. We now believe there is only one infected system, and that is at Spanergy."

Tank looked up from the note he was thumb-typing into his smartphone. “What if Spanergy puts that Control Center back online? Could this happen again? Could the malware take out another pipeline?”

“We don’t think so. But we still have more work to do in the analysis of the payload, the part of the worm that actually issues the destructive commands over the SCADA network. That doesn’t matter though, because we already know how to remove the software. Spanergy doesn’t have Industrial Shield installed—that’s our SCADA security solution—but even without installing Industrial Shield, we can deploy our removal tool. We just need permission to access their system in Charleston once more.”

Tank spoke up. “We can use my contacts again. I’m pretty sure they will want to get the local system up and running safely as early as possible.”

Barbara shook her head vehemently. “We are going to have to hold off on that.”

“Why?”

“Chain of evidence. This thing is blowing up. It’s now a criminal investigation.”

“And very soon it’ll be alphabet soup.” Krebber started ticking off with his fingers. ”DHS, US-CERT, FBI, CIA, NSA, DIA—.”

“Defense Intelligence Agency?”

“Yeah. The Pentagon is just down the road a piece, as you know, and they seem to know whatever Homeland Security is involved with, so as soon as US-CERT was alerted on this—”

“What? Who in hell alerted the Cyber Emergency Response Team?” Delacroix spread her hands in dismay.

“Our Threat Analysis team. It’s policy. And both Microsoft and Siemens were alerted regarding the zero-day exploits. We do that as a matter of course.”

Delacroix stood and leaned on the table. "What a bunch of . . . This is the biggest damn fuck up I . . . You have no idea how bad this is. Everybody on the goddamn planet is going to know about this now. If I can't see you all in jail, I will do my best to see that you and your company go down in flames. Come on, Arkady. Let's get out of here. Are you coming, Parsons?"

"No, I still have responsibilities on my investigation. Until I get orders otherwise, I'm going to push ahead to find out as much as I can about what caused that explosion. I have some more questions for these people."

Delacroix's gray eyes drilled into him, but she left without saying more.

Tank watched through the open door as the two FBI agents strode past the receptionist in the outer office and turned down the hall. "Is there some way we can get our consultant in on the discussion?"

"Your consultant?" DB asked.

"Yeah, we brought in a SCADA security expert to advise us. He was the one who recommended we work with you."

"Well, good for him. Who did you get."

"Guy named Lustig."

"You talking about Karl Lustig?"

"Yeah, you know him?"

DB was excited. "We sure do." Krebber looked less enthusiastic but nodded.

"That's great. Could we set up a conference call? He's in Israel, but he might still be reachable at this hour."

"Yeah, we could do that. Our video conferencing room is just down the hall. DB, can you get it set up?"

DB gathered his papers and left the room.

═

As they entered the teleconferencing room, Karl Lustig's face appeared, life-size, on a large-screen monitor at the end of the conference table.

DB waved them into the room. "I just got through. The video's a little pixelated and jumpy because he's on a laptop and using Wi-Fi." He looked toward a camera mounted at the top of the monitor and waved. "Hi, Karl. It's great to see you again. You're looking good."

"And you're looking more than good, DB. Moving up in the world has been good for you."

"Thanks. How's your son, Bini? He was quite the young computer hacker last time I saw him."

"Well, he's not a young hacker anymore. He's all grown up and his hacking days are over—at least I think they are. He's in the IDF, the army. Right now he's in training, but he wants to move into military intelligence and maybe do intelligence work when he finishes his three years."

"That's awesome. Following in your footsteps, huh?"

"Hey, I'm not in intelligence work. I'm just a consultant and technology blogger, remember?"

"Right, and I'm just a database specialist not the CTO of Scenaria."

"Chief Technical Officer? Really? Congratulations! So, what prompts the honor of a video call from the Scenaria CTO?"

DB signaled for Tank to come into the camera view. "I think you already know Tankut Parsons, with the NTSB. And, of course, Harry here." The men nodded to the image on the screen which returned the nod after a short delay.

"Before you begin, DB, if it's about the investigation in West Virginia, I'm afraid I can't help you."

"What?"

"I've been told to stand down."

"What do you mean? Who told you?"

"I'm not permitted to say. I can only tell you that I will not be allowed to work with you. I have orders to stand down."

"I thought you were an independent consultant."

"I am, but that doesn't mean that I can do whatever I please. Look, I wish I could help you, but it's not going to happen, so we probably should end this conversation."

═

In the parking lot, Delacroix slipped her cell phone back into her jacket. "We have a stop at Langley for an interagency briefing before we head back out to clean up the mess in Charleston. Some junior analysts aided by NSA sigint think they have a handle on where the malware originated."

"Sigint? Those damn signals intelligence people have their monitoring fingers in everything. It amazes me that they can ever find anything at all in the terabytes of data they are always gathering."

Chapter Twenty-One

Delacroix and Pohl were already waiting for Greely at the front entrance of the Spanergy Control Center when he arrived, out-of-breath and making a show of hurrying across the parking lot. He tucked his shirt in with one hand as he unlocked the door with his other.

Inside, he flicked several switches in the row beside the entrance, and the buzz of fluorescent lights in need of new ballasts filled the room. "Don't know what the damn hurry is. The computers hain't goin' no place. This could've waited until morning. Or ya could've gotten here during regular hours."

"We just returned from Washington, and then we had to get a judge to issue a warrant. Procedure."

"Yeah, well this hain't Washington damned DC, ma'am. We let people sleep 'round here. 'Less they work the shifts, ya know, like Len and Smitty do . . . . Did."

"We're just here to verify the status of the systems. A truck and crew are coming by in the morning to take actual custody of equipment. You have the list there."

"So, right now, what do ya need me for?"

"We want you to give us full access to all the systems and files and to assist us in finding the information we need."

"Well, I can log you-all in all right; then ya can do your thing, 'cause I aim to get home and get some sleep."

"Mr. Greely, we'll need you to stay here, if you don't mind."

"I do mind, but I'm gettin' the idea that I hain't got a lotta choice in the matter. So let me log you in so you can get at it."

He sat down in a posture chair and reached for the nearest keyboard.

"Hold on there, Mr. Greely. As I said, we need to follow procedure. We can't let you actually touch the system. Just tell us the credentials needed for complete administrative-level access: ID and passphrase."

"Now I hain't s'pose to do that. That's highly confidential."

"This has all been cleared. Didn't your superiors tell you? You are required to cooperate with us."

Greely's mouth opened and the corners turned down. "Guess ya gotta do what ya gotta do. Okay, sit there. Start with a three-finger salute to get the login screen." Arkady sat down, pressed and held Ctrl-Alt-Delete, and waited for the prompt. "Now type ADMIN and MERCAPTAN, all caps."

"You use ADMIN as the ID for root access? Not terribly secure."

Greely shrugged. "It's what the new system was set for when they installed it. I mean, it's not like this is some damn kiosk in a shoppin' mall. The building and this room are alarmed and guarded."

"Guarded?" Barbara made a 360-degree scan. "Really?"

"Well, yeah. Reid Security people patrol here, make regular checks, monitor the alarms and locks—all that stuff. 'Bout every hour or so."

"Sounds real secure, Mr. Greely, real secure." Her sarcasm did not seem to penetrate. "Go ahead and login, Arkady."

Arkady typed the credentials and watched. A confirmation screen with the Spanergy logo popped up. He waited for his next instructions.

"Let's go directly to the log files for the morning of the incident. How do we do that, Mr. Greely?"

Greely walked them through getting into the data logger archives and pulling up the right file. Barbara watched as

Arkady paged through the file to get to the end of the shift. Suddenly he stopped and stared at the screen. "This file is incomplete. It ends abruptly about ten minutes before the explosion. The rest of the data is gone."

"What do you mean it's gone?"

"Just that, the file must be corrupted or something. It just ends."

Greely gestured for calm. "I don't rightly know what happened, but there is automatic backups made of everything. We can pull up the backup copy." He reached for the keyboard, then stopped himself. "Be a damn-sight faster if ya just lemme do it myself, but okay, we'll do it your way." He described the rather clumsy process of using a completely separate system to access the backup copy.

After pulling up the file, Arkady jumped directly to the end. "It's the same story here, Barbara. The data's been deleted."

"What in blue bloody blazes is going on?" Barbara Delacroix's voice shot up in decibels and went from alto to soprano. "What do you mean, the data's been deleted?"

Arkady replied quietly. "Just that. The entries covering the tail end of the shift have been erased."

"Then we unerase them, damn it. We'll get a data forensics team working on the disk drives. We . . . What the hell is that?" She pointed to a number in the status line at the bottom of the screen.

Greely snorted. "Like it says, ma'am, that's the number of users logged in on the system."

"I can read, Mr. Greely. But why in hell does it show two? How can anyone else be logged in?"

═══

DB had never broken himself of his tendency to get so completely caught up in work as to lose all track of time. Aside from the cleaning staff and the overnight analytical crew down in the shielded underground Vault, DB was the only one left in the building. It had taken him all afternoon to get approval from the Spanergy corporate headquarters in South Carolina to study the payload of the malicious software that was now being dubbed PipeSmoke among his people. The negotiations had stretched to the point that DB ended up promising Spanergy a free one-year corporate-wide license for Scenaria's Industrial Shield product.

He was puzzled, and when DB was puzzled, he probed deeper. Karl's sudden withdrawal troubled him. It seemed obvious that Karl's wording of his precipitous separation had been carefully chosen. A consultant doesn't stand down; a consultant fires a client or gets fired. A military officer might stand down. And Karl said he had been ordered. This also had a martial ring to it. At the time, DB had said nothing, but it was beginning to seem like Karl's old contacts in Israeli intelligence might be somehow interested in the PipeSmoke virus. Why was Israel interested in a cyber attack on US gas transmission? If he couldn't get answers from Karl, perhaps he could get answers from the virus code itself.

DB had been about to siphon off a fresh copy of a piece of PipeSmoke from an engineering workstation at Spanergy when he got an error message: "Invalid path or incorrect file name." He opened a directory again to check the path and the spelling of the file name. The file was gone. He tabbed to another window displaying a directory where he had found another piece of the malicious code. According to that directory, the other file was still there. He took a screenshot of the directory and saved it before refreshing the window. The file did not appear in the refreshed list. He spent the next hour searching the system, looking for pieces of the PipeSmoke software or its data files. All the widely scattered pieces were gone. He finished by running a remote scan of the entire

Spanergy system for the signatures of PipeSmoke. The scan reported: “No Infections Found.”

Chapter Twenty-Two

Len's cellphone buzzed when he picked it up from the dresser to slip it into his pocket; a voicemail that he had missed was waiting. He swiped the phone and tapped on the message icon. "This is Doctor Johnson at Cabell Huntington Hospital. Your friend in the BICU is awake and has been asking for you. You might drop in when you're in the neighborhood."

"The only way I'm going to be in the neighborhood is if I drive all the way from Charleston, Doctor." Len knew it was pointless talking to the voicemail message, but it gave him satisfaction, like snarling at Windows whenever his laptop gave him a Blue Screen of Death. He deleted the message and started debating with himself about whether to go or not. In the end, he figured that if Smitty was asking for him, he probably should drive over and find out what it was about. After all, it was not like he had a job to go to.

At the Burn Unit, the doctor started talking the moment Len stepped off the elevator. "I'm sorry, but your timing is bad. You should have come earlier."

"Is he awake?"

"In and out. He just came from surgery and he's still fairly groggy."

"And he's been asking for me?"

"Yes, that and talking in his sleep. Mostly gibberish about wind and dragons and long fangs—nonsense. But he does call your name, keeps saying 'tell Len' or just your name."

"He talks when he's sedated? I thought knocked out was knocked out."

"Yeah, it's not common, but with these new meds we're using it does happen. Do you want to see him? Because of the risk of nosocomial infection, we'll have you wear a mask. And don't touch him or the bed."

Len ignored the medical jargon but made a mental note to consult Google later. "Sure, I'll see him."

═

The man in the bed was without eyebrows, and his head was wrapped in bandages that covered part of his face and one ear. His chest, open to the air, was a carpet of raspberry-red bubbles.

"Smitty? You awake? It's Len."

Smitty opened one eye and blinked. He had no lashes. "Lo . . ."

"That's okay. You don't need to try and talk. I just wanted you to know I was here. Been worried about you." He looked over his shoulder out through the glass wall of the room. "This pipeline thing has exploded, if you know what I mean."

"I . . ."

"Yeah, so." He lowered his voice and leaned closer to the bed. "It was an attack, Smitty. Malicious software. Man-in-the-middle."

Smitty licked his lips. "I know. Dragon." His voice was a whispered rasp.

"Yeah, the nurse says you've been having nightmares, talking in your sleep about dragons."

Smitty turned his head away slowly then back, then away and back."

"No? Not nightmares?"

Smitty nodded, a tiny nod that clearly hurt and took effort. He took a breath and licked his lips. "Long." He strained to get the word out. “F . . . F . . . ng . . . F . . . ng.”

“What? Long fangs? The nurse said you went on about that.”

Smitty shook his head slowly again. “Code. In code.”

“It’s in code? No? In the code? Yes? Okay, long fangs in the code. Yeah, I guess that’s one way of putting it. You always did have a poetic way about you.”

Smitty turned away in frustration. As Len waited for a response, his friend drifted off into sleep again.

═══

The boring drive on the long straightaways of the Interstate back to Charleston demanded little. Len kept thinking back to Smitty’s words and what the nurse had said. Whatever it all meant, it was important to Smitty. Long fangs, dragons, wind, code—in code or in the code. Len no longer had access to the Spanergy system, but he had downloaded copies of the data and much of the associated code. He was thinking it might be worth taking a second look when he got home.

Impatient, he was speeding as he approached his house. Suddenly alert, he braked sharply as he rounded the last curve. A half-mile ahead there was a blue-and-white parked in his driveway behind a car that Len recognized. His two favorite FBI agents were standing by the patrol car, facing the other way, chatting with its occupant. Len hit the brakes and turned a block early onto Chestnut Drive, then pulled over to wait. A lime green VW Beetle turned onto Chestnut and drove past, but no police car suddenly made the turn.

Len pulled out and drove down Chestnut to the first right, then took another right hoping it would bring him back to the main road. He mentally plotted a round-about route to Kat’s place.

═══

Kat greeted him with a hug and hurried him into her house. As she made coffee, he told her about the weird conversation with Smitty.

"What's it all about?" she asked.

"You know as much as I do, but if we could get to my laptop, we could go through the code. Maybe some of this will make sense in terms of the code."

"Why don't we just swing over to your place and grab your laptop?"

"Because the FBI and the police were waiting for me when I returned from Huntington. Even if they've gone, I'm sure they have the place under surveillance."

"Then they are probably watching me, too." She craned her neck to look out the front window.

"What next, then?"

"Maybe we can go to Tank."

"The NTSB guy."

"Yeah. Something tells me that he might help. And if the FBI really is after you . . . us . . . they would hardly expect us to go running right into his arms."

The metaphor bothered Len, but he nodded agreement. "All right then, let's go out to the airport again and see the man."

Tank seemed happy to see Kat, less happy when he saw Len behind her, especially after Kat explained the situation. "For some reason, the FBI is after Len here," she said.

"For some reason, that's for sure." Tank's voice overflowed with sarcasm.

"What's that supposed to mean?"

"I would imagine it's about the disappearing files."

"What files?"

"The data files covering the time of the Sadler Creek incident and the code for what the security people are now calling the PipeSmoke virus. I got a call from Agent Delacroix. When they checked the Spanergy computers last night, the relevant data was missing from the log files and the malicious software had been scrubbed from the system. At first they thought this anti-virus company they've been working with might have cleaned the system, but those folks were as surprised as she was. Now Len is the obvious suspect. All traces have vanished from the Spanergy system and, apparently, no other systems were infected. Looks like tampering, destruction of evidence, at least to them."

"And what do you think, Tank. Do you think we did it?"

"Well, I think you're innocent, Kat. I now am pretty certain you didn't cause the Sadler Creek explosion. And you did come to us with the evidence of the software failure. I don't know about him."

She gave Tank a stern look. "*We* came in with the evidence, Len and I did."

Tank seemed hesitant to extend the benefit of doubt to Len. Len reached out and put an arm around Kat's shoulder. Tank stiffened. Len broadened his smile. "You see what's going on here, Kat?"

"No, I don't. We have a serious threat to deal with, a threat to Spanergy, to the state, maybe to the whole damn country. We've been handed a clue by your friend Smitty. Now we have a mystery to solve, and you two seem to be playing schoolboy games with each other. Tank, we helped you. Are you going to help us?"

Tank scratched at the short hairs at the back of his neck. "Yes. I'm going to help you. We'll work together, at least until the FBI puts out a formal bulletin on you two, which I don't think they are likely to do, given how much they seem to want to keep a lid on things. But if they do, I can't shield you. Understood?"

"Understood."

"Good, then you tell me about what your friend Smitty has said, and I'll tell you about what the anti-virus people found."

They had just finished their mutual update when the rest of Tank's team came rushing into the hanger. Tank seemed surprised to see them all together. "Grant, Evan, Jess, what's up? Why the hurry?"

Jess eyed Len and Kat with undisguised suspicion as he spoke to Tank. "You haven't heard?"

"Heard what? Don't just stand there acting like a damned consultant, get to the point."

"There's been another explosion, also a thirty-inch aerial line, this one crossing a stream in Western Pennsylvania. This time there was damage to an adjacent highway and at least a dozen casualties."

PART THREE
Chapter Twenty-Three

Arkady held up his smartphone so Barbara could see the video. "Take a look at this. We missed the news this morning, but . . ."

"Holy . . . I don't get it. How did they get Sadler Creek on YouTube?"

"Didn't. This is Western Pennsylvania. A motorist shot it with his iPhone, posted it, and now it's gone viral. From the first reports, looks like this could be a carbon copy of Sadler Creek, right down to the time of day. They're still fighting the forest fire."

"I think it's time we drop in on our NTSB pals and see what they have on this. If they are still around, that is."

When they arrived at the hanger, Tank was busy with a cellphone in each hand, one pressed against his chest. "Right, got it. Hold that thought for a moment." He swapped positions of the phones. "I'm still here. Yes, I know, but just hold on a minute. I have visitors."

He looked over at Barbara and Arkady and motioned toward some crates near the door. "Have a seat, I'll be with you in two shakes." As he turned away from them, he put one of the phones to his ear and resumed talking while walking across the now empty hanger. He switched ears and said a few words, then continued with the other phone. The conversations alternated, and one call followed another for several more minutes before there was a lull.

"Sorry about that," he said as he approached the two FBI agents. "As you can tell, we're breaking camp. I assume you know about the new incident."

"We do, but not much. We thought you might be able to fill us in. What do you know?"

"Second wave? Copy cat? This time we do know what we are looking for, so it should be easier, but we're trained not to jump to conclusions. Are you heading up that way, too."

"Don't think so. We still have the messes right here to deal with."

"What's up?"

Barbara hesitated. "Not much. That's the official word. We're working more than one lead but can't say anything more."

"Law enforcement or more spook stuff?" Neither Barbara nor Arkady responded. "Okay, I understand. But if I can help you, do send up a smoke signal."

"We'll do that."

"Good. Right now I have to run back to my motel and take care of a couple of things in town before I fly up to Pittsburgh at the crack of dawn tomorrow—too late to get there tonight. Good luck with whatever you are working on."

"Luck has little to do with it, but thanks anyway."

Tank waited until they were gone before making another call. He was crestfallen when he was transferred to voicemail. "Hi, this is Tank. Sorry I missed you. I have been pulled to work on another investigation. I was hoping to see you before I left town. If you pick up this message before, say, midnight, give me a call. We can grab a late bite to eat or a drink maybe. I have to catch the early bird through Dulles first thing in the morning. I . . . I am sorry I missed you. Hope you get this."

═

Despite having reached the ranks of upper management, DB

spent little time in his office. Most days, when he wasn't hanging out with his Threat Analysis crew down in The Vault or practicing the time-honored techniques that he had garnered from a book on "management by walking around," he could be found beavering away on some technical problem at a borrowed desk on the main floor. He had traded his band merch tee-shirts for a sports coat and tie, but he was still a propeller head through and through.

DB was staring at a screen in a disused cubicle when Sami Huang interrupted him. "Oh, there you are."

The only furniture was a posture chair facing the built-in work surface, and the only equipment was an ancient desktop computer that was still running Windows XP. Sami looked with contempt at the furnishings and equipment but still approached DB with deference. Sami was a recent multilingual recruit drafted from Kaspersky Lab, the Stateside facility of the Russian Internet security giant. Sami specialized in forensic analysis of coding style, was fluent in Russian and Mandarin Chinese as well as English, and wore his straight black hair in a long braid that made DB think of a traditional Chinese Queue from the nineteenth century.

"And there you are yourself, Sami. What's up?"

"I've been poking around some more in the code samples from the pipeline company. It was a pretty sophisticated effort, not the work of some script kiddies. I even have some guesses about one of the authors."

"Yeah?"

"Yeah. I recognized a coding trick that I associate with a notorious hacker who goes by the handle of DigiAxe. Nobody knows exactly who he is, but he hangs out online with a group traced to Tokyo. And I found a text string repeated several places: the name Deming, which supports my guess."

"Deming?"

"Like, W. Edward Deming, I figure. You know, the statistical quality control guy, worked with Japan after the War, big hero there. I'm guessing this is some group of Japanese hackers. I'm now doing searches for certain signature coding tricks."

"That's very interesting, but it also makes no sense. Why would a group of Japanese hackers launch a cyber attack on a US gas pipeline?"

"Do hackers always need a reason? They're like mountain climbers. Because it's there, because it's doable: that's really all some of them need to set them off. Then again, maybe PipeSmoke is a work-for-hire. Could be some Qaeda branch is renting the brainpower they don't own. I don't know. I analyze code, not international politics. Maybe it's Russian or Brazilian cybercriminals behind it. The attack could have been a prelude to extortion or someone just trying to show up Kaspersky. Who knows?"

"Okay. Anything more comes out of this, let me know."

"Oh, one more thing: I thought you might want to involve our Tokyo office."

"I don't think so, Sami. It's just a sales office. All the brainpower is here in Reston. Have you talked with Tom Hishikowa about this? You should. Might have some angles on it if it's really made in Japan."

Chapter Twenty-Four

Len pushed through the scrub at the edge of Kat's backyard and hurried across the lawn. Seeing Kat in her kitchen, he tapped on the back door. She was barefoot and still wearing a lemon-yellow Turkish bathrobe, which she cinched tighter around herself as she let him in.

"You might have called ahead, cowboy, and let me know you were on your way."

"Took the battery out of my cellphone. I emptied my rainy-day fund, got extra cash back at the grocery, and then spent the night in a hunting cabin I know about, off the grid, as they say. Now we need to get our hands on another copy of the malware to figure this out. Your friend has the connection with those anti-virus people; they should have a copy."

"My friend? Do you mean Tank?"

"Whatever. That NTSB guy. Can you call him?"

"Of course, I can. Should I? If they're watching your house and tracking your phone, they're probably tracking my calls, too. Remember, thanks to Snowden, we now know the NSA taps just about everyone and everything."

"It's the FBI after me, not the NSA, as if it makes all that much difference. But you're probably right. Let's pick up a couple of prepaid phone cards just to make it a little harder for them to trace us, at least until we get this software virus business figured out."

"What about your friend, your partner from the Control Center? Maybe he can tell us more than just about dragon fangs."

"Good idea. I should check in with him anyway. The question is, how do we get from here over to Huntington without a bunch of feds and police tailing us?"

"I can probably help with that, if you don't mind riding on the back of my bike and taking a few bumps. We can go the off-road route out of town and do some back roads I know to pick up the Interstate nearer Huntington."

"I'm game."

"Good. Let me get dressed and we'll head out." She grinned at him. "We'll see just how game you are."

Ten minutes later, Kat emerged from the house in her road gear. "Here's a brain bucket that ought to fit you." She tossed a helmet to Len. "Put it on and climb on." She mounted her bike and inserted the key. Len adjusted the spare helmet as he straddled the bike behind her. "You sure you don't want me to drive? I used to ride myself, back in college."

"I'm sure. I'm better, and it's my bike. What's the matter? You think there's something wrong with having the chick in charge and the dude on the bitch pad?"

"Well, you don't see it very often."

"So what? Are you ready? Hold on." He tightened his arms around her waist and pressed into her. "Not what I meant, cowboy. Keep your hands on the tank." She twisted the throttle and leaned into the acceleration with Len pressed against her back.

"I could get used to riding to work this way."

"Just keep those hands low, cowboy."

The ride took over an hour and they arrived lightly frosted with road dust. "Fun, huh? Good thing it's been dry," she said, as she brushed the worst of the dust from her legs.

"I haven't been on a bike in a coon's age. That was some ride. You really know how to stitch a line with this thing."

"Thanks." She slipped off her gloves, stowed the helmets, and gave Len a broad smile. "Shall we go see your friend?"

═

The charge nurse on the burn unit shook her head. "I'm sorry. Mr. Jackson's been discharged."

Len looked skeptical. "I thought he was in, like, critical condition or something. How could he be discharged so soon?"

"I can't say. If you want to—"

"Can I help you?" It was the uni-brow Asian-American doctor from Len's last visit. "Oh, it's you again. Mr. Bergen, right?"

"Right. Can you tell me what's this about Smitty getting discharged?"

"Well, Mr. Jackson was transferred to the VA hospital up in Clarksburg yesterday."

"Really? I thought . . ."

"He needed extended care and rehab that the Johnson Center can better provide. We're an intensive care unit. Our work is done."

Len stared at her but the doctor made no move to add anything. After a few more seconds, she picked up a chart from the nurses' station and turned away.

In the elevator on their way out, Kat looked at her watch. "I'm already late for work. I need to call in sick at the garage. Should I just call them or do we switch phones?"

"Let's buy those prepaid cards first, then we'll figure our next move."

"I think our next move is to see Tank."

"So, back to Charleston. Seems like your bike has become a shuttle bus."

"Not Charleston. He left me a message before he left town.

He's up in Pittsburgh."

Len scrunched his face in concentration. "Okay, this might work. If I remember right, Clarksburg is right on the way to Pittsburgh. You ready for a road trip?"

"You're talking, what, 300 miles? I should've known you were trouble when I first saw you, cowboy."

"Ditto. Except I knew right from the get-go that you were trouble with a capital *t*." He dodged the fist that was aimed at his shoulder.

On the way out of town, they pulled into a drugstore and paid cash for new SIM cards for their phones. After switching cards, Kat put through a call to Tank's cell phone. "How would you like a visitor from West Virginia?"

"Kat, is that you? You really are thinking of coming up here?" Excitement rippled through his voice.

"Sure, I am; it's only a few hundred miles to Pittsburgh. It's pipeline business. Can't say more over the phone."

"Oh." The single syllable response dripped with disappointment. "I'm not in Pittsburgh. We set up shop in Johnstown, on the University of Pittsburgh campus here, closer to the site of the explosion."

"Okay, I think we can be there around dinner time. I'll ping you."

"We?"

"The cowboy's with me. I'll explain when we get there. Cheers."

"Yeah, cheers."

They took a different but equally circuitous route back to Kat's place for her to pick up some spare clothes and toiletries. It took her only a few minutes to gather what she needed and stuff it into the panniers on the motorcycle. "What about you, cowboy, need anything?"

"I got my toothbrush and clean socks in my backpack. A cowhand on the trail doesn't need much more."

"And I'm supposed to let you ride behind me after a remark like that?"

"You want to see what I got? Okay." He unzipped the outer pocket of his pack. "Got my Axe spray, my shampoo, toothpaste here. Plus a clean shirt and under—"

"Okay, no need to supply a detailed inventory, cowboy. You ready for a real road trip?"

"As long as you stay on the road, a trip with you sounds fun."

"Then hang on!"

Len hung on as she whipped around to the back of the house and headed out on a rabbit run through the woods.

Chapter Twenty-Five

Once on the Interstate headed north, Kat watched her speed and kept checking her mirrors. At midday, they took the exit for Clarksburg and found their way to the sprawling yellow-brick building of the Louis A. Johnson VA Medical Center. The admissions desk had no information for them, but the grizzled clerk agreed to check again when Len explained that he and Smitty Jackson had served together in the army. It was like a secret handshake to the clerk. "I was a medic in Nam. Where did you serve?"

"Iraq, Quartermaster's Corps. Spent two tours trucking supplies and dodging potholes and IEDs."

"Really? Which outfit?"

"Look, I'm not big on revisiting that chapter of my life. Besides, we don't have a lot of time on our lunch hour. I'd like to spend as much of it as I can with my buddy."

"Sure, thing. I understand. What was your buddy's name again?" They tried every variant of Smitty's name they could think of, but the queries all came up blank.

"I am sorry, but it doesn't look like your buddy is here. Too bad." The man gave them a well-practiced look of sympathy.

"Can you check about recent transfers from the Huntington Burn Unit?"

"I don't have to check that one. I can tell you, we haven't had any transfers from Huntington this week. I would know."

Len looked skyward as if for inspiration. "Is there anyone else we could talk with?"

"You can make an appointment to meet with our Interim Associate Director. She might be able to see you later this week."

"We just rode 175 miles to get here to check on my buddy. He was burned real bad."

"I am sorry, but there is nothing else I can tell you. Your buddy is not here."

═

Crossing the parking lot, Kat strode on ahead. "Come on, cowboy, let's go. We still have a long ride ahead, and I could use some lunch before we hit the road." She handed Len his helmet. "Did you believe the clerk?"

"Why shouldn't I?"

"Hey, it's your government, cowboy, not mine. I'm Canadian, remember. Doesn't this sound like the All-American run-around to you? First your friend has an accident, then he's suddenly transferred from the hospital, then he's not at the hospital where they say he is. Or maybe he's here but they won't let us know."

"Maybe, but I don't know what to do next. I don't know who to call."

"We'll think of something. Were you really in Iraq with your friend?"

"Naw, I made that up, which is why I dropped the conversation. But Smitty was there, in the Quartermaster's Corps, so at least that part would check out."

"Quick thinking."

"Yeah, us cowboys get to be fast on our feet. Comes from all that line dancing."

"Speaking of lines and fast, let's find someplace to get in line for some fast food before I faint from hunger."

Kat nixed the Dairy Queen they passed on the road back up from the VA hospital but decided that Vito's Pizza just off the highway on a cobblestone street to the right looked to be worth a try. It turned out to be a local hot spot, with a long wait for service. Over slices of olive-peppered Sicilian pizza that Kat pronounced were perfect, Len asked her how a Canadian ended up in the heart of Appalachia.

"We Acadians are everywhere. Who do you think the Cajuns down in Louisiana are? It's the diaspora. We're like the Jews."

"Not like the Jews."

"Oh, yes, like the Jews. The Acadians were French-speaking Catholics surrounded by Anglophone protestants: persecuted, kicked out of our homeland, our lands taken. Historically, we were this highly successful religious minority keeping our traditions and language alive in our own strong, tightknit communities. Any of this sound familiar? In Nova Scotia, we had developed systems of self-draining dikes that allowed us to turn marshland into some of the richest farmland in the world. The British coveted what we had, so they just deported us and confiscated our property in *le Grand Dérangement*, the expulsion, in the mid-eighteenth century. A little like the Jews being expelled from Spain, then Portugal. A third of our people died as a result, but, like your people, we survived and returned."

"I had no idea. So, you're a farm girl?"

"Genealogically speaking, but I grew up in Halifax and went to university there. Still, I think I've always been drawn to the countryside. My dream would be to someday return, buy a vineyard somewhere in the Annapolis Valley, not too far from Wolfville and Acadia University, and grow grapes and kids."

"Really?" He dabbed at the corner of his mouth with a paper napkin.

"Really."

"I wouldn't have guessed. So you're Catholic?"

"Raised that way, anyway." She took another bite of her

pizza. "Mmm, so good, huh? Where was I? Oh yeah, Catholic. But I haven't been to mass since moving down here. It's a little bit like my winery dream. I want to believe there's something more, that there's life after monitoring pipelines. I'm probably more catholic with a little *c* than Roman Catholic, a Universalist at heart. Whatever there is afterwards, whether it's heaven or the void, I think we all share the same ultimate fate."

"Only heaven or nothing? No hell?"

"People might reap their just rewards, but eternal hellfire for one mortal sin? I know that's the dogma, but who would call that just? Not me, not any god I would buy into, and I told our priest exactly that when I was sixteen after concluding that the Pope didn't know what he was talking about."

"Gutsy. You were pushy even as a teenager. What did your priest say?"

"He said I was grievously in error and risking my immortal soul by entertaining such blasphemy. I told him it was my soul and my life and walked out of the church." She reached for another slice of pizza. "Your turn now. You're Jewish, right? So what does that mean to you?"

"Same. I grew up in a Modern Orthodox enclave in New Jersey, another misunderstood and often maligned bunch. I toed the line—mostly—until after my bar mitzvah, but my parents, for whom the neighborhood was more a real estate decision than a religious one, were none too observant in the first place. Except when it came to riding herd on me, that is. So when I stopped going to temple and no longer muttered blessings in Hebrew, their disappointment was perfunctory and passing. Unlike you, I didn't feel I had to confront anyone else with my disillusionment."

"That's where you were; where are you now?"

"In Clarksburg, West Virginia, savoring a pizza that mixes meat and dairy—strictly forbidden under the rules of *kashrut*.

I'm also enjoying getting to know maybe the brightest and toughest shiksa I have ever bumped into and wondering whether it's entirely coincidence that we met."

"If you think I'm part of some conspiracy—"

"No, no. I meant in the sense of Fate, Fortune. I don't believe we're down here with some unnamed god sitting up there pulling strings, but I have never been able to shake this sense that things do not happen for no reason at all, that life—my life, your life—makes some larger sense."

They looked at each other for a long moment before Kat smiled and spoke. "Brightest? Toughest? Really?"

"Really."

"And shiksa? What's that?"

"That's you. Trouble. A temptation. A non-Jewish woman, technically, but more than that. Let's just say that my mother, of blessed memory, would not have approved of you."

An unsettled silence spread over the space between them. Finally, Kat glanced at her watch. "We really better get a move on. I'd rather not be on two wheels, after dark, on roads I don't know, with a passenger perched on the back of the bike to add to the challenge."

═

They were paralleling the Pennsylvania border on Interstate 68 in Maryland when Kat caught sight of a car rapidly gaining on them. "Hold on," she yelled as she slowed, left the pavement, and carefully ran the narrow grassy median strip that separated the highway from the long, straight off-ramp of the exit they were passing. She turned south at the end of the exit road and accelerated.

Chapter Twenty-Six

Len shouted to be heard above the rush of air and the rising whine of the engine. "Where are we going?"

"Sign back there said we're headed for Swanton. Guess that's somewhere in Maryland."

"Aren't we going the wrong way, then?"

"Only until we shake that heat behind us." She sped up as the road curved gently to the right, then abruptly slowed as it turned left. Just beyond the curve was a break in the guard rail on the right shoulder. Kat braked hard, barely maintaining control of the bike, and slowed enough to make the turn, then gunned the engine again to straighten out onto an unpaved road. Well before the next car passed by, she had pulled into a grove of trees and cut the engine.

"Were you speeding?"

"No, definitely not. We'll know in a minute if they were actually after us." Not fifteen seconds later, a Maryland State Police patrol car whizzed past on the road toward Swanton. "At least they didn't have their flashers on, so we are technically not fugitives from the highway patrol."

"What next?"

"Use your smartphone to figure out where we are and how we can get to Johnstown by an alternate route."

Len fiddled with his phone for a couple of minutes. "This works out. We can continue on this little road back under the Interstate to pick up US 40 to Maryland 699, which eventually gets us up to Johnstown. Costs us an extra twenty minutes, thereabouts."

"Not if I have anything to do about it. Hang on, cowboy, we are going to hammer down."

"Okay, as long as you stay vertical. See, I know the lingo, too."

"You, my friend, are no more a biker than you are a cowboy. Lingo indeed!"

═══

It was after seven when they rolled into Johnstown and rode down Main Street past the famous corner of the old stone City Hall. Len looked up at the high-water marks of the city's multiple floods, the topmost some thirty feet above his head. Opposite a small park farther down the street, Kat found a generous space between two parked cars.

Len staggered off the pillion. "I think I have lost all feeling in my butt, and I don't know if my knees will ever hold me upright again.

"What's the matter, cowboy, a little saddle-sore?"

"No." He arched his back, then bent over and rubbed his knees. "I'm a *lot* saddle-sore." He started pacing back and forth.

"The weather's still good. Let's walk around town a bit to stretch. First, let me try to reach Tank." After seven or eight rings, she was forwarded to his voicemail. She left a message, then got a call back within seconds of hanging up.

Tank's voice rang with an echo. "Sorry about that, Kat. My phone was on the other side of the garage. We're inspecting a pipe section for evidence of erosion."

"S'okay."

"Have you eaten? You said you're downtown, near the City Hall, right? There's a Szechuan place a few blocks up the street from where you are that I am told is quite good. I'm over at the Pitt Johnstown campus. I can meet you in about fifteen minutes."

"We can walk up the street and meet you at the restaurant."

"Sure, good. The restaurant will be on your left. Can't miss it. See you there."

═

The service at the restaurant was faster than expected, and they were still working on their spring rolls when blue-and-white bowls of orange-flavored crispy beef, kung pao chicken, and steamed rice filled the table. As Kat spooned spicy beef and rice on her plate, Tank turned to her. "So what is this all about that you ride all the way up here?"

Len answered the question. "We want to get access to computer files, particularly the code that triggered the Sadler Creek explosion. You're working with that antivirus company, and we figured they would have a copy."

"Didn't you already grab the files you needed?"

"Len's computer has been, shall we say, confiscated."

"The police or the FBI?"

"Both, I suppose."

"Are you two fugitives?"

"Not that we know. It's not like I was resisting arrest or anything. We just decided to take a road trip."

"Shit. If you think I'm going to become an accessory . . ."

"We're working on the same problem as you, on the same side."

"I oughta just make a phone call and turn you in, Bergen."

Kat folded her arms. "Fine, you just do that, Tank. You can tell them to pick up both of us, because I drove Len here. If you're going to pull that on Len, then count me with him."

Tank expertly tweezed a piece of chicken with his chopsticks. "I suppose I would not be breaking any laws if I gave you a phone number and a name."

"No, we certainly wouldn't want you to take any unwarranted risks on our behalf." Len curled his lip in well posed disgust.

Tank ignored the dig. "I still don't get why you two came here in person. Why not just call?"

Kat and Len looked at each other as if waiting for permission to speak. "Go ahead, Kat, you tell him."

"No, you. Smitty was your friend. And you're the one who decided we should go off the grid."

Tank laughed. "Off the grid? You called me—twice. And I would bet you bought gas on the way up here. If the feds are seriously after you, they're on their way into town even as we speak."

"We got new SIM cards for the phones, and we paid cash for the gas and lunch."

"That's all amateur stuff that might make you feel better but is hardly effective against the eyes and ears of the clandestine services. Did you make any stops other than for lunch and gas."

"Just the VA hospital in Clarksburg."

This time Tank doubled over with exaggerated laughter. "Just a stop at a government-run facility. And then you call a government employee during an active investigation related to the one that got you into trouble. Oh, you are being so careful. They'll never, ever track you."

Len bristled. "Do you want to talk about the pipeline attacks or do you just want to ridicule us amateurs?"

Tank savored a morsel of crispy beef as if seriously weighing the choices. "All right already, let's talk about the pipeline explosions. Tell me what you got."

They explained about Smitty's sudden disappearance and his confusing talk about long fangs. Tank was reluctant at first, but finally gave them the gist of what Scenaria had worked out about the software used in the attacks.

"Look, I need to get back to the temporary lab we set up at the University. Why don't you come along, and we'll see what we can do to get Scenaria to help you."

Chapter Twenty-Seven

Tank led the way into the garage at the edge of the campus and flipped the switch by the door. With a dull metallic clank, the overhead mercury lights kicked in and brightened slowly, filling the room with harsh, cold light. "I just had an idea. Why don't I call this guy at Scenaria and grease the skids for you. I'm just as invested as you are in clearing up exactly what happened here and at Sadler Creek. The guy works late; he might even be at his desk now. What do you say?"

"Sure, why not. You okay with that, Kat?" She nodded.

"Let's go into my temporary office here; it's a little better than the digs down in Charleston. The Engineering Department here has been very generous." He led them into an alcove with a semi-circle of small offices and opened the door to the second one. "Modest but cozy. And it has a speakerphone. So let me try to call Mr. Botteneau at Scenaria."

DB picked up on the second ring. "Hi, Tank. When I saw the caller ID of the University, I guessed it was you. How is the investigation going?"

"By the book, DB. It's looking like a clone of the attack at Sadler Creek, but don't quote me on that. Nothing is ready for release yet."

"Do you have any code samples from their control system yet?"

"I don't do code; one of my guys is working on it. This section of pipeline belongs to another company that is being just a tad less cooperative than Spanergy. They are strangely protective, but I suspect they'll come around when the marshals serve them with a warrant. And speaking of code samples, that is what we are calling about."

"We?"

"Yeah, I have two Spanergy people with me here on speakerphone. DB say hi to Kat Gaudet and Leonard Bergen."

"It's just Len, not Leonard. Hi, DB."

"Hi, Len. Hi, Kat. Actually, I know about you two from my online research. You were both there at the beginning, right?"

"Right. Smitty Jackson, my supervisor, and I were on duty at the time of the explosion. Kat was actually at the site. Smitty was the one who put me onto taking another look into the data logs. Then he was in an accident, got burned pretty bad. He told me something about the code, but it's pretty weird. We thought maybe if we could look through the code again, we might figure out what the heck he was talking about."

"What did he say?"

"Something about long fangs. Does that mean anything to you? You're the cyber-security expert. Is that some kind of insider cyber slang?"

"Not that I've ever heard of. You want me to take a look at the code for you?"

"Yeah, sure."

"Okay, give me a minute here. I'm up at my desk and the copies of the malware and data files are down in The Vault. We don't allow any regular network connections into or out of The Vault for obvious reasons. Quarantine, you know. I'll put you on hold and pick up when I get down there. Just hang on a minute."

It was just over a minute when DB, a little winded, was back on the line. "Okay, I'm here, I'm opening a folder with quiescent copies of everything we pulled from Spanergy. Now what was it that we are looking for?"

"Long fangs. I know it sounds weird."

"Okay, let's start with the simplest thing, a text search. I'm typing 'long fang' into an incremental search box and . . ."

"Yes?"

"I already got something; hadn't even finished typing. It's in a header record left by a compiler. It's a path name for some of the source code for this block of binary. I'll read the whole path to you:

/PROJ17S/LONG/MYBLOX/LONG/FENG/CLOK/WIPER/

"That's it. F-E-N-G, long feng, not long fang. Hmm." DB hummed a few bars of Leroy Anderson's "Syncopated Clock" before continuing. "Long feng. Makes me think of that flaky West Coast nonsense. What's it called? Feng shui? Could it be this was some group of California hackers doing a little too much funny tobacco?"

Len tapped his lip as he concentrated. "Hang on there. Feng shui. I remember Smitty telling me about it once. It's some sort of a Chinese mystical philosophy. Something about wind and water. Maybe long feng is also Chinese. Smitty studied Mandarin. He would probably have known what it means. Shame he's not here when we need—"

"But," DB interrupted, "Sami Huang, who works in The Vault, might know. Let me call him at home."

"It's after nine, we shouldn't bother him."

"Oh, it's okay. Everyone who works on the Threat Analysis team knows they are always on call. Besides, Sami loves knowing and figuring out stuff. I'm going to put you on hold again." The speakerphone switched to a music loop that repeated several times before DB was back on the line. "Okay, here's what Sami says, and this is good. In Chinese, long means dragon and feng means wind, so dragon wind. Together, long feng, they can also mean phoenix. Get it? Dragon wind? Dragons breathe—"

Tank supplied the answer. "Fire. And the phoenix is consumed by fire but rises from its own ashes. So it makes sense for malware that explodes a pipeline. I—"

Len cut him off. "And what is natural gas, really? Dragon wind. Okay, so we know what the words mean, but what do we make of all this?"

"Sami has some guesses; he's coming to the office to check them out."

"Tomorrow?"

"No, tonight. He's on his way. Us geeks are at our happiest working through the night."

"Len's like that, too," Kat said, "prefers to work the hoot-owl shift. Me, I'd rather rise with the sun and retire with the sun."

DB chortled. "Sounds like you two would make a great team—twenty-four hour coverage built in."

"Yeah, that might work." She gave Len an elbow to the ribs. "That way we'd never have to actually see each other."

"Well, I'm going to let you two work it out. I need to start digging with Sami on this Chinese angle. Can you guys sit tight for a while? From what Sami has in mind, we might need a day or so to follow up.

Kat and Len looked at each other. "I guess." Kat spoke hesitantly. "We'll have to find someplace to stay."

"All right. Thanks for calling, Tank. Good to meet you, Len and Kat, even if it's just by voice. We'll talk again tomorrow. Let's say same time, same place, unless something comes up."

Chapter Twenty-Eight

The city was awakening. Dangerously high pollution already blanketed the area despite the coastal breezes that had historically cleansed the port. Hazy sunlight, browned by the low-hanging atmospheric grunge, filtered through an unwashed window, backlighting the nearly bald man seated behind a large desk. Like a teak aircraft carrier that filled half the modest office, the desk was arrayed with carved figurines and cast models of tanks and planes, mementos and small gifts collected over an extended but undistinguished career. Over the years, Deming had not advanced as he had planned, nor had he been recognized as he believed he deserved. His Mongolian mother had always pushed him toward success, to rise above others, but he blamed his mixed parentage for the discrimination he had experienced. He was determined that, with the new endeavor he had started on his own initiative, this would now change.

Deming was not happy. It showed not in the practiced passivity of his face but in the rigidity of his posture and the quiet tension of his voice. "Again you are here. You will recall that you were told to develop a proof-of-concept program; you were not told to deploy it. Still, you did. I may value initiative on this team, but not recklessness. We are not sanctioned; we must not display our initiative until the proper time."

Kai, whose thick, dark hair was cropped in a military cut, felt as if his legs might give out at any moment. "Yes, sir. But, as we said, without proof, sir, there is only concept. One cannot debug code without testing it."

"Testing code is one thing, but what you did was another matter altogether." He turned the display in the corner of his desk to face the pair standing at attention and tapped on a video downloaded from a foreign news site. "This was your concept, your proof, in action. This does not look like a computer program."

Kai stole a glance toward the young woman beside him, desperate for support. "We did that, yes, together. To prove the concept."

Lee straightened her back. "I was following orders," she said. Sweat was forming at the nape of her neck beneath coarse, black hair that was almost as short as Kai's. She was the taller of the two, and the smarter, but she had been conditioned since babyhood to be defensive and self-effacing.

"Following orders? Were you, now?" Deming knew that she had a tendency to spice her inbred deference with impulsiveness. He steepled his hands and placed them carefully on the desk, pointed toward them like some kind of weapon. "And what orders said you should set this thing loose in the wild? Tell me that?"

"None, sir. No orders. We . . . we thought you would be pleased to know that this was real, that it was truly possible. It was only a most modest and controlled demonstration."

"I asked you to build it, not to launch it. Not yet."

"But," Kai protested, "we thought, who will believe us if we only make claims or threats. Anyone can brag that their code will do this or do that. We thought, we have the proof. We are the best. We can now show those who call themselves the A-team—"

Deming slapped both hands flat on his desk and leaned forward. "They do not call themselves that."

"But the article in *Forbes* said—"

"You read *Forbes*?"

"We have been working on attacks against news websites using the new database hack. *Forbes* was a target."

"Does the creation of these Web Wasps, as your programming compatriots refer to them, do they require you to read the content on the website?"

"No, it does not, sir. Still, on the websites we must study the HTML—the markup code and the content are connected. They—"

"Focus. Discipline. These are what you need. In any case, your real work, is not designing attacks on news sites, most certainly not reading *Forbes*. Your real work is what you do for me, part of our private strategy to move beyond harassment to engagement. Stealing secrets from technology companies and hectoring the Western media will accomplish little beyond irritation—and a warning to our adversaries. It is time we show that it is possible to put the terabytes of data our Unit has pilfered over the years to some real purpose with real impact. We are capable of so much more than the Unit has yet been asked to do."

He pulled his shoulders back an extra centimeter. "We are the true elite, not the sailors in our navy, not the troops who play games with assault rifles. We are the future of military superiority. With your skills and perseverance guided by my vision, our project will become the noble demonstration of that, and we will lead the way into a new era for our nation." He rotated the display again and began to study the papers on his desk as if they might help him decide what to do next.

The two stood at attention before him, silent through his pompous speech, waiting to be dismissed. But Deming's eyes remained fixed on the papers, which he paged through slowly before putting his chop on the last page. He slid them to the side, placed a carved ivory elephant on top, and stood. He did not look at them, but turned to face the dirt-fogged window behind him. “What you did was bad enough; now, this is treason.” He bowed his head. “If I were to report you, you would be shot.” It was an empty threat, for he knew he could not expose them without exposing himself.

“But you were the one who—”

“I was the one? The one who what? I did nothing except to ferret you out and expose your dangerous, treasonous actions, your acts of purest egoism.”

“But—”

“Silence. I am not finished. I was describing a scenario, a scenario that will unfold if you do not bring this thing under control in time. Although this operation is not official, it has been a long time in the planning and execution, a very long time. But you had to push forward the hands of the clock.”

“But sir, we have already remedied the situation, the code has been deactivated.”

“Deactivated? If that is so, what is this?” He slapped a folded printout of a wire service report against his desk with a smug smile that betrayed he had been waiting for the moment.

Lee appeared to be on the edge of panic. “What are you talking about?”

“The second attack, you idiot. There should not have been a first attack. You already knew that. And then you pulled this.”

“I don’t understand, sir. There was no second attack. We used the backdoor we had installed in the computers to deactivate the code and wipe all traces.”

“If there was no second attack, then tell me what the hell this report is about.”

“I don’t know, sir. I haven’t seen any reports of—”

“Read this. And tell me what happened. It better make sense and it better be good, unless you like the thought of a new career—shorter, perhaps, and a lot dirtier."

Kai accepted the printout and started to read. As he skimmed through it, the color drained from his face. "It has escaped into the wild, sir. There must have been some interaction between Lee's updates and the modified commands I posted to the C&C servers. I think . . . yes, I think I know how it could have happened. It should have been obvious that—"

"Yes, it should have been obvious. Why is it so obvious now and not before? Why did you not work together so there would not be 'some interaction' between your code and her code?" Deming stood suddenly. "Now I must decide what to do next, and there is probably not really time for you to train replacements. I will have to trust you for now, which is madness, and I am not mad. I will have to watch you—myself, if necessary. The stakes are too high."

"I will take care of it, sir. We will, sir."

"When is that? When will you have this thing you have unleashed under control again?"

"Well, it might—"

"Now!" He sliced the air with his index finger. "Do you understand? Now! That is the correct response to my question, the only correct answer. I ask you once again, when will you have it under control?"

"Immediately, sir!"

He turned away again and continued to speak to the tall towers of the city outside the window, barely visible through the dense smog. "This time work together. And listen to your stammering supervisor who always counsels you to avoid error in the first place rather than creating defects that you must later find and correct. You have been trained as software engineers. It is time you draw on that training and act like engineers. Just because what we are doing is unofficial is no excuse for being unprofessional."

He faced them with an expression that was enough to make the two programmers tremble. "Go! It is time for you to return to your work. Continue to play the games you must play, but fix the proof-of-concept. And do not get caught. I have restrained my hand with you only because my own actions might draw more attention to us. Right now, it is our enemies abroad who you may have alerted. We do not want to wave a banner in the faces of those here at home." He was thinking of the afternoon briefing with his own commanding officer, but said nothing more of it.

"Remember that there are others who would sacrifice a hand for the honor of working on such a project." He dismissed them by turning again toward the window. "Some would kill for the honor." He could hear the soft shuffle of their steps as they backed toward the door. Before they closed it behind them, he added an amendment. "I am not finished with you, Kai."

Lee took her place in the long row of programmers seated at the series of carrels. She carefully positioned her keyboard, logged back in, and started typing. She would set things right, then Kai and their leader and the others, the men in their cadre, would respect her. She would create updated code for when next the remote program was scheduled to check into the Command and Control computers. She had several hours to prepare her modifications and deliver them to the C&C server. She would be ready.

Lee rested her chin in her hand as she scanned through the source code looking for the correct hook onto which to attach the improvements.

"Is . . . is there a p-problem?" Her supervisor leaned over from the other side of the string of workstations and peered down at Lee's monitor screen, squinting as he attempted to read it upside down.

"No, sir. I am still working on the database attack for news websites."

"B-be sure that you are working on Advanced Persistent Threats." He laughed. "That is what their security community calls our work: APTs. Remember: advanced, persistent. And threats, not merely p-persistent d-daydreaming."

"No, sir. I am reviewing my code, looking for errors."

"You would not have to look for m-m-mistakes if you did not m-make them in the first place."

The man known behind his back as the Stuttering Strutter straightened up. He signaled for Lee to carry on before folding his hands behind his back and resuming his slow march up and down the aisle between the rows of tables and terminals.

═

Lee shifted gears and threaded her bicycle between the closely packed cars to catch up with Kai. He was on his way back to the apartment complex where most members of the Unit were housed. "Your talk this morning," she said as she pulled alongside, "it went well?" The air quality was still poor after an afternoon rain shower, and even this short ride made her short of breath.

"It went. Our Leader now feels trapped between our actions and his superiors. Our hand has been tipped, our cards showing to those across the table. It is no longer possible to bluff, but perhaps he can force their hand. It is now up to us to slip our cards back into the deck unnoticed. I have already—"

"I have already taken care—

"—taken care of it."

"The modifications have been uploaded to the C&C server." They finished the final words together. As they eyed each other, they nearly ran into a woman crossing the road, a basket of produce in one arm, and a well-wrapped infant in the other. She cursed after them as they narrowly missed colliding with each other.

"Your initiative, Lee, is what embarrassed us in the first place. Cooperation and coordination are our true strength, not the coding calisthenics of a single player out to prove something. I just hope we have not brought more shame upon ourselves and our Leader. In the morning, you will arrive early to review the modifications and ensure that there is no conflict."

He stood and pedaled hard to pull away from her. Her face reddened with the rebuke and the stinging dismissal. She wondered whether he would, as usual, tap on her door after dinner.

Chapter Twenty-Nine

Sami swiped his card on the badge reader and swung open the heavy door to The Vault. Beneath plaster, tan paint, and a papering of movie posters—Star Wars, Avatar, Ender's Game, and a few obscure cult classics—the walls of the windowless room were lined with metal to prevent stray signals entering or leaving. The assortment of computers in the room were isolated from each other and from the company network. A single diskless workstation with all its ports sealed shut gave the room access to the Internet and the company network when that was needed for research.

The Vault was a controlled environment where the dirty detective work of analyzing malicious and capricious software was carried out without fear of a runaway infection. A single telephone connected by armored and shielded cable was the only other link with the outside world. Cellphones, tablets, and wireless devices of any kind were prohibited. Removable media, such as USB sticks or DVDs, were carefully monitored and controlled.

Three members of the company's industrial security team were busy at workstations arrayed along the walls when Sami checked in. DB was at his preferred desk just to the left of the door, scrolling through a block of decompiled code. The code was part of a program that had been retrieved from Spanergy in the obscure binary form understood by computers but had since been converted back into something closer to what humans could read. At least it was readable in principle if the humans were computer programmers and puzzle addicts like DB and his Threat Analysis people.

"Any luck, DB?"

"Some. I was finally able to get access to the malware from the system up in Pennsylvania. Pulled the old voice-of-God routine on the poor night-shift network admin I got on the phone. Threatened him with everything short of bodily harm and promised him the moon. You know, the usual."

"What's the sample look like?"

"I ran comparisons with the code recovered from Spanergy. The most recent time-and-date stamps are different, and this block of code I'm studying now was not even in the Spanergy attack. Whoever is doing this, they keep working on it, modifying the code on the fly."

"What does this block do?"

"I'm still deciphering it, but it seems to pull IP addresses from an encrypted file and to pass them on to a communication module. I'm guessing to contact a C&C server.

"So this thing is connecting to a Command-and-Control system, getting what? Instructions? Updates? Does it pass back local data? Have we cracked the encryption on the file yet?"

"Too many questions. The answer to the last is no: we have not cracked the encryption yet. But the older version from Spanergy has the IP addresses stored in a plaintext table. Maude over there is working on who those addresses belong to and where they are located."

Sami sat down and started to work without saying anything more. DB returned to the code displayed on his screen.

Maude Girard, the only woman on the industrial security team, clopped over in her bright green clogs and handed DB a piece of paper.

"Shanghai?" he asked her.

"Several of the addresses, in a block owned by a Chinese provider in Shanghai. Says a lot."

"Not to me, it doesn't."

Sami grinned over at them. "Maude's right, says a lot. I should have known from the coding style in the blocks I reviewed. Some of the newer stuff is a bit ad hoc, but most of it is old school, very disciplined."

"Hell, I'm old school, Sami. But tell me what this tells you."

"Many of the current generation of Chinese software professionals were trained in classic software engineering techniques by disciples of the old masters—pioneers like Bertrand Meyer, Grady Booch, Ed Yourdon, that crowd. Unlike so many of today's self-taught hackers who are rather loosey-goosey in their approach, these guys are very methodical, almost stilted in their programming."

Maude was grinning and nodding in agreement with such force that it made her bangs flap like a fan. "Unit 61398," she said.

DB did a face-palm. "Of course. Let's see if we can get any independent confirmation. But if that's the who, we are still left with the big why."

═

Tank, who had driven into Pittsburgh to meet with people from PanPenn Energy in the hopes of getting some insight into what might link the two incidents, was surprised to find Thadeus Greely from Spanergy there. "You trying to help out a competitor, Greely? Or are you here to gloat over their misfortune?"

"I'm here because my boss says to be here. Probably same's you. We are having ourselves a consult, we are. This here is—"

"Willem Fassberger, Vice President of Operations here. We talked on the phone earlier." He held out his hand to Tank.

"Oh, right. And I'm Tankut Parsons, NTSB, as you already

know."

"Yes, I already know, and I have been looking forward to meeting with you. I hope I can speak freely."

"If you mean off the record. I'm not exactly a reporter for the *Washington Post*. I'm an investigator with the NTSB. The Board bases its findings on facts and analysis as well as formal interviews with all pertinent parties to an incident. If you have something to add to the record, let me know and I'll get out my phone and fire up the recorder app."

"Quite the contrary. I certainly would not want to attempt to influence your investigations or conclusions. I am just hoping you will be able to take into account the enormous complexity and the far-reaching impacts. We are not dealing with just one company, here, or even two. We are talking about an entire industry, one vital to the US economy."

"Yes, and a vital industry that seems to be under attack."

"We don't know that, Mr. Parsons, now do we? We have a couple of accidents, that's all. The laws of statistics guarantees that sometimes accidents cluster. Random chance can look like a pattern."

"This is a pattern. These are not accidents. They were deliberately caused by a hostile party or parties unknown."

Fassberger feigned surprise. "I haven't seen the final report from the NTSB yet. Has it been issued and nobody told me?"

"It has not been issued, no, but the evidence is becoming persuasive; these were not accidents."

"I am afraid I am not making myself clear here. Whatever your guesses, that simply cannot be the case. On the one hand, even linking these two events in the public mind will have a detrimental impact on the financial health of our two companies and on the economic well-being of the industry. Think about it, Mr. Parsons. What will be the public reaction to wild-eyed speculation that the transmission network of the nation's natural gas industry is under attack, that the next target might be the pipeline that runs past their farm or through their neighborhood. The result—"

"But this is not wild-eyed speculation, sir. Of course, I cannot give you details in advance of the release of my report. Besides, we don't yet know all—"

"You don't yet know. Exactly! And I think your resources may be overstretched on this one. Mind you, I am not questioning your credentials or competence, but, surely, you can't be an expert on everything. You are a metallurgist, if I am not mistaken, and now you seem to be speculating about machine code for industrial control systems, if I am to understand what Mr. Greely here has told me."

"That is precisely why we have a team approach to these investigations. Metallurgy, fluid dynamics, mechanical engineering, industrial engineering—my team covers the gamut."

"I note you do not include computer programming in that list."

"No, but we are collaborating with an FBI team specializing in cybercrime. And we have access to more resources and expertise if we deem it prudent."

"Prudence would dictate erring on the side of caution, even understatement, when it comes to what might rightly be termed exotic scenarios. Believe me, my company stands ready to counter any erroneous, erratic, or irresponsible reports, and I have spoken with counterparts at Spanergy who share our concern and our commitment to keep this matter from, shall we say, exploding out of control." He paused as if waiting for a reaction. "Forgive my attempt at a little humor in a serious situation, and it is serious. But remember, we stand with Spanergy, ready to take action as needed."

"You stand wherever you want and do what you will," Tank raised his index finger, "*after* my report comes out. Until then, let me remind you that interfering with an ongoing investigation, including applying public pressure, could prove costly to you and your company."

"My company—make that our companies—have reputations for being proactive. We do not wait for things to happen, we take the initiative. That's how we have done so well and grown so fast. As I am sure you know, the industry and regulators, like DOT, work closely when it comes to ensuring an uninterrupted source of energy to power commerce and meet public demand. In the final analysis, the interests of the regulators and the industry are the same. We know that, and the people above you know that. I just want to make sure that you know it as well."

Tank narrowed his eyes as though he were trying to bring a distant object into sharper focus. "I hear what you are saying, Mr. ..."

"Fassberger. Think fast burger, like what you would get at McDonald's."

"Right. Fassberger. I hear both what you are saying and how you are saying it. Now, please hear what I am saying. Regardless of what you and your company do, my report will be as complete, consistent, and accurate as I can make it within the limits of our methods. Period."

Fassberger smiled the purse-lipped smile of a man who knew more than he was saying and did not take too seriously what he was being told.

Tank sighed. "In the interest of cooperation, or at least the semblance of it, can we get access to the PanPenn network so we can examine the SCADA and PLC programming?"

"No, not without a court order. And even then, I would expect that Corporate Legal will chime in with something to say before anything can happen."

"I already made the request through channels but have gotten no response."

"Nor will you, unless it is a simple no. Get your court order, Mr. Parsons—if you can find a sympathetic judge, that is. Then watch our people go into action."

"You do know that we already have copies of the Spanergy code."

"I know pretty much everything that you know—and a great deal that you don't. That code is connected with a completely different incident, and its function is subject to interpretation. Besides, I understand the code seems to have disappeared. Is that not right, Mr. Greely?"

"Yeah, 'sright. Least wise our copy. Seems as it's been deleted."

"There are other copies," Tank said.

"But, what a pity there is no chain of evidence for these other so-called copies." Fassberger seemed to be enjoying the exchange. "Who knows where they really came from or how they might have been doctored?"

Tank's face reddened in anger. "We'll get our court order, and we'll get access to the code. In the meantime, need I remind you that destroying evidence in a criminal investigation is a crime?"

"Criminal? I thought you were with the NTSB. Have you suddenly gone Dick Tracy on us?"

"No, but if they haven't already been in touch with you, I am sure the FBI will be calling soon, as Mr. Greely here can attest."

Greely worked his jaw but said nothing.

Tank closed his briefcase and stood to leave. "Thank you for your time, Mr. Fassberger. And good to see you again, Mr. Greely."

═

Greely caught up with him as Tank reached the elevators. "I

know you have a job to do, Parsons, but maybe you should know this is a mite bigger than you were thinkin' it is."

"What do you know, Greely? Tell me what I don't know."

"Well, I shouldn't 'xactly say, now, but, see, Spanergy is in negotiations to take over PanPenn. They don't want word leakin' out, but they been lookin' into how to merge operations. That's really why I was up here, following up on what our technical team did last month. But don't tell nobody I said any of this. Okay?"

"There was nothing about this in my materials; nothing has been filed."

"It's all very hush-hush. And when this second incident—er, accident—happened, well, it got even more quiet-like. Top management is 'bout as nervous as a long-tailed cat in a rockin' chair store."

"I can see why." Tank's mind was racing ahead as the elevator doors closed.

Chapter Thirty

Severson knew that he was still being watched by Arkady Pohl and his partner, but he didn't care much about the FBI and its targets. By this point he had bigger fish to fry, and one of the fish was swimming within sight. While desk demons back at Langley prowled the Internet in search of a digital trail back to the perpetrators, Gil Severson had been pounding the pavement, trying to locate a ghost. The ghost had been haunting West Virginia since the explosion at Sadler Creek, and now was taking on Pennsylvania. Severson would have preferred to have made his move at the sleepy passenger terminal back in Charleston, but his quarry had been too fast. Pittsburgh International was going to be tougher. Still, Gil felt good, confident that he himself had not yet been spotted by either his quarry or the FBI.

With the swarthy ghost heading for the airport, the pressure was on. Severson checked into headquarters with a brief coded message that his target was within reach, then quickly changed clothes and identification. Dressed in jeans and a black tee-shirt, he looked the part of the high-flying FAA technician that was one of his favorite covers. Before leaving the airport hotel for the quick hop to the terminal, he slipped a handgun into the back of his trousers and covered the fact with a camel-hair sports jacket.

At the Main Terminal, he spotted the ghost in line at the long row of US Air ticket counters. Severson was about to make his move when he heard a familiar voice from behind.

"Are you following us, Severson," Arkady said to his back, "or are you still on vacation? After the bright lights of swinging Charleston, now you've decided to take in warm and sunny Pittsburgh. What a fun life you lead. I'm envious."

Severson kept walking and didn't turn. "I thought it was you who were following me, Pohl, though your surveillance lacks finesse. Are you two still on that pipeline case?"

Delacroix paced him. "Severson, you are just not convincing when you are playing dumb."

"Really? I guess it's the problem with casting against type. Less of a stretch for Arkady here, though."

Arkady ignored the barb. "From what we heard, Langley is in overdrive and the NSA is flat-out.

"The NSA have nothing. We know more than they do."

"Really? Not the way we heard it at a recent briefing."

Severson stopped and turned to face them. "It's all technology with those spreadsheet spies at Fort Meade. Search algorithms, petabytes of data, Bayesian statistics, and low-pass filters: that's what it's all about for them. They're stumped because this is something new that requires actual thinking rather than just vacuuming up data and crunching numbers. And you guys? The FBI couldn't pull off an effective tail even with an invisibility cloak, and the NSA can't think unless they are handcuffed to a computer keyboard."

"That so? Speaking of tails, Severson, isn't that your target over there? Better get a move on before you lose him."

Severson whirled just in time to see his man handing a passport to the TSA officer in front of a row of x-rays and metal detectors at the security checkpoint. "Hmmm, not my man, I'm afraid. Bad call. As it turns out, I am actually on my way out of the airport. I have a meeting in town that I will be late for if I don't cut short our scintillating conversation. I'll leave you two to your own pursuits." He glanced at a departure schedule display as he marched away toward the exit. He had counted on reaching the ghost this side of security. Going through the checkpoint with a handgun in his jacket was a no-go. He needed to rework his plan.

He trotted toward the short-term parking lot to retrieve his car, then forced himself to slow down and become more casual. There was time, he told himself—at least an hour before the flight. He drove out of the airport, then turned into the service road leading back into the maintenance area. He flashed his FBI badge to the guard at the gate, who waved him in after scrutinizing the badge and questioning him about his business at the airport.

Without stopping, Severson drove completely around behind a row of hangers and headed across the tarmac, back toward the passenger terminal. As he cut across marked lanes and dodged luggage trains, he reached through the open window and clapped his blue flasher to the roof of the car. At the foot of one of the passenger gates, he showed the FAA badge to the airport ground-crew member who approached him, then trotted up the stairs on the outside of the jetbridge. Without hesitating, he slid the FAA badge down the slot in the card reader beside the door and punched a code into the keypad. The door unlocked and he ran up the gangplank. Once inside the terminal, he slowed to mingle with a group of passengers exiting for the baggage claim.

His quarry, a tall man in a sports jacket standing in the gate area, did not turn to look as Severson passed him and then looped around to approach from behind in the swirl of passengers.

"I think you just changed your mind about flying today," Severson said, leaning in close and barely moving his lips. "And don't turn around. As I am sure you have guessed by now, that's not a pen poking in your back. An incident in the airport would be most embarrassing to us both—and most fatal to you."

"Don't be stupid, Severson. I'm with the Company, too. I've been ordered back to Langley. I need to catch this next flight."

Severson, improvising at every turn, firmly pushed the man to one side. "I think you just got that irresistible urge to use the toilet before you board. Let's head that way." He increased the pressure of the gun in the man's back and steered him toward the men's room.

US Air Marshal Daniel Gomez detoured to make a quick pit stop on his way out of the airport for a short stopover before his next assigned flight. The incoming plane had been delayed on the tarmac after landing, and now everyone on the flight seemed to have the same idea. Daniel charged past the lines at the urinals and entered the only open stall, next-to-last in the row. He lifted the seat and looked down. There was a hand reaching under the partition.

Chapter Thirty-One

Agent Pohl looked up from his coffee to see two airport police officers pushing past passengers waiting in line to get through security. He nodded to Barbara. "If it isn't one damn thing then it's another. What do you think that's about?"

"I'll go see if I can find out."

Delacroix returned from talking with a security guard for a couple of minutes.

"What is it?" Agent Pohl popped another French fry in his mouth.

"Took some schmoozing, but it seems we got a body at the airport, in a men's room on Pier A. It was discovered by a passenger, an Air Marshal off an arriving flight."

"Well, then, I think we ought to go check it out, see if we can be of assistance."

The restroom was cordoned off and guarded by Airport Police. Delacroix and Pohl showed their badges and were greeted by Marshal Gomez.

"I was on a flight from Dallas and stopped in here on my way out of the airport. I saw a hand under the partition of the last stall. When it didn't move, I checked it out. The stall was locked from the inside, but the victim was dead."

"Identification?"

"I checked, didn't find any. I thought it might have been a heart attack or something, but then I noticed this small spot of blood in the center of his chest. It was almost invisible against the black tee-shirt, but it caught the light. Must have been fresh."

"Let's take a look."

Gomez pushed the door of the stall open with his foot. "I didn't touch anything except to see if he had a wallet or something before I saw the blood."

Pohl leaned around the partition and then turned back to Delacroix. "It's him."

"You two know this man?"

Delacroix answered. "In a manner of speaking. We know who he is and who he worked for."

"Who, then?"

"His name is Gil Severson. Gilbert, I think. We'll notify his office; they'll want to know about this."

"His office? What did he do? And how do you know him?"

"We couldn't say more. I think you understand." She gave the Air Marshal a look like a secret handshake, but he didn't seem to catch the message.

"What do you mean?" he persisted. "Is he with the Bureau?"

"Look, saying more could get us all in hot water. Take the hint."

Pohl was now kneeling half in, half out of the stall. "Could be robbery. His wallet and ID are gone, along with his watch. He might have been carrying a piece, but if he was, it doesn't seem to be here now. And I lifted his tee-shirt. There's a spot of blood and a pin-prick in his chest, like from a hypodermic needle."

Gomez was watching over Pohl's shoulder. "Drug overdose?"

"You don't shoot up in the chest." He backed away from the stall and gave Delacroix a raised eyebrow signal. "Thanks, Marshal Gomez. We better be going and make room for the real crime-scene pros."

As they walked toward the airport parking lot, Delacroix asked what Arkady had made of the whole thing.

"Well, I don't think we have to wait for an autopsy report to rule out a heart attack. It looks like a very sophisticated hit, something a professional might pull. I'll lay odds the autopsy will find potassium chloride. It stops the heart in seconds."

Delacroix gave him an open-mouthed smile. "I didn't realize you were such a crime-scene pro yourself, Arkady."

An embarrassed look spread over his face. "I read a lot of murder mysteries."

"Good for you. I don't know where you get the time."

"Lonely nights in cheap motels. But it seems everybody reads murder mysteries and watches 'CSI: NY' or some other television fabrication, including our eager Air Marshal."

Arkady kept shaking his head as they continued on toward the car. When they reached it, he stood beside it without opening the door. "There is something else that bothers me, though, something weird."

Delacroix looked across over the sunroof. "What's that?"

"The rose in his lapel. I just never thought of Severson as the boutonniere type. I mean, what was that about?"

"Maybe just him dressing for the part. You saw what he was wearing."

"Yeah, but I don't remember him having it when we saw him earlier. I think I would have noticed. And a rose. It just doesn't go with the camel-hair jacket and the black tee."

"You are hardly one to comment on fashion, Arkady, considering how you dress."

"What's wrong with it? I dress not to be noticed—goes with my work."

She gave him a skewed-mouth look as she got in. Before starting the car, she dialed her contact at Langley to deliver the news. When she announced what the call was about, she was passed to a liaison officer whom she didn't know.

"I don't believe we have anyone named Gilbert Severson," he said, his voice had the measured rhythm of officialdom. "But we do appreciate your call in the spirit of inter-agency cooperation. Enough said. We would not want to fuel speculation or rumors."

"No, we certainly wouldn't want that, now, would we?"

"Right. And, of course, there are severe penalties for revealing the identity of a CIA employee operating under cover, although in this case that would be irrelevant, since we had no one working for us under that name."

"Right. Under that name. Okay. The FBI has done its bit. We'll be moving on to other matters." She disconnected.

Pohl waited to be enlightened about the conversation.

"Well, Langley disavows Severson, who probably isn't really named Severson. But we do know he was watching us and, from the strength of his protests to you, was clearly here because of Spanergy and now PanPenn. He's dead and a technician is on the burn ward. The evidence has vanished, and—"

"And we have other business here in Pennsylvania, remember."

Chapter Thirty-Two

By the time Len and Kat showed up at Tank's office in the evening, he was already on the phone with the Scenaria team. They recognized DB's slightly squeaky voice over the speakerphone.

"It's been a productive day," he was saying. "We have confirmed—at least to our own satisfaction—that the source of at least some of the software in both of the code samples was Unit 61398."

Len turned to Kat. "That number sounds vaguely familiar. Wait, wasn't that the number on the haiku about dragons that we found at Smitty's place?" She nodded.

Tank shrugged, then remembered DB couldn't see him. "But what the hell does it mean?"

"The Chinese Army," DB announced dramatically, "hacker central in Shanghai on Datong Road. Unit 61398 is the so-called Military Unit Cover Designator for a Bureau in the People's Liberation Army dedicated to cyber espionage and cyber warfare. Sami thinks it may have been accidental that the header got left in the file. That Unit used to leave all kinds of clues behind but has gotten more careful since our cyber sleuths revealed that they had been tracking some from the Unit for years. The time-and-date stamp on that particular block makes it just before the Sadler Creek explosion. Maybe they were making some last minute mods, in a hurry, and forgot to strip the header. Or maybe it was an unofficial action, because he said the army guys on Unit 61398 are usually very methodical."

"So, you are saying the Chinese army might have done this?"

"Yes. After we called his attention to that compiler header, Sami said he saw other clues in the section he was working on: the name Deming appears in another file path. At first he thought it was a reference to some Japanese QC guru, but now he thinks it's a Chinese given name written in Latin letters. And the coding style reflects how Chinese programmers are taught. All in all, not enough to be conclusive in itself, but we also were able to trace back several embedded IP addresses to C&C servers in Shanghai. Sami has been talking with some of the people at Mandiant who in 2013 released the definitive report on Unit 61398. He has also been doing some digging with the help of some old contacts from his Kaspersky days, looking for more evidence and further clues as to what this is all about. He's catching a nap at the moment after working through the night and all day, but he'll be back at it soon.

"One big question we still have is how it is that we have these two, virtually identical, infections—and none others."

"I have an idea, DB. I was in town at PanPenn offices today and got wind of a possible merger or takeover. A guy up from Charleston, West Virginia, was visiting. There had previously been some preliminary work on how to merge operations."

"That could do it. If a technician brought a USB stick with him either to bring files or pick them up, it could have been infected. One of the zero-day exploits we identified allows access through fully-updated Windows by way of USB ports."

"Is there a way to confirm that this was the route into the PanPenn system?"

"Not definitively, but we might find code traces in the samples we have that point in that direction. We'll dig into it."

"Thanks, DB. We'll let you get back to digging. Cheers."

"Bye."

A double click and dial tone punctuated the call, and Tank tapped the hang-up button on the speakerphone. "Well, that's an interesting development, the link to Unit 61398. I wonder what our FBI pals would make of that, or their pals at the CIA or Homeland Security."

Kat had a worried look. "Shouldn't we report this to somebody? If this story checks out, the United States has been attacked by a foreign power. This could ultimately be as big as 9/11, maybe bigger. Do you realize how many miles of pipeline thread the East Coast? Spanergy alone has 9,000 miles."

"DB and his company are already working with the FBI—or were." Tank did not sound completely convinced or entirely reassuring. "I would imagine they will keep the Bureau apprised. Plus, their procedures call for sharing such information with US-CERT. This will all be online by this time tomorrow and in the newspapers soon after."

"No it won't!" Agent Delacroix stood in the open doorway. She and her partner had their guns drawn and pointed into the office.

Chapter Thirty-Three

Tank stood up slowly behind the desk, keeping his hands in front of him. "What is going on here, Agent Delacroix?"

Delacroix signaled to Pohl, who started to cuff Len. "We're taking these two into custody. You are being recalled, we understand. You should be getting a call from your boss any minute now. I would imagine there will also be people making contact at Scenaria about this time."

Kat squirmed as Pohl tightened the flexi-cuffs on her. "How did you find us?" She kept her eyes on Tank, an accusative look forming on her face.

Delacroix laughed. "How could we not? You were the one who installed the anti-theft system on your motorcycle. Law enforcement can activate and track it, you know. We, honey, are law enforcement."

Tank's cellphone started buzzing in his pocket. "Parsons here . . . Yes, I think I understand. The FBI is here right now." There was a long pause as Tank nodded and kept glancing side to side. "I don't think that will be necessary. I can complete the investigation and then return at the end of the week. No, I absolutely understand the need for discretion. But . . . but . . . Can you hold a minute?" He put his hand over the phone and turned to Delacroix and Pohl. "Why don't you go ahead with those two. I have official business to take care of myself." He caught Kat's eye; she gave him a withering look and turned away.

"Sure, Parsons." Delacroix smiled at him. "Seems like we

are all, at the moment, waist deep in more 'gaters than a Florida swamp." She and Arkady escorted Kat and Len out of the office and toward the exit.

Len stopped in his tracks just outside the door. "What are the charges?"

"You'll be charged later, but let's just say our warrant covers a lot of territory and circumstances give us a lot of latitude as to how you are questioned."

"What about my bike?" Kat asked.

"It'll be impounded. In any case, there's probably not a lot of use for motorcycles where you are going. Come on, let's go." She took Kat's arm at the elbow and steered her toward a black Cadillac that looked as if it had seen better times. Len followed with Arkady guiding him from behind.

"Where are you taking us?" he asked.

"We're headed into the FBI field office in Pittsburgh for the time being. Eventually . . . who can say."

"We have rights, you know."

"We know all about the rights you have and do not have and how acts of terrorism figure into that equation."

Kat stopped and turned. "Look, I'm a Canadian citizen; I can show you my passport. I have a right to contact my embassy. I insist on the use of a phone."

Delacroix placed her hand on top of Kat's head and pressed down as she maneuvered her into the backseat of the car. "You'll get your call . . . but not yet." Behind her, Arkady let out a sharp breath, a one-pulse laugh at a private joke. "Right now you two are wanted for questioning. Let's get on the road, Arkady."

Kat and Len were silent as Delacroix drove out of town, both of them deep in anxious thought about what might lie ahead. As the car slowed, Len, suddenly alert, strained against the seatbelt. "What's happening?"

“We’re stopping for gas and a bio break. Anyone back there need to use the toilets? No? All right, Arkady, you pump the gas and keep an eye on them; I’ll be back in five.”

While Arkady worked the pump, Kat surveyed the surroundings: a two-pump gas-and-groceries shack on a country road lit by bare fluorescent tubes that stayed steady for ten or twelve seconds, then flickered and restarted. Delacroix returned and stood by the car as Arkady went into the small building to settle up.

As they pulled back onto the two-lane highway, the lights in the gas station winked out. “We’re the last customers of the night, I guess,” Delacroix remarked.

“Yeah, that mountain mama in the store looked only half awake when I paid. Had to use cash. She said the phone line wasn’t working. No phone and no credit card machine. She told me, ‘Yins have a good’n.’” He snorted. “Just gotta love these dialects.”

“I wouldn’t talk, Akady. Your accent is not exactly middle-American neutral.”

“What? Are you saying I have an accent?”

“As thick as Putin.”

“Putin doesn’t even speak English.”

“And your point?”

“Besides, he’s Russian, not Ukrainian. Do I really have that bad of an accent.”

“No, I’m just ragging—” She swerved and skidded as she rounded a curve. A dark delivery van, lights out, was stopped, crosswise, straddling the double-yellow line a hundred feet down the road.

“What the fuck?”

Delacroix pulled over to the shoulder and aligned the car so the headlights were directly on the stopped van. It looked to be empty. “Stay in the car while I check this out.”

She stepped out of the car and reached for her sidearm as she walked slowly toward the van. She had halved the distance when two shots rang out. She dropped down, returned fire, and got off several shots before being hit a second time.

Arkady grabbed the walkie-talkie from the center console as he opened the passenger-side door and ducked behind it.

"Shots fired, officer down! Anyone copy?" There was only static in response. He peeked around the door to get a better look at where Delacroix was crumpled in the road. "Barbara! Barbara, you all right?" There was no response. Figuring the headlights would blind whomever was firing, Arkady edged forward, trying to position himself for a run out to where Barbara lay. Several more sharp cracks of rifle fire echoed off the surrounding hills, and both of the car's headlights shattered in quick succession. Arkady blinked, trying to adjust to the sudden blackness. "Barbara!"

Inside the car, Len heaved himself against the backseat door as bullets struck the windshield, turning it into a network of spider webs. The door had been locked from the front. Meanwhile, Kat was climbing over the driver-side seat. The horn blasted as she squirmed past the steering wheel and worked the door handle with her elbow. She slipped out. Two more shots rang out as she crouched and ran behind the car. "You coming, Len?"

"I'm right behind you." He scrambled out by the same route and joined her behind the car.

"What do we do?" she asked.

"We don't stay here, that's for sure. Looks like both our escorts are down, maybe dead. I think whoever is firing from that van may have night-vision goggles. If we run straight back and keep the car between us and them, we may be able to keep from getting shot."

"Okay, let's go."

They ran, keeping their heads low, to the sound of more shots, this time a mix of heavy-throated rifle fire and the sharp bark of handguns. Where the road curved, Kat led them through a shallow ditch beside the road, then over the rough ground that paralleled the highway.

"We should stay off the road but keep parallel to it." Len spoke between breaths. "We don't really know where we are."

"Yes we do. We're on our way back to the gas station."

"For what?"

"You'll see."

Chapter Thirty-Four

The first rounds struck the windshield of the highway patrol car as Officer Hegland rounded the curve. With sirens still screaming and dazzlers splashing blue, red, and white light over the scene, the car swerved and skidded to a halt, its right front bumper slamming into the left rear of the Cadillac stopped by the road. Without waiting, Hegland's rookie partner, Matt Zimmerman, was out of the other side with his service revolver drawn.

There was a shout from up ahead. "Agent Pohl, FBI. I'm pinned down off the shoulder to the right. My partner's been shot; she's in the middle of the road."

"Stay put. Keep your head down." Zimmerman strained to see around the rear of the Cadillac as Hegland exited the patrol car on the driver's side. Hegland reached back into the patrol car for the radio handset. "I'm calling for back—"

A high-power rifle shot cut him off. More shots split the night.

"My partner's been shot," Zimmerman shouted. "I'm going to check on him." He slipped around behind the patrol car but heavy firing prevented him from reaching his partner. Suddenly, the firing stopped, then the screech of tires filled the silence as a dark van headed straight for the patrol car, then swung past, ripping the driver-side door off and nearly running over Hegland.

Zimmerman rounded the back of the car and grabbed the mike dangling by its cord. "Shots fired. Officers down on Whitfield Road north of Debbis Road. Unmarked dark brown or black van headed south on Whitfield. Occupants armed and dangerous; approach with caution. And send the ambulances. Tony Hegland's been shot. At least one other gunshot victim."

═══

The country road was lit up like downtown Tokyo with the dazzlers of four police cars, two tow trucks, and two ambulances. Delecroix looked up from the stretcher behind one of the ambulances. "Are you all right, Arkady?"

"I'm good. Just scratches and a sprained thumb from when I hit the pavement." He held up a bandaged hand. "You're the one who took the bullets."

"I'll be okay. I just can't figure why they were after us. Then again, maybe it was not us but our prisoners they wanted. We were just in the way." She winced in pain. "Of course, if that's the case, we may have led them to their targets. Somebody wants those two—or wants them silenced."

"But we had them in custody. Who would they have talked to and what would they have said?"

"Check with the office and see if they'll tell us any more about what is really going on. Starts out we're on a cybercrime investigation, then suddenly it's a national security issue and we're rounding up people, then some bad guys are trying to steal our prisoners."

"Or kill them. Or set them free. What do we really know?"

"Not a hell of a lot."

The EMT standing patiently at her side cleared his throat. "We have to get you to the hospital."

"Okay. Arkady, meet me there. And don't report in just yet. I've got one of those worrying suspicions."

Arkady nodded and watched as she was lifted and slid into the ambulance.

The EMT climbed in, then leaned out and reached to close

the door of the ambulance. "She'll be all right."

"What about the patrolman."

The EMT flattened his lips and shook his head.

Arkady looked him in the eyes and dropped his voice. "I'm sorry."

"Me, too." The door closed with a loud thud and the ambulance pulled away.

Arkady walked over to where the other patrolman was watching while a wrecker hitched up the disabled police car. "I am sorry about your partner. I almost lost mine tonight. Had you two been paired up long?"

"No, I'm fresh out of the Academy, not even a year yet."

"Ouch. Well, you handled yourself just fine. By the book. There was nothing else you could have done." Arkady bent to pick up a piece of glass. "By any chance did you get a look at them as the van whizzed by you."

"Not really. Except, the driver was tall, kinda bent over to keep from hitting his head on the roof. And I got a partial plate: West Virginia, starting 67B or 678. I already called it in. The whole region will be on the lookout."

Chapter Thirty-Five

Through the trees, dim interior lights in the gas station were just visible. Kat stopped, held out her arm to keep Len from trotting past her, and struggled to get her breathing under control. "We have to work fast. Either the Feds or the assault team, whoever they were, are going to be chasing us down as soon as they settle their scores. We have to get into the garage and cut these cuffs off, then find transportation."

"How?"

"We'll see when we get to that point."

Kat approached the dilapidated building and tried to see in the dirty side window of the store portion. She jumped back as a face appeared in the window and the quiet was broken by a vicious growl and a burst of furious barking.

"Rottweiler. Don't think we're getting in here unless you are prepared to kill a dog with your bare hands—tied behind your back."

"No thanks." Len walked around to the front of the building. The dog followed from inside the office, alternately growling and barking as it stood with its front paws on the bar of the front door. Len continued over to the garage half of the building, but the dog stayed as sentinel at the office door. "I think the owners are more concerned with guarding the cash and cigarettes than whatever's in the garage. I'm going to check out the back."

Kat backed away from the office door and waited. Suddenly there was a crash and the banging of a door. When the lights came on in the garage, Kat followed around the corner. A side entrance was open and Len had his back up against a workbench, sliding himself up and down like a dog scratching its back against a post.

He pulled his hands around in front of him and sucked blood off his wrist. "There was a piece of metal in the vise. Let me find something to cut you free with a little less collateral damage." He took a hacksaw down from a peg board. "Turn around."

"You be careful with that."

"Yeah, we wouldn't want to nick those delicate hands." She gave him a teasing kick in the shins. "Raise your arms and pull your wrists as far apart as you can. And hold still." He worried the saw blade back and forth in short strokes until the plastic of the cuffs parted. "There you are, much better. And nary a nick."

She turned around into him and he instinctively put his arms around her. "I was scared," she said, resting her head on his chest.

"Me, too. Now, how are we going to get away."

"Maybe the car here?" She nodded toward a two-door relic straddling the grease pit in the garage.

"That's ancient, probably being worked on, might not even start."

"Looks can be deceptive. This looks like maybe an antique. People with classic cars tend to take good care of them. Let's give it a try, see if it runs." She opened the door and climbed into the driver's seat.

Len leaned in the open car window. "What is this thing?"

"A Plymouth. Late 1940s. And look at the odometer, less than 30,000 miles."

"If it hasn't been altered."

"No, it looks good, numbers all neatly lined up." She patted the chrome-trimmed dashboard. "This is what my father would have called a cream puff. Keys are in it. They must've just pulled it in here before closing." She turned the key and the car started after cranking several seconds. "Get the garage door and then let's get out of here." Above the rumble of the idling engine, the barking had become faster and more insistent.

Len swung the heavy overhead door up and waited as Kat backed out. He lowered the door again and hopped in the car.

Kat spun the wheel as she whipped the car around and squealed out onto the road. "Hold on, cowboy."

They were only a few miles down the road when Kat braked suddenly and made a hard right onto a dirt road.

"Where are we going?"

"Don't know yet, but this looks promising. The commandos don't know if we have a car and if they do, they are going to expect us to boogey on down the highway. I'm going to give them some time to get past us, and then we'll do the unexpected and head back into Johnstown." She pulled over onto a sloping shoulder. "Why don't you grab a few winks of sleep? I'll keep an eye out."

"Sleep? Who can sleep with the SWAT team on our tail?" He leaned against the door but obediently closed his eyes and slowed his breathing.

Chapter Thirty-Six

In stocking feet and carrying his shoes, Kai walked the length of the corridor, stopping at the last apartment to listen. No one approached from the steps. Through the thin door, he could hear a soft fluttering, like the wings of a house sparrow caught in a mist net, the bird now almost too tired to struggle. He tapped gently on the door. "Are you there? Lee, it's me, Kai. If you are there, please open up and let me in."

Between pulses of breath, the answer came, barely audible. "Go away."

"I will not. We must help each other. Let me in."

"There is no help for me and nothing that I can do to help you."

"You can help me by letting me in before someone hears."

She laughed through her tears. "You were always the better debater. You win every argument." She unlatched the door and opened it.

"And you were always a better programmer." He set his shoes beside the door, pushed it closed with his foot, and took her in his arms. She struggled against him, but he held her until she quieted and the soft, fluttering sobs resumed.

"I failed," she said, her mouth buried in his uniform, now dampened by her tears. "I should not have written those changes in haste. I should not have had the pride—or the fear—to act alone. It was my bug that sent *lóng fēng* into the wild to explode another pipeline. I was trying to recall it and wipe the footprints."

"I know. But it was not your code. I studied it at the Unit. Your code was perfect. It was my code that failed. I used the name of a flag without checking it and stored a value in the wrong place. It reversed an action of your routine. It said 'go' when your code had said 'stop'. If I had looked to see what was there, it would not have happened."

"Will we be shot?"

"Shot? Why would they shoot us? We are the best. We have proven ourselves. The Leader knows this, whatever threats he may make. They will give us medals when this is over."

"There will be no medals for me. They have sent me to the countryside. I am to be a farmer."

"Then I will be a farmer's husband."

"I do not want to go; I do not want you to go."

"Then we will get away."

"There is no 'away'; where could we run?"

As the classic blue Plymouth coupe approached the edge of the Johnstown campus of the University of Pittsburgh, Kat turned off the headlights, cut the engine, and coasted in neutral down the hill.

"Why are we back here? We should get away."

"Where can we get away to? We are back here because Tank might be able to help. And see, there are still lights on in the garage, so he is probably still around."

"It's always Tank, isn't it. Tank this, Tank that."

She let the car roll to a stop before confronting him. "Look, cowboy, Tank might be able to help us. The fact that he has the hots for me merely stacks the odds in our favor. So don't act like a jerk in front of him. Let me handle it, you stay cool." She leaned over and gave him a peck on the cheek.

Len blinked. "Are you saying . . . ?"

"I am not saying anything except for you to stop worrying

and behave yourself."

At the side of the garage, Tank was startled when Kat rattled her fingers on the window. He searched for the latch, then raised the sash. "What the . . . ?"

Kat grinned at him. "We forgot to say goodbye. Be a love and open the door for us."

"They let you go? No, of course not. You got away somehow. What on earth have you gone and done?"

"Just let us in, Tank, and we'll explain. It's cold out here."

"Ah . . . okay. Go around to the other side."

At the rear entrance, he let them in, looked around anxiously, then closed and locked the door behind them. "So, what happened?"

"We were ambushed."

"What? Ambushed? Who would ambush you?"

"No idea. Don't know who and don't know why. There was some kind of a road block, a van. When the shooting started, we ducked out the back way, borrowed a car, and now we are here."

"You should give yourselves up. You can't run from the feds. Where would you go?"

Kat chewed on her lip lower. "Not sure, but we'll think of something. Right now we need tools and transportation."

"Tools?"

"I have to remove an anti-theft transponder. Forgot it was there. I can't believe I was that stupid not to think of it. That's how they tracked us down, but I still need my bike. And we need to get something similar for Cowboy Len here. I figured that at a college campus there must be a bike or two we could borrow."

Tank dropped his chin to his chest and closed his eyes. "I don't . . ."

"Please."

"Okay, take what you need from the garage, including some cable ties. You're going to cuff me and tie me to a chair before you leave. And remember, I never helped you."

Kat stood on tiptoe and kissed his forehead. "Thanks."

"Right. Better get a move on. A SWAT team could come through the garage door any minute now."

Kat made a quick tour of the work area, gathering tools then rolling them into a small tool pouch. Back in the office, she used cable ties to cinch Tank's legs to a chair. "Now, hands behind your back. No, not like that: hooked through the chair back."

"Oh, lady, you do know what you are doing. Are you sure you're not a career criminal?"

She tightened the tie around his wrists. "Looks like I am now. How's that?" She leaned around and crinkled her nose at him. "Too tight?"

"Yeah, but I'll survive."

"Okay, I'm going to shove you over near the phone so you can later knock the handset off and dial the operator with your long nose."

"Hey, I'm not the one with the schnoz. Have you checked out your cowboy friend's face lately?"

Both Kat and Len laughed. He tugged at her elbow. "We gotta go, Kat."

Tank twisted in the chair and smiled up at them. "Be careful. And good luck . . . both of you."

"Thanks. I hate to do this, but, you understand." She held out a short length of duct tape and placed it across his mouth.

"Mmm hmmm," he said, nodding.

═

It took Kat two tries to undo the security screws and dismount the anti-theft system from her bike. "As soon as it's disconnected, it will start screaming for help over the airwaves, so

. . ." She placed it on the curb and smashed it into small pieces with a ballpeen hammer. "That should do it. Now let's find a steed for you, cowboy."

"Why not keep riding two-up? Works for me."

"No, for several reasons. First, they will be looking for a bike with two riders. Second, we lose speed and maneuverability. And third, with you hugging me for dear life, we can't split up if need be. So, let's pick something you can handle on your own—like maybe a nice little Moped."

"How 'bout a Hog?"

"How about we check out behind the dorms and see what the residents ride. We need something which is not chained, not alarmed, and which I can hotwire."

They ended up picking a hot little Kawasaki with the keys and a helmet tucked in an unlocked carrier on the back. "You remember how to ride this thing, cowboy? Clutch left, accelerator right, gear shift—"

"Yeah, yeah, I know. Just try to keep up."

"You're on, cowboy, you're on. But we roll to the bottom of the hill before we hammer down."

"Well, maybe not. If we hammer down, we attract attention."

"Then just follow me and do what I do."

He rolled the Kawasaki down the road behind Kat's BMW. "Just where are we going?"

"North. I figure they expect us to head back home, to Charleston." She tromped on the starter. "Let's go somewhere that's not connected with either of us. Just stay on my tail." She waited for him to get his bike started, then pulled out onto the street. Above, the growing crescent moon shimmered behind scudding clouds.

Chapter Thirty-Seven

The cloudy sky lightened with predawn glow as Arkady exited the Conemaugh Hospital parking lot and turned his rental car toward the Pitt campus. He was eager to check in with the NTSB crew, particularly Parsons, who had been with Gaudet and Bergen when they were taken into custody and, when last seen, had been on the phone with his NTSB superiors.

Lights were already on in the garage itself and two of the offices when Arkady arrived. He knocked on the front door but got no answer. Walking around to the side, he stretched to see in the office windows. In the second office, a man was visible, slumped over and tied to a chair, his mouth covered with tape.

Arkady ran around to the back door and tried it. Locked. He was debating forcing the door when he heard a vehicle roll up behind him.

"Looking for something?"

Arkady turned slowly to face a skinny campus patrolman, chewing gum, with a two-handed grip on an outstretched service revolver. Arkady raised his hands, palms forward. "I'm with the FBI. There's a man tied up in there, possibly injured."

"Is that so?" Chew, pop. "You got identification?"

"On my belt. Can I get it for you."

"Yes, slowly." Chew.

Arkady retrieved his badge and held it out toward the patrolman.

"I'll be dang. FBI for real. You know anything about that FBI woman brought into Conemaugh Hospital last night?"

"Yes, she's my partner. We were escorting prisoners when we were stopped and fired upon."

"And what brings you over this way?"

"This is where we picked up our prisoners. I was checking back."

"This here building is off limits. Being used temporarily by the National Transportation Safety Board. Investigating. You know anything 'bout that?" His gum chewing speeded up.

"Yes, we were working on the same case. Can you open this door so we can check on the NTSB guy?"

The patrolman hesitated, but opened the door, then insisted on going ahead, handgun still at the ready. "Clear!" he called back, trying to emulate the tone of the point man on a Navy Seals team. Arkady smirked and followed him toward the alcove with the offices. The patrolman pushed the first door open with his foot, looked around, and said, "Clear!"

The door of the second office was locked. The patrolman told Arkady to stand back, then kicked at the door, planting his foot just above the doorknob. It rattled but didn't open.

"No master key?" Arkady asked.

"Oh, yeah, sure. Didn't think of that." The man fumbled with a big ring clipped on his belt as he chewed furiously. "Ah, here's the one. Nope. This one." He opened the door.

Tank Parsons, now fully awake, talked at them through the tape over his mouth. "Mmm, hmm-hmm hmm hmm-hmmm."

I'll bet you are." Arkady tugged at the corner of the duct tape. "This might hurt." He jerked the tape free.

"Ouch. I'd hate to be interrogated by you."

"Well, you might yet get that opportunity, sir. What the hell happened to you?"

"Those two came back, tied me up, rummaged through the garage, then hightailed it out of here."

"Did they say anything about where they were headed?"

"No, but this was hours ago. Could be anywhere—halfway to Arkansas by now."

"Arkansas? Did they mention Arkansas?"

"No, just an expression. Look, are you gentlemen going to untie me or what?"

"Sure." Arkady nodded to the patrolman, who pulled a nail clipper from his pocket and started cutting through the cable ties holding Tank.

Tank rubbed at the red marks on his wrists. "I see you got a new partner, Agent Pohl. What ever happened to your lady friend?"

"She's in the hospital. Gunshot wounds. Shoulder and neck."

"She going to be all right?"

"Yeah, I guess." He stared at Tank. "You wouldn't know anything more that you're not telling me, would you?"

"Like what?"

"Like why this thing is such a stew pot and boiling over."

Tank shook his head. "Look, I'm as clueless as you. What I mean is . . ."

" 'S'okay. It's all probably above our pay grades, anyway. If you learn anything, do tell me. If you can, that is."

"Right, if I can." Tank waited in silence as the discomfort grew. "You both probably have work to do. I know I do. I have just two days to wrap up here, then scurry back to DC, tail between my legs." He turned to his desk and pretended to be busy with papers.

═

Arkady sat thinking in the car for several minutes before dialing a number on his cellphone. He waited as it kept ringing.

Finally it was answered with a grunt. "Pohl here." The voice on the other end was hoarse and heavy with sleep.

"Dmitry, it's Arkady. Where are you?"

"San Fran. Stopover on my way overseas."

"China?"

"No, Taiwan."

"Anything I might know about?"

"Perhaps. But you know how this business works."

"I do, dear brother, I do."

"So, what's the occasion for the call? It's not my birthday."

"They tried to kill us. Barbara Delacroix, my partner, is in the hospital."

"Is she all right? Are you?"

"Yeah, she'll mend. I got away with a sprained finger. I don't know about the *schwarzer* driven off the road down in West Virginia, though. He's vanished from a burn ward. And we got a dead CIA NOC we found in a toilet—appropriately—at the airport." Arkady waited, but there was no response. The silence was eloquent. "When do you leave?"

"Tomorrow afternoon."

"San Francisco, you said. You should try that kosher Chinese place for dinner tonight."

"Kosher?"

"Yeah, the Shangri-La. Great food. Definitely do it before you leave."

"That good, huh?"

"Yes, an absolute must. Kosher."

"Okay. Watch your back."

"You watch yours." Arkady stared at the phone until the screen saver timed out and it went black.

Chapter Thirty-Eight

The thermometer said that San Francisco was warmer than Pittsburgh, but it did not feel that way to Arkady. He used the hike through a windy Golden Gate Park and a stroll around Slow Lake to make sure he wasn't followed. He deliberately walked a block too far, then doubled back to the small restaurant on Irving Street. He entered it and knew immediately where to look for the familiar face—the face he saw in the mirror every day. Dmitry, in a brown leather sports jacket and French-blue button-down shirt, could have been Arkady's twin with better taste in clothes. He was seated toward the rear at a table for two, back to the wall, pretending not to be constantly checking his surroundings. Arkady nodded, approached, and sat down without removing his sunglasses.

Dmitry sighed. "This place is vegetarian. You didn't say it was vegetarian. You know how much I like meat. How can anyone eat just vegetables?"

"I love you, too, Dima. At least it's kosher."

"When did you go Orthodox on me, little brother?"

"Never. I was just using an old trope to get your attention. We can go someplace else if you want."

"No, this is fine. But next time, remember: I like to eat. Real food. In my work, well, it could be pork roast, cheeseburgers, whatever. Not kosher. I eat what the people I am with eat. You know how this works." It was a timeworn passphrase between them: a universal explanation and an all-purpose excuse.

"Yes, I know how this works. And I know you. Shall we

order?"

"I already did, an assortment. The spring rolls will be here any minute."

"How did you know when I would arrive."

"How could I not know? I knew what flight you would have to take and when it arrived, what car you rented, where you parked. Hey, I do the same kind of work as you; I am just better at it than you are." He looked askance at Arkady. "You are clean?"

"Yes, I took my time through the park. No tail."

"And yet . . ."

"Yet what?"

"I could follow you."

"Perhaps. But I am not here to restart the competitive sports of our school days. I want to know what you know. Or what you have heard."

Dmitry's expression did not change as he waited and said nothing.

"Dima, you have to talk with me. If you know something, tell me. You are my brother."

"Yes, and we parted company many years ago, brother. You would not make *aliyah* to the homeland. I did. You chose to join the bench-warmers at the Bureau. Now you are American, and I am Israeli. You work for them. I do not."

"We are both working for the same things."

"Are we?" Dmitry looked up. "Ah, here are our spring rolls. I hope you are hungry. I ordered double. It's Chinese food, you know, and vegetarian. Doesn't put much meat on the bones."

Arkady sat back and looked about in embarrassment while the waitress rearranged plates and deposited the rolls and shallow dishes of sauces. He followed with his eyes as she returned through the double swinging doors to the kitchen. "We work for different governments, Dima, but for the same principles."

"Hardly. I work for the Jewish homeland. I work to protect our future. You work for a fair-weather friend of the State of Israel."

"Look, I did not come all the way out here to debate politics or principles or to defend the policies of the current administration, for that matter. I came here for help. They tried to kill us. It was too crude for one of your operations, but the CIA agent killed at the airport, a needle to the heart. Quick, quiet, like one of yours. And the engineer, the *schwarzer*—that was slick. His car had been hacked into and the brakes disabled by remote control. It was like that attempt on the guy in Madeira, only this was much slicker. It had Mossad stamped all over it."

"Not mine, not ours. The stamp, maybe, but rubber stamps are easy to come by. No, it wasn't one of ours."

"How can you say that with such certainty."

"Because I am where I am."

"Who then? Who tried to take out Barbara Delacroix and me, and maybe our prisoners."

"Could be lots of people, any of the many parties who do not want it known how World War III was started in cyberspace. There are new alignments, new friendships for Israel. Taiwan now makes some of our military avionics chips, and we are growing as trading partners with China. They borrow from us; we borrow from them. Do your homework, Arkady. We're not in school anymore. I can't comb my hair back and fool the proctors to take the test for you."

"You just did. And like back then, you already had all the answers worked out." Arkady pushed his chair back from the table and started to rise.

"Remember, Arkady, not all the Indians stay on the reservation. Remember that."

Arkady scanned the room before fixing his eyes on his

brother. "I will. Enjoy the Chinese food. I hope there's enough for you. And thanks for filling me in. Shalom."

"You're welcome, I will enjoy myself, and shalom. Watch your back."

"You watch your back."

═══

Delacroix craned her neck to be sure the nurse was back at her station before putting the phone back to her ear. "Okay, Arkady, go ahead. We can talk."

"I can't tell you how I know, but I am now certain that we are caught between opposing teams. Our own people, at least some of them, seem determined to cover things up, to make sure that the true story doesn't get out."

"And what's that?"

"Didn't you keep up with the sigint on the exchanges between our NTSB hero and the antivirus people?"

"You mean that it's China, the army. And you believe that?"

"The weight of the evidence favors that conclusion. Since meeting with . . . someone, a source, I have been following up with other sources, sources at NSA."

"You said we were between opposing teams. And the opposition is . . . ?"

"There are rogue players on the field. Who, how many, where: these I don't know, only that they are there. Some, I think, are American, some Israeli. It's not clear. What is clear is that we had better be very careful who we trust about what. I've taken care of reporting in about the shooting, but I admit that I kept it to the bare minimum. How soon before you can be back on the case?"

"It was worse than they thought; I go in for surgery tomorrow. After, I'll know better. Thanks for calling, filling me in."

"Anytime. I'll see you after you come out of surgery."

"Thanks, Arkady. I better go, looks like nursey is about to

come back."

"Oh, one more thing. I talked with the sheriff. They finally ID'ed the body from Sadler Creek."

"And?"

"Just some college dropout on his way south. They now figure he found the tools and wire someplace along the way. He was just on the wrong road at the wrong time."

"Yeah." There was a thoughtful silence. "By the way, where are you?"

"On the road. Later."

PART FOUR
Chapter Thirty-Nine

Colonel Todd Whitcomb scanned the faces in the underground conference room at the Idaho National Laboratory. At forty-seven, he was the oldest person present, although tinting his hair kept his age from showing too much. Cyber security was a young man's game—with a few exceptions. He glanced toward the left side of the room where Cassandra Welke and Bridget Saunders were seated together as always. Cassandra, who was almost as old as Todd and didn't color her hair, had taken Bridget under her wing when the younger woman was hired right out of MIT. Only a few of the group were in their early forties, and those were veterans from early days in the Control Systems Security Program at the Laboratory.

Cassandra had come over from the nuclear side of research right after the control systems group was formed. Frank Gorham had become a rising star after Operation Aurora when he had helped hack into an electric generator to destroy it by remote control. And Dieter Kauffman was a holdover from the Siemens PCS 7 Cyber Security Assessment that had ultimately fed into the US-Israeli operation against Iran code-named Olympic Games. The only one in the group who wasn't native-born American, Dieter had come over on loan from the Siemens test lab in Karlsruhe, Germany, to help INL assemble their own test bed. He had married an American, stayed on, and was now a citizen.

Welke, Gorham, and Kauffman were his A-team of the A-team, the veterans who added maturity to the bull-headed brilliance and obsessive overconfidence that were the common currency of the rest of Todd's people. There wasn't an also-ran in the room, but there were fewer in the room than there should have been. The government funding sequester had hurt them along with the rest of the Lab. The baker's dozen present were the handpicked SWAT troops of cyberspace, a black ops team assembled from other INL groups, including the threat analysis group that studied malware, the Cyber Analysis Center that tested industrial control systems for vulnerabilities, and the top secret "watch-and-warning" center. Whitcomb's group itself did not exist on any org chart or budget spreadsheet. It was the ultimate black ops program, so deeply buried that even the Snowden disclosures had not blown its cover.

Whitcomb stood at the head of the table and clicked the remote to switch on the projector mounted on the ceiling; the group hushed in anticipation. They had been summoned on short notice to a crack-of-dawn meeting, so there was little doubt in anyone's mind that something substantial was up.

"There's no elaborate PowerPoint today, people." He pointed to the projected image with the US Department of Homeland Security seal, the Idaho National Laboratory logo, and below, the team's acronym, COAST, spelled out: Cyber Offensive Actions, Systems, and Tactics. "That's it, folks. My complete PowerPoint deck."

"And that's a relief." Hassim Peterson, the only black on the team, clapped his hands. "Punishment by PowerPoint at this hour in the morning would be ruled cruel and unusual by any court."

"Amen, brother." Rick Chan, seated next to him, slapped him on the back. "So, Colonel, is there a briefing packet?"

"No. And there is no PDF file posted on the server. This is a verbal-only briefing. There will be no emails exchanged internally or externally regarding this meeting or its subject matter. This stays here, strictly within the COAST team present. Understood? Any breach, even the smallest, could have serious consequences—for you and for the country. And yes, I know that goes without saying, but I am required to say it anyway. Those of you who are not military may not fully understand, but the Marine guards outside the door of this room are not there for decoration and their sidearms are loaded. From here on, you will be escorted at all times, and all work will be carried out here and in the COAST ops center. No unescorted trips to your offices or even to the bathroom."

Bridget Saunders looked anxious. "Are you going to tell us what this is about or is that above our pay grades."

"I am going to tell you what you need to know."

The tension in the room was rising to the point that those toward the far end of the table could almost smell it.

"Okay, okay." Gus Eggleston, who had just joined the team after leaving the Air Force, did not look up from his doodling. "Just tell us what you can."

"Actually, I can tell you just about everything I know, because you will need to understand the context in order to accomplish the mission we have been tasked with. Just over a week ago, a natural gas transmission pipeline in West Virginia ruptured and exploded, killing one person. Because of the location, the only other damage beyond the pipe and the suspension bridge carrying it was a bunch of trees and a drop in the share price of Spanergy Holdings, the gas company operating the pipeline. You probably already knew all about that. Some of you got pulled in to help analyze what looked like a Windows-to-SCADA injection scenario alleged to have been used to trigger the explosion. You may also know that there was a second, similar explosion approximately two days ago, this one on a transmission line in Pennsylvania that took out part of a farming community with at least a dozen casualties."

"What's that got to do with us? Strictly speaking, pipelines are DOT territory." Paul Michaels was ex-Army. He liked to stick to protocol and color within the lines.

"Well, it also comes under the Department of Energy. And in the never-ending campaign of our government to confuse issues and confound responsibilities, pipeline cyber security belongs to DHS, anyway. Be that as it may, where we come in today is that we now know it was a cyber attack traced to professional hackers within Unit 61398 in Shanghai: the People's Liberation Army."

Gorham, poker-faced as ever, straightened up in his chair. "We know this for certain?"

"As certain as it is possible to be in these circumstances. Israel's Unit 8200 sigint has confirmed the US Cyber Command conclusion that the malware originated with the Chinese."

Eggleston looked up from his doodling. "Are we supposed to try and stop this thing?"

"No, that's now with US-CERT. The Cyber Emergency Response Team is already taking action to identify other compromised sites and to protect them from further attacks. We have been tasked with providing the President with a set of offensive options. Non-kinetic, that is."

"Does that mean kinetic options are actually on the table?" Eggleston asked. "Are we considering nuking somebody or launching a drone strike?"

"I am not in a position to know that, but we can assume the President and his advisors are at least considering military options. That is not our concern. Our job is to offer a range of actionable offensive cyber initiatives. We are constrained by very specific criteria. Anything we propose must be based on proven capability using only fully operational technology and tested software components. Not-invented-here is not a problem, as long as any borrowed or requisitioned components or technologies are fully understood and field-proven. Anything we offer must be amenable to a short-cycle agile software development project for final assembly and deployment."

"How short is short-cycle?" Hassim had a look that said he already suspected he wouldn't like the answer.

"Forty-eight hours, people."

Hassim whistled and Eggleston flipped his pencil in the air.

"That's right, forty-eight hours from Presidential order to deployment, that's the objective. We have already lost more than a week, and the Pentagon and Whitehouse want there to be no doubt that whatever we do is in direct response to those attacks. So let's get started, people. We're going to begin by brainstorming ideas, then start to tear them apart and pare them down."

Hassim offered the first suggestion. "Okay, what about classic tit-for-tat? We pull the same stunt on them, blowing up a main natural gas transmission line somewhere in China using a similar software attack vector."

Cassandra Welke shook her head in disapproval. "That's just going to escalate things."

"Maybe, but we know the technology works—they did it already—and we can probably even borrow code from their attack."

Whitcomb tapped on the table for order. "Hang on, people, hang on. This is brainstorming. Let's get the ideas down before we start critiquing them. So, that's one idea. I'll call it 'Tit-for-Tat' for short. There." He wrote it on a flip chart. "What else?"

At the far end of the table, Paul Michaels raised his hand. "We could knock out the servers at Unit 61398. That would teach them. And it would, at least temporarily, cut their capability."

"I'll build on that idea. We wipe the disks in the process.

That'll put them out of commission a lot longer." Frank grinned at the thought.

"Great! Keep 'em coming, people. What else?"

"We respond in kind but not tit-for-tat. Maybe an attack on some other piece of critical infrastructure."

"Yeah, building on that, we use what we learned from the Bluedog.Win64.sys virus and attack their electric generation capacity or the power grid itself."

"That's going too far, Rick," Hassim countered. "I say we do something high-profile but without causing actual physical damage. Let's say we hack into Chinese government websites and substitute our own message on the home pages."

A mixture of boos and laughter passed around the table as Whitcomb scribbled quickly on the flipchart.

Chan picked up the thread. "Okay, Hassim, but we could make it more personal. Just selectively hit personal computers of government officials and known senior officers of Unit 61398 and see how they like that."

Eggleston looked skeptical. "This is pretty tame stuff and not very painful."

"We're just brainstorming," Whitcomb reminded them. "What would you do?" Eggleston returned to doodling.

Dieter Kauffman, who had been listening and taking his own notes, responded. "Take down the Chinese stock exchange, maybe cripple their banking system. You want it to really hurt? Set their economy back a few notches."

Eggleston looked up. "How about some gain with the pain? We could do electronic funds transfers from Chinese government accounts. Maybe better to suck funds from various offshore accounts of the government or Chinese companies."

Rick Chan smiled. "I like that. Do we get to keep whatever funds we siphon off? That would be divine justice: the first war with a negative cost."

Dieter circled something in his notebook with a flourish. "Right, Paul, so now we're international thieves."

Casandra Welke waited until it was clear no one else had anything to offer. "I want to return to Unit 61398. How about a surgical strike?"

"I thought this was supposed to be in cyberspace, not a kinetic attack."

"That's what I meant," she said. "We could cripple part of the IT at a factory or business in Shanghai, preferably located near the Unit headquarters on Datong Road in Pudong. The message would come through loud and clear. It's doable."

Frank Gorham cleared his throat. "I want to go back to an earlier suggestion. Instead of actually damaging power plants or the grid, we could trigger an extended nation-wide power outage. That would be huge but temporary."

Rick Chen's face lit up. "How about launching a distributed denial-of-service attack on Chinese government websites, a cyber outage."

"No," Hassim drew the word out. "Instead, we direct the DDS attack to Chinese industrial and commercial sites. Hit them in the pocketbook. We want to hurt them, not just embarrass them."

"I say we do what they have been doing to us and the Canadians for some time. We hack into various industrial, military, and government computer systems and extract state or trade secrets."

"And you think we are not already doing that? Besides, where's the attack? You've got to do something with the secrets for it to mean anything."

"Give 'em all to WikiLeaks!" Rick Chen shouted. Everyone laughed. "Of course, the trade secrets they do have are all stolen from the West anyway."

"While we're on the subject of old-standby techniques,

what about a malware attack on Chinese government computers with selective destruction of files?"

"Or launch the same attack on the Chinese embassy here."

"Better yet, how about we hit all their embassies around the world?" Gus slammed his hand flat on the table.

"Great, this is a good starting point. Any more? No? Then let's start discussing this list and turning it into a small set of fleshed out proposals."

Whitcomb numbered the ideas, then read each idea along with a quick summary for the group. "Understand, we are not constrained to just this list, and enhancements or elaborations of any of these scenarios is acceptable. However, I want to remind you that the clock is ticking. We have only about the next two hours to winnow this down to three top contenders in terms of realizable delivery and appropriately measured impact. I am looking for technical consensus on this. Everyone in this room must be comfortable with supporting all three options that we pass on.

"Once we have the three, we split into teams and start detailing the development strategies. Concurrently, I will be writing up our recommendations to forward to the President. Once he tells us his choice, we will review the implementation plans for the two rejects to see if anything might be salvaged for use with the chosen attack vector. Then we will begin the first sprint of a six-cycle agile development project. That's eight hours per sprint, boys and girls. Nobody goes home; nobody gets more than half-hour naps until we deliver the solution. I am and will remain open to suggestions, anything that will help, but I am ultimately calling the shots.

"When we know what weapon we are building, I will make assignments of project roles and responsibilities. There, too, I am open to suggestions but not open to volunteers. We do not have time for lobbying or campaigning. We are a team, the best in the world, and we will succeed as a team.

"Now, thoughts on these scenarios. Are there any we can strike off the list at the start."

Rick Chan spoke up without waiting to be recognized. "Colonel, some of these require intelligence that we may or may not have. For example, number five, attacking personal computers of selected officials. Do we even know who the targets would be, much less technical details that would enable us to attack their individual machines?"

"We have NSA and CIA liaisons to answer specific questions, some of which are already being formulated and submitted for confirmation. If and when we need the specifics, if there is anything we don't have ourselves, it will be given to us by the cognizant agency. The Tailored Access Operations group, the NSA's version of Unit 61398, also stands ready to hack into specific sites or systems if the need arises."

Gorham spoke up. "This highlights an issue. Number five is a problem for another reason. It could—almost certainly will—require customized attacks for each of a substantial number of disparate targets. That's not technically realistic given the short time-frame. And it could be very hard to synchronize for maximum impact. It also multiplies the chances for failure. I say we strike it from the list." There were nods around the room.

"Okay, is there anyone who absolutely could not support the decision to eliminate number five from contention?" He scanned the room. "Gus?"

"I really think we should stick it to the guys in charge."

"I wouldn't disagree, but there are other ways on the list that perhaps offer more straightforward ways to accomplish that."

"Okay, I withdraw my objection."

"Alright, people, we are on our way. Let's get it down to

three."

"Can we combine or merge options?"

"We can do anything we damn well please as long as we give the President three feasible, effective attacks to choose from within"—he checked his watch—"an hour and fifty-one minutes."

Chapter Forty

Arkady studied the latest paperback thrillers at the news kiosk as he watched his brother board a plane for Shanghai, not Taiwan. He suppressed a grin over having pulled off a surveillance coup. Mixed with the pride was the realization that Dima had been a good teacher. Now, however, the apprentice was as good as the master.

Arkady ducked into the men's room and called Barbara's cellphone, but there was no answer. He thought of leaving voice mail, but then changed his mind. How pervasive was the operation? How many agencies were involved? Severson was CIA but Severson had been taken out. So, not the Company, or at least not a sanctioned op. Which countries were collaborating?

His brother had essentially told him in code that it was a rogue operation, not Mossad itself, but possibly involving Mossad people. That had happened before, and there had even been previous instances of off-the-books operations in collaboration with the CIA or parts of it. But the Bureau? Could the FBI also be involved in suppressing the story of the malicious software and the China connection? Could the FBI have now adopted the covert tactics for which the CIA had become notorious?

He needed to trust somebody. Barbara? Yes, but she was out of commission, at least for the moment. Their boss? A long shot. Then he reminded himself that the enemy of your enemy is your friend. Who else was in the line of fire? Bergen and

Gaudet! It was crazy, but it made sense. And they would be in need of a friend, too. He would have to be extremely careful not to lead the assassins to them again. There was still plenty of time for him to call in, get some research done, and catch the red-eye back to the East Coast. The question was which lily pad to jump to. New York, DC, Pittsburgh?

"Okay, Pohl, let's see just how good you are. Pick one." He looked around, suddenly aware he was almost at the exit to the terminal and was talking aloud to himself amidst a river of arriving passengers.

═

The strip-mall motel just over the New York line was cheap, and the rooms were grungy, but Len awoke with a smile on his face and Kat's tight curls tickling his left nipple. "Wow," he said, his voice just above a whisper.

"Mmm, what?"

"Just wow. You are amazing. I thought we would never get around to . . ."

"You are a man of little faith, cowboy. And you worry too much about the competition."

"Admit it. You had your eye on Tank. And there is no hiding the fact that he was after you."

"He never had a chance. You really are a clueless cowboy, Lenny."

"Never? Really? You know, by the way, my mother was the only one I ever let call me Lenny."

"Well, I am not your mother, in case you didn't notice."

"Oh, I noticed, Kit-Kat, I noticed." He ran his hand down her back and gave her left buttock a squeeze.

"You, I will let call me Kit-Kat. But only in private and only if you let me call you Lenny."

"What a price, what a price! Okay, but also only between us."

"It's a deal, Lenny. Now, let's grab some breakfast at the diner next door and hit the road." She kicked off the covers and stood beside the bed.

Len propped himself up on his elbows and admired her compact, toned body. "You look . . . yummy."

"Yummy, huh? Well, you'll have to settle for eating bacon and eggs this morning, because we need to put some more miles between us and them. Maybe tonight."

"Maybe?"

"For a smart guy, you really do need to have some things spelled out for you. Patience, cowboy, patience and faith."

Over a short stack of pancakes with a side order of ham and drenched in syrup, Len asked Kat if she had figured out a destination.

"I have. Ithaca, New York."

"Why Ithaca?"

"The Pitt campus in Johnstown got me thinking about universities, about getting lost among students, about lots of little cafes with free Wi-Fi. You know, second-hand clothing stores and used laptops on bulletin boards for sale for cash—all the stuff that goes with a college town. Ever been to Ithaca, to Cornell?"

"Nope. And you?"

"No. See, that makes it perfect. Neither one of us have any connection with it. We're going to blend in while we figure out our next move."

"We look a little old for students."

"You, maybe. I can do something with my hair, my clothes, and bingo—I'm a twenty-something grad student." She lowered her head, smiled to bring out her dimples, and looked up at him demurely.

"If you're the cute grad student, can I be your lecherous

thesis advisor?"

"We have to get there first. So, finish your plate of maple syrup with pancakes, and let's ride, cowboy." She looked again at Len's breakfast swimming in syrup. "You know, you would be right at home in Nova Scotia. Up there, they put maple syrup on and in everything, even make maple-flavored wine." Len made a face. "Yeah, my reaction, too. But who knows, you might like it."

Chapter Forty-One

Tank tapped rhythmically on his leg as he sat in the outer office. He was unsure why Dean Phelps was stalling him, but he knew it to be a tactic the man valued. Phelps's secretary touched the cordless headset she wore, a fixture of her hairstyle as much as the silver clip at the back, and nodded to an unheard voice. She looked up to smile mechanically at Tank. "Dr. Phelps will see you now. You can go right in." Tank had to admire the man for his comprehensive control of the situation. The big boss was not even going to come out to greet him.

The inner office was the dress-down government equivalent of modern business décor, with functional metal cabinets to one side and a utilitarian horizontal file serving as a credenza behind an L-shaped desk. Dean Phelps rose and held out his hand but did not come out from behind his desk, forcing Tank to cross the room and lean forward to shake hands. "Welcome back, Tankut. I hope your trip was uneventful."

"My trip was eventful, as you know; my flight back was routine."

"Yes, of course. How is Dorothea these days?"

"Remarried these days, living in San Diego."

"Oh, right, of course. I should have remembered. But you're looking well."

"I'll recover."

"They tied you up, I understand."

"Not for long. I was rescued by the FBI after a few hours.

Look, can we move directly to the bottom line? The final draft had to be typed out in rather a rush, I know, but why was my report rejected?"

"It wasn't rejected, Tankut, it was superseded. Our senior team did a thorough review and an independent analysis and simply concluded that your findings were in error. To save the Board any embarrassment—and avoid damage to your reputation, I might add—we are issuing the revised analysis as our official findings. Your report is, shall we say, vacated."

"Vacated. And replaced with what? What whitewash did your senior lackey team come up with."

Phelps tensed at the word lackey. "Oh, it's no whitewash. There will be consequences, changes in practices, heads may even roll. I called you in because I wanted to alert you, give you the benefit of advance notice. We would not want you saying anything that might cast a bad light on the NTSB or make you appear ill-informed."

"No, we wouldn't want that, would we? So what cockamamie conclusions did your revisionists reach?"

"The right ones, Tankut, the right ones."

There was an extended pause, as if Phelps were waiting to be asked something or were reconsidering what to say next. Tankut decided to wait the man out.

"You will, of course, get the full report and the opportunity to add your signature as lead on the preliminary team, but the gist is fairly simple. The two incidents were both, as we now know with near certainty, the result of faulty software supplied by a subcontractor to the German firm that provided industrial control system components. The same incorrect code was in control of both pipelines. As is so often in such cases, it was, at the heart, human error, even if mediated by control computers."

Tankut worked his jaw as he shook his head in disbelief.

"What bullshit, what clever bullshit. Blame it on the software. Even better, blame it on a subcontractor. Better still, blame it on an offshore company. I can even see the forthcoming Fox television special report on why we should always buy American when it comes to critical infrastructure technology."

"It's what happened." Phelps stared him down. "And I am confident that you will agree with the corrected interpretation once you read the report and sign it. You are not a computer specialist; your beat is pipeline networks, not industrial control networks. When you got in over your head and out of your element, you had the good sense to call for expert help. It's even in the phone logs. You got that help, in spades, doubled down, through interagency collaboration, a unified assault on the problem. That will sell well in an era calling for more cooperation and less duplication of effort. And you were man enough and professional enough to admit when you were wrong. More than that, you are enough of a team player to put the best interests of your government and your country ahead of your own ego."

"Cue trumpets, stirring martial theme."

"Read the report."

"I'll read the report, all right, and then prepare a line-by-line response based on material from my own report."

"Your report is classified, Tank. You will not quote it or even refer to it."

"I have clearance."

"Not that high, you don't."

"What is this really about? Who got to you?"

Phelps tapped on his desk blotter. "What I am telling you and what is in the report is the official position of the NTSB, of the Department of Transportation, of the Secretary—everyone all the way up the line. All the way. This is what really happened: programming error, plain and simple. It was the same software controlling both systems. They were different lines operated by different companies in two different states. No other explanation makes sense. Software error."

Tank nodded slowly. "Now I get it, how you can say all that with a straight face and will be able to be convincing in front of the cameras or testifying before congress, if need be. You are clinging to the notion that you are telling the truth, not a cover-up. You get to tell yourself the face-saving lie that, in a sense, it is the truth you are reciting, just a long way short of the absolute truth. Maybe that's how you interpret your job and the allegiance you swore, maybe that's how you would talk under oath, but that's not the way I see it and not the way I would tell it."

"Tankut, you need to listen very carefully. I want you to stay with us; I do not want to see you leave NTSB in disgrace."

"Is that a threat? Is that from you, Dean, or does it come from . . . where? Higher up?"

"Just read this." Phelps passed Tank a folder. "Commit it to memory. And sign it. This is an official NTSB document. This is what happened. Your career depends on putting reality above your own pride."

"And what if I no longer work here? I can take this to the press. Fox news would be in a frenzy. David Sanger at *The New York Times* would turn it into a Pulitzer-nominated book."

"I don't think so. And I don't think you want your epitaph to read that you were a wing-nut conspiracy theorist. You start selling some line about government cover-ups and you will find only the lunatic fringe will be buying it, because you will be all alone in your delusion. No one will stand with you."

"There were others, witnesses, reliable sources. Good citizens."

"Loyal citizens, good team players."

"I . . ." Tankut blinked slowly, then stood.

"Don't forget your report." Phelps held out the folder.

Tank looked down at the cover and the list of authors. His name was first. "I don't understand. You said my report had been withdrawn, that it was now top secret or some such."

"This report is your report. You get the credit. You will be surprised how much a brilliant investigation like this will help your career. In a few years, when you retire and become an overpaid consultant, you should have no difficulty seeing plenty of action on the most interesting cases."

Tank looked as if he would melt into the floor. "My career . . ."

"Just please don't take the report from the building. Read it, sign it, and bring it back to my secretary. Remember, we want to follow procedure and the law. No leaks, no going rogue. The report will be released tomorrow at noon. Be ready for an onslaught from the media. And show them how proud you are to be part of a team that takes on challenges like this and comes up with the right answers."

Chapter Forty-Two

The Bahá'í gardens on the slopes of Mount Carmel overlooking Haifa, Israel, were one of Karl's favorite retreats, a change of space and pace whenever he felt in need of soul-healing. There was something both ordered and other-worldly about the broad green expanses of the layered lawns offset by neat patches of bright color. These appealed to Karl, whose own need for order and sense of not belonging were the inbred forces that shaped his journey through life. He was an eternal outsider in his adopted country, Jewish but not a Jew, a novelist with no books, and here, at the Shrine of the Báb, a pilgrim without belief.

His writing was not going well, and a familiar malaise had settled over him, like the morning fog over the lake in Upper Peninsula Michigan near where he had spent his childhood. He knew the fog would lift, eventually, but not when. He could not hide his moodiness from Shira—they had been married too long for that—but neither could he explain what he was feeling when she asked him about it.

He made his way up the central stairs bisecting the eighteen terraces of the gardens. At each level, he would pause and turn around to catch his breath and look out toward the sea, past the vast, beautiful bowl of Haifa, his home since marrying Shira. Boston, where he had spent most of his life before, had no similar vantage point, but he could not look out over the Mediterranean without thinking of his other home—"somewhere beyond the sea, in that direction"—where he had attended college, settled down, and finally been launched on the extraordinary voyage that would end in Israel.

A devout agnostic whose liturgy of logic was always up front and yet was always being undermined by unlikely events and by the mystical devotion of his wife, Karl would be the first to admit that he admired the Bahá'is. In a region torn by thousands of years of interfaith struggles, the simple, all-embracing belief of Bahá'í, with its foundation of faith in the spiritual unity of humankind, was like the fresh breezes blowing up the hillside from the harbor below.

He was halfway up the kilometer-long climb, which had become decidedly less easy in the two years since his accident and hip replacement. The new hip gave him no trouble, but his knees complained with the exertion. He stood looking seaward, waiting for the burning behind his kneecaps to subside, thinking of far places he no longer visited and journeys he no longer made. His three-score-and-ten loomed just ahead, a box on the calendar in his study, a way-marker on his long hike through the world.

His cellphone rang.

"Hi, it's DB. We need to talk."

Karl's heart raced and the bright sun overhead dimmed. "I can't. I told you. And how did you get this number?"

"You gave it to me, years ago, when we were working on that software attack together. I figured you were a man of habits and would have kept the same cell number."

"Well, I did and I didn't. Now the number you have just forwards to my phone in Israel. But I can't talk with you."

"Even as a friend?"

Karl glanced around. He knew he shouldn't be talking on his phone in such a sacred setting, but no one was near. "As a friend. Okay."

"I just texted you a tiny URL. Download the app you find and call me back." Click.

"Oh, shit! I don't want this." Karl spoke to the phone in a low growl as he clicked through on the URL; it took him to the BathyFone site where he found the app he needed. He downloaded and installed the app, enabled it, then returned DB's call.

"DB here. Can we talk now?"

"I don't know. And I don't know this BathyFone app. But let me guess, we're talking with end-to-end encryption."

"Better than that. You're actually not even calling my number. The calls redirect, then get sent over the Internet, voice-over-IP through layers and layers of indirection. The only thing traceable about this technology is that you can't hide that you are using it, so just having the app can be suspicious. Forewarned, as they say."

"How do you know about this stuff?"

"Look, to keep up with the bad guys, which is our job here, we need to get down in the gutter with them. This system was designed by malevolent hackers and is used by the scum of the Internet underworld. We know that the cyber cavalry is working on cracking it, but we are also pretty sure they haven't succeeded yet."

"Encrypted or not, I still can't talk with you."

"Karl, I need your help. I got a call from Tank Parsons, the lead investigator on the NTSB inquiry. You met him by video conference. He's been told to bury the truth about the Spanergy and PanPenn incidents. My boss—you remember Harry—told me essentially the same thing. We have consistent evidence that points back to Unit 61398 in Shanghai. This was an attack by China. As you know, not the first cyber attack from that quarter, but the first to actually do physical damage to us. People died. This is a significant escalation of hostilities in cyberspace, tantamount to an act of war, and now we are being told it never happened."

"China? You're saying China attacked."

"Yes. What do you know?"

"I keep telling you: nothing that I can say anything about."

"We need your help, Karl. A Spanergy technician was forced off the road by someone hacking into the onboard computer of his car; now he's disappeared. A CIA agent is dead, assassinated, and an FBI agent has been shot."

"Who? Who was the FBI agent? Not Barbara Delacroix."

"Yes, that's right. I forgot you know her. She and her partner were escorting prisoners when they were fired upon; now their prisoners have also disappeared."

"Is Barbara all right?"

"She's in the hospital, recovering from gunshot wounds. Abe is with her, flew out from Florida."

"How do you know all this?"

"You forget, it's my job to know things. Parsons filled me in on some of it, although I got the feeling he wasn't telling me everything he knew. I may not be a super spook like you, but I'm good at digging and putting things together."

"Are you? Then look into the crash of an Israeli F-16i jet in the Negev a couple of years ago. Oh, yes, and you might talk with Shawn McCauliffe, author of that literary tour-de-force, *Zombie Zoo Rampage*."

DB laughed. "Really? Zombies?"

"Really."

"Thanks, Karl."

"Thank me by not calling me again, with or without encryption. Good luck." He disconnected and stared at the screen of his phone. He realized that his heart was pounding; his depression had lifted and been replaced by fear. Karl disabled the BathyFone app and dialed another number. "Hey,

Lev, how the hell are you?"

"I am great, Karl. Just got a three-book deal from Sentinel-Victor for a new series of thrillers."

"Mazel tov! But who is Sentinel-Victor."

"I think it's a spin-off from DAW that was bought up by Penguin, then sold and merged with . . . Oh, hell, I don't know, but they actually sent me an advance. The check even cleared. And how is your writing coming?"

"Don't ask. I've been in a gray funk of late, so don't remind me. How about you and Anat coming up our way for dinner? You can cheer me up, the gals can schmooze about being married to writers, and we can talk shop."

"What makes me think this shoptalk is not going to be concerning the finer points of story construction."

"Oh, it is, it is. All about thrillers: plots, characters, intrigue and betrayal. We'll have fun."

Lev's breathing came through clearly in Karl's ear. "Okay, but don't let on too much with Anat. She likes to keep me on the fiction side of our division of labor. Until she retires from her position at the Institute, you know."

"Same for Shira. You and I will go out for an evening walk after dinner."

"Sounds good. See you tonight. Is eight good?"

"Yes, great! See you."

DB, intrigued by Karl's hints, began researching immediately, starting with the Negev plane crash because it was a specific event that would make formulating search queries easy. The older news stories he located referred to it as "unexplained" or contained references to "unspecified pilot error," but a later article in *Military Avionics* referred to a hardware or software glitch in the onboard computers that led to a loss of control of the aircraft. Some early reports even mentioned

Bedouin witnesses claiming that the plane had been struck by a missile, although Israel's Air Force denied it. The deeper DB dug, the more confusing the story became. One Al Jazeera item even cited Jordanian sources describing debris, recovered near the border with Israel, that supported the case for a missile attack or an explosion of some kind.

Nothing recent had been written on the incident other than a comment posted to the Al Jazeera story claiming that anything with avionics chips from Israel Tactical Systems, generally known as IsTac, could not be trusted, implying that this was the source of the chips in the crashed F-16i. To DB, the comment sounded like it had come from one of the numerous conspiracy-theory trolls who haunted the Internet, but it also had the ring of an element of truth to it.

He did a quick search on IsTac and found, to his surprise and confusion, that Karl had once been a consultant to the company and was named as one of the inventors in several patents filed by them. Two of the patents related to hardware security features manufactured directly into microchips. Further searches turned up several ads for IsTac avionics chipsets and offers for resale in various quantities. There seemed to be a vigorous global trade in the chips.

Turning to Shawn McCauliffe, he quickly located the man's Facebook page and his author profile on Amazon. *Zombie Zoo Rampage*, McCauliffe's debut novel, was currently ranked 19,126 on Amazon, putting it in the top two-percent of Kindle editions. DB read a few pages of the book using the Look Inside feature but quickly gave up. The guy could actually string words together into intelligent sentences and coherent paragraphs, which was more than ninety percent of self-published authors could do, but the opening scenes were crude, cliché-ridden, and gross. Clearly, these qualities did not prevent readers from loving the work, which had accumulated over a hundred five-star reviews and an overall rating of 4.2 stars. Many of the reader reviews mentioned eagerly looking forward to the next book from the author.

DB was still in the dark as to why Karl had pointed him to the book and author until he got to the man's Wikipedia page, which mentioned that McCauliffe had worked for the CIA before retiring to become a fulltime writer. It took some clever Google searches, but eventually DB was able to retrieve McCauliffe's email address and home address in Alexandria.

He sat at his desk trying to put himself in Karl's shoes. If he couldn't get more help from Karl, he would have to do what Karl would do. He picked up his desk phone and dialed a Virginia number. "Hello, is this Shawn McCauliffe, author of *Zombie Zoo Rampage*?"

"Ah, yes, ah . . . How can I help you?"

"Sorry to call you at home. My name is Karl Lustig, I'm a blogger and journalist. You can Google me if you want to check my credentials. Anyway, I'd like to interview you—the back story on the author, that sort of thing."

"Yeah, sure. That would be great." He sounded both eager and hesitant.

"Can we set up a time? I'd like to do it by Skype. A podcast is really better with the video, you know."

"Sure, we can do that. The problem is I am stuck at home with my kids at the moment. The joys of being a single parent, you know. Can we wait until this evening, after eight when I get off duty?"

"No problem. I'll contact you then. Cheers."

DB set about creating a new Skype account with Lustig-Journalist as the ID and a headshot of Karl as the photo. Then he started planning the call.

Chapter Forty-Three

The small apartment in Haifa that had seemed crowded to Karl and Shira ever since Shoshi was born, had suddenly become spacious once their son, Binyamin, started serving in the Israel Defense Force. Karl looked up from his paper as Shira stirred a pot of soup on the stove. "It will be good to see Lev and Anat, again, won't it, dear. Nice to fill out the dinner table again."

Shira tucked a stray strand of graying hair behind her ear and smiled over at him. "Are you and Lev up to something?"

"No, nothing in particular, just a couple of old friends getting together." He watched appreciatively as Shira busied herself with the cooking. They were an unlikely couple: the older American and the middle-aged British widow, the journalist and the jewelry designer, the engineer and the artist. A confluence of forces had brought them together, forces that Shira regarded as Fate and that Karl called a roll of the dice. One thing Karl had learned through long experience was how smart and perceptive Shira was. Would she guess?

She noticed him looking at her. "Why do I not quite believe you, Karl? You've been awfully moody lately. Something's up."

"Moody is why I want to see Lev. My writing is stalled. I figured he would be an inspiration, a fresh breeze. He's already a successful author." She gave him a look that said she didn't exactly believe him but loved him anyway.

When Lev and Anat showed up a few minutes later, six-year-old Shoshi leapt into Lev's arms. "Uncle Lev, Uncle Lev,

Uncle Lev!"

"Shoshana Banana, Shoshana Banana, Shoshana Banana!" He tousled her tight, coffee-brown curls and gave her a squeeze before lifting her until her head brushed the ceiling. "Oof, you are getting big. Or maybe I am getting little."

"Old. You are getting old." She poked at his neck.

"Shoshi! Watch how you talk with your uncle." Shira put down her spoon and came over to hug Lev, then she turned to Anat. "It has been too long. It is not that far from Tel Aviv, you know. You really should get up here more often." There was a deep bond between the women, built slowly over the years and cemented by harrowing experiences. Lev and Karl were friends as men often were; Anat and Shira had become sisters. "Your work, Anat? It goes well?"

"Well enough. I must say it is good to be back at a desk and looking at retirement just over the horizon."

"It will be Mossad's loss. You have done so much for the Institute and for Israel." Shira took Anat's hand and held it. "And for me. We owe you so much, too. I will always thank you for returning Karl . . ." She noticed Shoshi watching and listening and decided not to finish her sentence.

Anat leaned in and whispered in Shira's ear. "We did it together. We brought Karl home."

Shoshi pulled at her mother's pant leg. "Let's eat!"

Throughout dinner, Shoshi, always the actress and always center stage, charmed her audience with extended summaries of her favorite books and TV shows, complete with acted out parts. Over coffee, however, Lev confessed that he could use a break from Shoshana Banana and suggested that he and Karl take a walk. "Let's leave the ladies to themselves."

Shira looked at Karl over the tops of her glasses. "I get it, a male conspiracy to get out of doing dishes. Right, Karl?"

"You caught me. I had to bribe Lev, though, because he so

loves washing dishes."

Anat dropped her jaw in mock amazement. "Really? A side of you I have never seen, Lev. I would hate to deprive you. From now on you can do the dishes every night at home."

"And did I tell you that I had just put a dishwasher on order?"

"Ooo, now we are talking. I will hold you to that, Lev."

Lev shook his hands in Karls face. "Now see what you've gotten me into? All this for a little fresh air. You are becoming an expensive friend."

The two men walked in silence until Karl finally spoke. "This is complicated and . . . well, complicated. I don't know quite how to put this."

"If it's about the affair you are having with my wife, I already know all about it."

"Be serious, Lev. This is serious. But it is about Anat, at least in a sense."

"Okay, let me guess. You are messing with Mossad again."

"Not exactly, but they may be messing with me."

"You know that Anat never talks with me about her work. We have an agreement. Since I left and retired, I am truly out of it. The only spy stuff I deal with now is in my novels."

"How many is it now?"

"Nine, not counting the three that were just contracted for. Your suggestion that I write in English for an American audience was the best advice anyone ever gave me."

"Then maybe it's time you returned the favor."

"Okay, my advice is that you finally finish your first novel. Sit down, and write it, right through to the last chapter. Finish it, damn it."

"That's not the kind of advice I need."

"Yes it is."

"No, just listen. I have been threatened. The implication is that my whole family is in jeopardy if I don't stay out of something and don't keep my mouth shut."

"National security?"

Karl nodded silently.

"Then stay out of it and keep your mouth shut. You and I are getting way too old for this action-and-adventure stuff. Keep it on the pages of a novel. Let the young and immortal put their lives on the line."

"That's so easy to say, but people are being maimed and killed, and I am not the only one being threatened. Remember DB, from Scenaria?"

"The fat guy, the geek with a gun. Is that who?"

"That's who, but he's lost weight—a lot of weight. And he's now CTO at Scenaria."

"Well, good for him."

"Not good. He seems to have scooped the NSA on something big. He—"

"Please, stop there." He held up his hand. "I don't want to put you at risk, and I don't want to put Anat and me at risk. If you've been told to stay out, stay out."

"I want in. I want you to convince Anat she should bring me in as a consultant."

"Curiosity killed the *katsa*. It almost killed Karl."

"I am no *katsa,* not a field operative, and it's not curiosity. I am pretty sure I have already figured this out. But if I am inside, I am not a threat, not the opposition. I am part of the team. And I can help."

"Modesty was never your biggest problem."

"Please, talk to Anat. Convince her."

"I can try."

Chapter Forty-Four

DB switched on the Skype plug-in to record the call. "You are looking good, Mr. McCauliffe. You say you can't see me? Only my thumbnail? I don't know what's wrong with my video; it was working this afternoon. I'll edit in some retakes of my questions later. Is that okay?"

"Sure. Go ahead."

DB started in as if he were introducing a guest for a podcast, then began running through questions about McCauliffe's first book, the writing, and his earlier career. Still channeling Karl, DB finished with an editorial flourish and a plug for the book. "Available at Amazon and other booksellers, in both trade paperback and various e-book formats. If you are into zombies, get your copy of this one."

He paused for effect. "That was great. Thanks for the interview."

"You're welcome."

"I can't believe you worked for the CIA. Amazing. You know, I sort of did some things like that myself."

"Yes, I know, Karl. Mossad, right? Your name did come up on our radar now and then."

"Well, I was just a consultant; you were the real thing. I am honored and impressed. What made you choose to write about zombies. You must have some good stories to tell from your days playing spy games."

"Don't we all? But I'm more interested in selling books. I think the market for spy stories and espionage tell-alls has been saturated."

"Maybe. But certainly that chipset caper, the Israeli F-16, that whole mishegas—certainly some version of that escapade would sell."

"So, you know the story."

"Yeah, pretty much all of it. China, the avionics chips, the CIA, you know." DB knew full well he was casting blindly, fishing without much bait.

"It wasn't exactly the CIA, of course."

"No, I knew that, figured it out, but I don't think everybody knew what was really going down, not even the ones in the center of things."

"No, you got it. But enough said."

"Enough said. That's how it is with these things. Especially the China connection."

"Well, they never knew they were working for us any more than the Israelis did. All of them kept spreading the doctored chips around, serving as our distributors. Our team was the puppet master."

"You said it: our team."

"You weren't . . . Wait a minute. You don't know what you are talking about. You . . ."

"No, that's right, and enough said. We both know better than to get to chatting about stuff like this. So, anyway, thanks for the interview. And, of course, none of this off-the-record chat ever goes anywhere. We are both professionals and patriots, both on the team. So, thanks again." DB terminated the call before there could be a response. His heart was racing as if he had just finished swimming five lengths of the lap pool at the gym. He was wondering how many alligators were in the pool with him.

═

Shawn McCauliffe pulled his second cell phone from the bottom drawer of his desk where he also still kept his automatic.

He was wondering whether this Lustig clown really had been part of the Operation Chipset team. It was hard to tell whether he was bluffing or really was an insider playing it cagey. He started to dial the DCI at Langley then changed his mind. He wasn't sure the Director would even take his call anymore. Instead, he'd wait and see what came of the interview. Maybe he could sell a few books while he waited. Publicity never hurt. He slipped the phone back in the drawer, locked it, and logged onto his Amazon Author-Central account.

Chapter Forty-Five

Colonel Whitcomb sat with the core team in his office. "We got our answer already. Washington rejected all three of our attack scenarios as non-responsive."

"What precisely do you mean?" Kauffman spoke in his controlled, Teutonic style. "We met every one of the objectives. Any one of those designs would be effective retaliation, and they were all doable. We already have enough of the code to be able to assemble and prove out before deployment. What exactly do they want?"

"Not these, Dieter, not these. We met the stated objectives but we didn't meet the unstated ones. Our proposals got them to rethinking what the criteria are."

Gorham put his hands on the back of his head. "So, what do they want?"

"They want something that is, and I quote, substantial, costly, unambiguous, and invisible. It must send a clear message that we know what they did and will not be fucked with. There must be no doubt about the source and the reason, that it is coming from us in response. At the same time, it must not be public. Public embarrassment would only put them on the defensive and provoke them into believing that a face-saving response is necessary. In fact, ideally, our action would be something that they would not even want to acknowledge openly. Washington is looking for a back-channel message with a clear text and real bite. A private, government-to-government exchange, not open warfare."

"I get it," Cassandra responded. "An escalation is the last thing Washington wants, especially since US-CERT and the industrial security community are saying that it will be months before all our pipeline systems can be sufficiently hardened to be safe from attack."

Gorham snorted. "There's no such thing as safe from retaliation. Even hardened targets can be vulnerable to a truly concerted APT. Months? A joke. It will be some quick-and-dirty solution cobbled together out of bits and pieces with more holes in it than the systems it is intended to protect."

"Right. Of course, Frank. But I was just referring to shifting the odds. I think that's all Washington wants."

Dieter Kauffman nodded slowly. "So, they are looking for an attack we can pull off that would stay behind the scenes and be difficult to respond to in kind."

"Exactly."

Gorham scribbled swirls on his notepad. "Do we call in all the troops again?"

"No, just the four of us. And we're going to drive the development with user stories that break the problem into small pieces so that none of the developers sees the whole picture. I want our very best programmers, and I want state-of-the-art best practices—test-driven development, pair programming, everything we know that works. Same schedule as originally planned, just a smaller team. I want this really focused and really contained."

"Now, all we need is to know what it is we are assembling." Gorham smiled.

Cassandra raised her index finger. "I've got an idea. I was thinking about what is different between the Chinese and us, what's different about their government, how things are run, and the culture within government there."

"So, tell us."

Chapter Forty-Six

The wind dropped and the rustling of the cornfield outside Ithaca stilled. Dmitry, on a small rise two hundred yards away, was counting on a startle response to allow him a second shot. Anyone with police or combat training would instinctively flatten, but civilians were more than likely to look up. He would take out the man, work the bolt action as he panned that tiny fraction of a degree, then take out the woman as she popped up in surprise at the rifle crack that she would hear a half second after the first bullet struck. He practiced the move several times as the two targets lounged on the berm at the edge of the cornfield.

There was the snap of a twig behind him, a twig that he had placed in the path and sprinkled with dry leaves. He froze.

"A hunting rifle, Dima? Doesn't the Institute have the budget for a decent assault rifle anymore?"

Dmitry did not turn. "When they recover the bullets, they will look for a hunter, not a sniper. Shalom, little brother."

"Hardly shalom. There is no peace with you. You're at war, Dima, as you always seem to be."

There was no sound behind him, but Dmitry sensed the move, the change of position, "A Glock, right? Your favorite, with a suppressor. You would kill me, Arka? You would kill your own brother?"

"Wouldn't you? You would kill those two, who have done nothing to you and are no threat to you or your beloved State of Israel."

"They know things. Knowledge itself can be a threat."

"I know things, too. I know who you are."

"I am your brother."

"I meant you plural, collectively. It is one of the odd ambiguities of the English language. You, plural, are *HaVered*. Are you surprised I know this? You see, we are not all bench-warmers at the Bureau. You have your tendrils in too many places. The conspirators are many, and each is a resource as well as a source of mistakes or disclosures, intentional or not. China, the German BND, the American CIA, Israel . . . where else? And where do the loyalties ultimately lie, Dima?"

"I know where my loyalties lie, that is enough to know. We use the others as we need or find convenient. They are, like us, invested in stability, in maintaining a world order that works."

"At the expense of family? Of innocents?"

"It has always been so, brother: civilian casualties, collateral damage. Don't bore me with that high-minded American moral posturing. Your President uses drone strikes that kill whoever happens to be in the building or the car or the neighborhood. We, at least, are willing to dirty our hands. We do not sit safely in a control room in Nevada while a mindless drone takes out tribesmen in Afghanistan."

"You are the drone, Dima."

"I have my orders."

"A mindless drone. Tell me, drone, how did you get here? I thought you were on your way to Shanghai. I saw you get on the plane."

"I did. And I got off the plane in San Francisco right afterwards, right after I got a text message. One of our *sayanim* had seen them. We are lucky to have our Assistants everywhere. And, you, little brother, still have things to learn about surveillance. You should have watched until the plane left the gate, until it was airborne."

"I was—"

"Be still a moment. I have my shot." He fired, worked the bolt, steadied his weapon, and fired again. He laid down his rifle and looked up into the barrel of a Glock 17. "As I guessed, brother. You are so predictable."

"And you, you are so despicable. I should take you out myself."

"Then do it. Or have you gone soft? Or perhaps you merely act without thought, without knowing what is happening?"

"You killed them."

"I missed my shot." He lifted the rifle toward Arkady. "See for yourself, through the scope. They are running across the field. At this moment they should be mounting their motorcycles at the far corner. Check it out."

Arkady holstered his pistol and raised the rifle, steadying the scope and scanning the far side of the field. "You are not the sharpshooter you once were, Dima. You failed."

"What a pity. I shall have to cover my incompetence, report that the targets were taken out so the file can be closed."

"I don't understand."

"There is much that you do not understand. Israel is the one nation in the world that allows its pilots to refuse, on conscience, an order to take out a target. I made my choice—on conscience. Now, you can turn me in: to Mossad, to your government, or to *HaVered*, if you really do know who they are. You must act on your conscience. But I know you, and I do not think you will say anything about me to anyone."

"You think because I am your brother that—"

"No, I think because you are good man and know another good man when you see him in front of you."

"You took out Severson, the CIA agent."

"We did. It was not me but one of us. He was an insider but

with divided loyalties and devious methods. He had a tendency to act without orders. And he deceived his own."

"The CIA?"

"Yes, that of course, but also Mossad and *HaVered*. He manipulated a *kidon* team into believing they were the assassins who had been directed to take out the *schwarzer* technician. Severson, as you knew him, could not be trusted. We may be off the reservation, but we are not rogues; we still maintain discipline."

"And those two?" He gestured with the rifle.

"They will be allowed to get away. You will find a way to impress upon them how much it is in their best interest not to be a threat, not to become talkative."

"Why is Israel protecting China? This pipeline attack was cyber warfare, an act of war."

"War? In cyberspace? The terms haven't even been defined yet, and no one really wants them to become too clear too fast. Certainly, no one wants to start a war where the capabilities and consequences are completely unknown and the risks so far outweigh the potential gains. Just because it is not physical does not mean this is a replay of the Cold War. There are no safeguards, no precedents. One explosion becomes two, two becomes a conflagration.

"But Israel has led the way in cyberspace, this ether filled with flitting ghosts, and we want to keep our lead, to know what everyone else is doing and to keep everything under the table, under the ground, out of the hands of the amateurs and opportunists, beyond the reach of extremists and insurgents. Suppressing all this is self-protection, particularly as we save the very best for ourselves: the best avionics, the best cyber weapons—the best. We do the same in other areas, all the while denying that we are even players in the game. Keep in mind, we do not have nuclear weapons, we do not have chemical weapons, we do not have biological weapons, and we did not work with the US and Germany to develop and deploy Stuxnet against Iran."

"But Israel actually . . ."

"Exactly. And both our countries want to keep the genie in the bottle. Genies, I should say. China as well, the EU, all the real players. At the same time, we in the West, we of the putative democracies, want to be first and best—just in case."

"Are you . . . is this *HaVered* everywhere? What an odd name: The Rose."

"We are an odd group. Some of the early core were fans of Umberto Eco. Plus, our thorns are very sharp. We entice people with our color, and, whatever happens, we will come out smelling like . . ."

"A rose. Of course. So, do you have your people even in the FBI?"

"Perhaps. I couldn't say. No one knows everything. For all I know, you could be one of us and playing dumb to keep me off the scent. You know how this works." He winked.

Arkady thrust the rifle back to Dmitry.

"And I have something for you." He handed Arkady a small packet. "Shalom."

"Shalom, Dima."

Arkady turned slowly and walked away. He did not pause or turn around when he heard the sound of the bolt on the hunting rifle being pulled.

Chapter Forty-Seven

Kat shifted the bag of groceries to her left arm, wiggled the key in the reluctant lock, and elbowed open the door of the motel room. "I got some deals at the Ithaca Market," she said, as she set the bag down next to the door. "They were closing up when I got there, willing to deal to sell everything. We are going to have to start thinking about how to get some more cash soon. I'm just about tapped out. I did managed to get us a blueberry-apple pie for dinner, though—a discard that's a little smushed but it'll still be good." She smiled at Len, who was sitting in a chair next to the microwave on the kitchenette side. "What's up?" She closed the door behind her. Len gestured with his head toward the other side of the room where Agent Pohl sat with his handgun in his lap.

"Please, come in, Ms. Gaudet. Have a seat. Next to your friend will be fine. Nice and cozy, so I can keep an eye on both of you."

Kat gave him a defiant look but turned the other chair around and sat down.

"Please, move a little closer. I don't think he'll bite."

"How did you find us?" she asked.

"Oh, you were quite resourceful for rank amateurs, but you have no idea what you are up against. We are persistent, professional, and we have more friends than you do. A brotherhood, you might say."

"Are we under arrest?"

"That depends."

"It depends on what?"

"It depends on your priorities."

"On our priorities. Don't you mean yours, the FBI, Washington?"

"No, it's up to you two. What is important to you? Do you want to get away? Or do you want to be heroes? Do you want to champion truth and transparency, like Chelsea Manning or Edward Snowden? Or do you believe that discretion and studied silence may sometimes have their place in the grander scheme of things?" He folded his hands in his lap and leaned toward them. "Do you see where I am going with this? Manning is languishing in prison and Snowden is languishing in Russia. Where are you going, and do you really want to languish there? Or . . . ?"

Len narrowed his eyes. "What exactly are you saying?"

"You are one of those people who has to have it spelled out for you, aren't you, Mr. Bergen? You are smart enough and probably are a good engineer. However, you should probably not consider a career change into my line of work, which is all about guesses and unspoken uncertainties."

Kat put her hand on Len's leg. "That's my Lenny, Mr. Pohl, but maybe I should make sure we all understand these, uh, unspoken uncertainties. You want us to keep quiet. This is a cover-up. Nothing is going to be done about an attack on US soil by a foreign power. Am I right?"

"Mostly. It's entirely your choice to keep quiet or to run naked down Pennsylvania Avenue screaming about suppression and conspiracies. Keep in mind, though, which is more likely to get you locked away—or shot. And don't conclude that nothing is being done just because you don't know about it. A lot happens in this world that you don't know about, particularly on the international stage."

Len narrowed his eyes again. "So what is being done that

we don't know about?"

"I wouldn't know. And if I did, I couldn't tell you. That's how these things work." He stood up and slipped his gun into a shoulder holster. "I need to be going."

"What should we do?"

"You are a smart woman. I am sure you will think this through and come up with a good plan. For the moment, no one is looking for you, thanks to an unexpected benefactor who will remain anonymous. For the moment. Oh, and you might want these." He reached into his breast pocket and then placed two passports on the coffee table. "A going away present." He started to leave.

Kat rose and placed herself between Arkady and the door. He stiffened. "How do we thank you?" she said.

He put his finger to his lips and shook his head, then reached for the door handle. Kat stepped aside but, as he passed, put her arms around him. He stiffened again, then gently placed a hand on her back. "Stay out of trouble," he whispered. "And watch your back."

As the door closed behind him, Kat was already fishing in her purse. "It's still here. Look." She held up a Canadian passport. "This is my passport, in my purse, where I always keep it. So what is this?" She picked up the top passport from the coffee table and opened it. "It's the same. It looks just like mine, even the picture is the same. Only it's one of the new ones, with biometrics. What about yours?" She reached for it, but Len grabbed it first.

"I don't have a passport. Never needed one. Maybe this is a hint."

Kat gave him a hug. "Maybe? Lenny, you can be such a clueless cowboy. If it were spelled out in any bigger letters it would blind you."

═

Arkady scanned the bottom of the FM dial looking for the local NPR station as he drove south out of town. It was the top of the hour, and the local and regional news was just coming in. The second story got his attention.

"Police responded to a report of shots fired at a farm not far from Treman State Park yesterday. Several .30-caliber shells were recovered from a trampled area. The farm and surrounding lands are all posted, but owner Brent Allenberry said that illegal hunting has been a growing problem over recent years. No arrests were made and police say they have no suspects."

Arkady turned the volume down. "Shalom, Dima, and safe journeys."

Chapter Forty-Eight

Anat turned from her desk at Mossad headquarters in Tel Aviv and gave Karl a look that told him she was not happy to see him. "I let you in because I didn't want to make a scene or to have this conversation on the street or in some café. You are a friend, which is why I am telling you this. Go home, Karl. I don't need your help, and I don't want it."

"Maybe I need yours."

"No, you don't. Just go home. Write your book. It's time to stop playing espionage games."

"I want to know what is happening and to help out some friends Stateside."

"Your friends don't need your help."

"That's not the message I got."

"What? You mean that phone call from Douglas Botteneau at Scenaria Security Systems?"

"You knew?"

"Karl, you are getting slow and maybe starting a slide into senility. Remember, essentially everything of interest that crosses our borders gets monitored by Unit 8200. What we don't catch, one of our partners will. Stuff gets flagged and passed on. Privacy is an illusion. Certainly, you of all people should understand that. You worked in high tech."

"What about DB, Doug Botteneau?"

"He's being watched, but he'll be all right. He's a clever guy, even impersonated you to interview a former CIA case officer."

"He what?"

"Relax. Nothing is going to come of it."

"What about this other guy, the pipeline investigator?"

"Karl, please, go home. I would have thought the avionics caper would have taught you something, that it's always bigger and more complicated than you think."

"But China has launched a deliberate cyber attack on the US. People died, property was destroyed. What the Chinese accomplished is scalable. Much of the Eastern Seaboard of the US could be turned into an inferno. I researched this stuff online. The pipelines go through cities, along major highways, through tunnels, under harbors—"

"Slow down on the litany of targets. Even there, you don't have it all correct. But the real thing for you to understand is that China did not attack the US."

"Who did, then? You have information? Are you ready to share it with me?"

"I am sharing nothing with you, only getting you to think. Think what would make sense. Why would China attack the US, their best trading partner? Why would they destroy cities or bridges or pipelines, risking crippling the US economy? The US loses and they lose. So, by definition it was not China, not a deliberate attack."

"You're telling me that?"

"Karl, I am telling you nothing. You are out of the loop. This is just what you would have figured out on your own if you stopped to think about it. Politics was never your strongest suit. You are—or were—a technology journalist."

"But my friends, these people . . ."

Anat turned away with her head tilted back. "That's why you could never be Migdal, you could never be a *katsa* and do what he did as a case officer. Not even what I do." She talked to the ceiling. "It just always becomes too personal for you.

You are smart, you love the intrigue, but you could never pull the trigger."

"But I did."

"Once. You were much younger and your hand was forced. Maybe any one of us can do it once. But again? Regularly? As a matter of course, as part of a job? Because you've been ordered to or because your country depends on it? I don't think so, Karl. You can't live the lies, be an actor on stage every minute in everyday life, deceive or abandon your friends because it's required. That's not you."

"Is it you?"

"Maybe not. Maybe even just saying that word—maybe—says it might not be so, not anymore, at least." There was a long silence between them. "You are not going to let this go, Karl; I know that about you, so I will tell you this one thing so you don't keep pushing until you get hurt again. The people you are worried about are being taken care of."

"Taken care of—that covers a lot of territory."

"So do we. We cover a lot of territory." She reached toward the vase on her desk and extracted a flower, a yellow-and-peach Peace Rose. "Here, take this. But mind the thorns."

"What's this?"

"A token, a message. Give it to Shira with my love for all of you." She turned away from him and started typing. "Go home, Karl, go home."

Chapter Forty-Nine

Frank Gorham looked over the cork board covered with index cards. He used a felt-tip marker to put a large green checkmark on one of the cards, a so-called user story that specified a small piece of functionality, one of the last bits to be programmed. "That's it." He pulled down several cards with red Xs. "These are out. Everything else is complete. The last regression tests confirm that all the code works together exactly as designed. Most of it was stuff we already had on hand, anyway, developed as part of Operation Shotput and Olympic Games. We had a rich component library to draw on."

Todd Whitcomb gave him a slap on the back. "Well done, Frank." He turned around and smiled at Cassandra and Dieter. "Well done, everyone. We'll pass the atta-boys on to your programming and testing crews once we wrap up our work."

"Now what?"

"Now we wait for the final Presidential order and the call from Cyber Command. Then we deploy."

"How will we know that it worked? I mean, when it works."

"We have flags on all the accounts. A piece of code embedded in the monitoring software previously put in place by the Tailored Attack people at the NSA, which is how we know about the accounts. That planted software will send a coded packet to our C&C server in Taiwan. Immediately afterward, the server will be taken down—and I do mean literally, not just taken offline but physically dismantled. The Trojans that gave us backdoor access to the banking systems will erase any footprints, then wipe all their own code. We don't want the Chinese to see exactly how it was done, particularly not let on how we have had our fingers in their banking system and offshore accounts for so long."

"But they'll trace the IP addresses back to the server, which they know to be one of ours."

"Exactly. We want them to know who did it. But we also want plausible public deniability."

"Do we know who is on the list? I mean, the coders obviously had to know bank routings, IP addresses, and account numbers, but it's all just digits. Who are the people or agencies we hit? Just curious."

"Right. 'Just curious' could be the epitaph carved on the gravestones of some of the people in this business. At any rate, it's above even my pay grade. What I understand, off the record, is that there are several top party officials, corrupt, who had accumulated private wealth and squirreled it away in offshore accounts. We are talking about billions of dollars in total. The idea of targeting the Chinese government's sovereign dollar reserves was rejected because it would be too hard for China to cover up and too likely to roil the world economy. But the government itself had some funds that they weren't supposed to have, money siphoned off from 'The People'. Those will be cut by nearly half a billion dollars—not enough to hurt the economy, particularly as these funds were set aside, but enough to hurt.

"It was your idea, Cassandra, to target the bureaucrat in charge of natural gas resources to make absolutely sure the message was unambiguous. I understand he was not as corrupt as some, but we can assume he will be suddenly much poorer and less powerful. Some of those who were targeted might even lay low and stay quiet about their losses, but sooner or later they will no doubt be ferreted out.

"Any more questions?"

Dieter, always the one to be a stickler for details, spoke up. "The packet to our C&C server only tells us that the targets were taken out. How will we know that the real message was received?"

"We, here at COAST, might never know. The response could come in a diplomatic pouch or a private meeting or even as a side comment at some public speech. In any case, the NSA analysts and the White House will know. That's the game they are good at. Hell, whatever we may think of ourselves, we're all just glorified computer jockeys."

Chapter Fifty

Ever since the release of the official report from the Sadler Creek and Johnstown investigations, Tankut Parsons had become a news junky, closely following the online channels, particularly those associated with industrial security. He now started each morning with hope and dread as he reviewed the various news feeds that he had subscribed to. Sometimes his keyword settings turned up unlikely stories that made little sense in isolation but took on a shape in combination. This morning, three stories formed a triangle.

> *Beijing, China.* Sources in China close to top Party officials confirm that a government official was found dead in his apartment last night, an apparent suicide, following disclosures yesterday that he had been charged with corruption and misappropriation of state funds. It was alleged that he had accepted substantial bribes from foreign companies seeking to do business in China and had accumulated funds in excess of ten million dollars in offshore accounts. No official comment has been made.

> *Jingbian, China.* A speech by the Assistant Vice Chairman of China's National Energy Commission, speaking at the dedication of a new pipeline completed by China Natural Gas Ltd. in Shaanxi province, called for increased attention to the security and reliability of natural gas transmission and distribution networks. Noting recent

explosions at two sites in the US, he stated that safety was an issue that did not respect national boundaries and that greater international cooperation to develop standards and systems for protecting critical infrastructure would be in the interest of all. China, which relies predominantly on coal for its growing energy needs, has been making a slow transition to greater use of natural gas as part of its efforts to cut its greenhouse gas emissions.

Shanghai, China. Although ridiculed by software security experts as nothing more than posturing to mollify the international community, a recently announced Chinese government crackdown on computer hackers has produced its first results. Two programmers, both soldiers and not identified by name in accordance with Chinese military practice, have been court-martialed and found guilty of "sabotage through gaining unauthorized access to government computers and implanting malicious computer code." No appeal of their conviction is expected and sentencing has been deferred, but they could be facing long prison terms or even the death penalty. In a possibly related story, an officer at the notorious Unit 61398 here has been publically reprimanded for misconduct. Unit 61398 is part of the Chinese army and is alleged to be the source of a number of malicious software offensives, including penetration of the networks of major US and Canadian energy companies. Details of the charges against the officer are not known at this time.

═

As Tank nibbled on his breakfast bar and continued to read,

others pondered the same stories. Anxious, and already in his Idaho office two hours early, Todd Whitcomb checked his email and phone messages, then started scanning the Lab's already qualified and approved world news summary broken down by region. Three stories from the Far East immediately caught his attention.

"We did it," he said, his voice barely audible.

Cass Welke stepped in from the hallway. "I see you couldn't wait either. Even after two days without sleep I was wide awake at four this morning. Message received, huh?"

"Yeah. Seems so. And we did keep it under wraps."

"I'm still not completely clear on why this had to all be kept so quiet."

"Think about the method of attack used by the group at Unit 61398; it is so simple. Think about the code; it is so easily copied or adapted. Think about the vast army of competent hackers around the world. Remember, after Stuxnet pieces of the code and revamped versions of the techniques started boomeranging back at us. That's the biggest problem with cyber weapons—once they are out there, they can so easily be recycled, revised, repurposed. We don't want that. Think about all the hundreds of thousands of miles of pipelines that are wide open, that can be turned into gargantuan incendiary bombs. In the hands of terrorists . . . well, the results could make 9/11 seem like a mere pipe bomb in comparison."

"Bad pun, Todd."

"Unintentional. Anyway, instead of all-out war in cyberspace, we seem to be at digital détente, mutual assured destruction. We know they could do it, they know we could do it, and we have both agreed not to. Crisis averted."

"For now. Isn't there still the possibility the story will get out?"

"Possibility, yes. At least the anti-virus company has agreed to keep a lid on it. Noble of them. Of course, they were helped by mention of several hundred million in fresh government contracts. I also understand that Washington had some dirt on the company from incidents of earlier skullduggery. That probably made the government case all the more persuasive."

"I would think so. But don't forget the people from the gas company. I understand that three of them seem to have vanished; rumors have it they may be dead. We won't speculate too much further. Not a pretty business we're in."

"The world isn't pretty, Cass. There are casualties. That's the way these things work."

"Yes, of course, I know, but it seems the collateral damage is always the little guys who happen to get in the way or the young people with too much enthusiasm or the middle managers muddling through. The real big shots never pay. Like that army officer in China: reprimanded. Like the CEOs of the predatory lenders who get a wrist slap and a hundred million dollars in severance bonus."

"There's a lesson in that."

"Yeah, what?"

"Don't be a little guy or a young enthusiast or a middle manager."

Epilogue

The sun was already slipping behind the hills when Len returned to the house. He paused to look back out over the Annapolis Basin, the flat expanse of the rich Acadian lands spread out below, outlined by the system of dikes and neatly sectioned into fields. He rinsed his hands under the outside faucet, shook the water off, and entered through the kitchen. The sight of Kat chopping vegetables brought a smile. "Hey there, Kit-Kat. Didn't expect to see you yet. You must have come home early. How was work?"

"Same as yesterday. Good clean fun. After the long shift out on the water, they let us off early. I stopped at the Market in Wolfville before coming home." She kissed him lightly. "You better wash the dirt off your face, my Lenny, if you want more than a peck."

He made a half-hearted sweep of his cheek with the rolled up cuff of his shirt. "I am so glad this research project is working out for you. I know tidal power in the Bay of Fundy is not exactly what you thought you would be working on, but engineering is engineering."

"So says the man who went from controlling thousands of miles of high-pressure gas transmission pipeline to digging ditches."

"I was not digging ditches. I was trenching for the conduit to bring power down from our new wind turbine."

"When will it go online?"

"Sometime after the harvest."

"Are you excited?"

"About wind power or the grape harvest?'

"Well, both."

"I don't know. I'm no farmer, darling. Grapes is grapes."

"These are not just grapes. These are l'Acadie blanc, the finest cold-tolerant wine grape on the planet. Wait until you taste our first vintage."

"It's not exactly the first vintage, because the winery was six years old when we took it over. And it's not exactly ours, because we have a humungous mortgage, so the place still mostly belongs to the bank. And don't forget, we also pay the geniuses over at Domaine de Gran Pré to supervise everything. They want to buy the whole crop, by the way. We're negotiating on price. If I can dicker enough, we will just about recover what we pay them for running things here."

"It's only until we learn enough to do it ourselves."

"And then we can be dirt-poor Canadian grape growers and winemakers without any help from anyone."

She swatted at him with the corner of a towel. "You want out, you can always leave Nova Scotia and go back to whatever is waiting for you south of the border."

"No thanks. Everything I want is right here. In this very room, in fact." He put his arms around her and kissed her passionately over her renewed protests about his dirty face. They were interrupted by the front doorbell. Len reluctantly pulled away and hollered. "It's open. Come on in." He tore a square from the roll of paper towels by the sink, stuck it under the faucet for half a second, and swirled it over his face. "Be right there!" he called out.

He rounded the corner into the front parlor where a black man with a scarred face stood, a suitcase in his hand and a broad smile on his lips. "Hey, cowboy, you know anything about pipelines or SCADA security."

"Nope, not a damn thing, Smitty. Not a damn thing." Len cracked a lopsided smile as he strode over to Smitty. "And that's the way I intend to keep it. Know what I mean?"

"I do. That I do." Smitty set his suitcase down as Kat entered the room. "And who is this pretty thing?"

"What? You don't remember me, Smitty?"

"Course I do." He lowered his gaze to her bulging white apron. "I just didn't remember you being quite so big and round. I see you two been busy."

"That we have. That we have." Len shook his head in disbelief, then put out his hand. The two men held the two-handed shake for many seconds as they studied each other's faces. "How?"

"How what?"

"How did you get here, Smitty?"

"Bus. Shank's mare."

"Not what I mean. You disappeared. We looked for you at the VA hospital in Clarksburg where they said you had been taken, but we were told you weren't there."

"Oh, I was there, all right. Didn't even find out myself right away, but turns out I had been admitted under my mother's maiden name, McIlroy. False transfer papers to boot. Somebody was lookin' out for me, seems."

"Did you ever find out who?"

"Not so's you could take it to court, no. But I got my suspicions. Same somebody as talked with the staff at the hospital. They passed on the suggestion that I might consider gettin' out of the energy sector altogether, find a less dangerous profession, lead a quieter life."

"They said that to you? Just like that?"

"Occupational therapy and lifestyle counseling is what they called it. I got the hint. Anyway, 'fore they finally kicked me out, I found myself with lots of time on my hands, time to work on my Mandarin and Japanese and write more haiku. You ever figure out what I was tryin' to tell you?"

"Yeah, we figured it out. Got us into trouble, too. But somebody was looking out for us, too. Maybe the same somebody as you."

"Maybe. I guess we were both lucky. At least we're alive. I read a piece in the *Washington Post* once about a couple of programmers in the Chinese army who were court-martialed and faced a firing squad. I assume they were part of the story."

"I missed that one. As you say, we were lucky. Still, there's no going back." He looked down at Kat and grinned. "Not that I'd want to."

"So how is it up here for you?"

"You want to know something about up here? The people are different. They are nice. I mean, like, *really* nice. Friendly, welcoming, polite, generous. Until we settled in here, I had no idea how uncivil we Americans had become. Down in the States people don't even seem to be aware of it, how habitually hostile they can be with each other."

Kat looked up at him with admiration. "Spoken like a real Canadian, my darling, even if you don't have the right accent."

"I'm working on it."

"Are you, now?" She turned to Smitty. "I hope you know you are welcome to stay for awhile, if you have the mind to. We have an extra room—until the baby arrives, that is. So, welcome to our home."

Smitty scanned the room, nodding with approval. "I see somebody is into calligraphy."

"That would be me." Kat smiled as Smitty walked over for a close-up look at three ideographs in an elaborate frame.

龙卷风

"Yeah, I reco'nize this. Same as on the base of the wind

turbine I passed on the way in."

Kat's grin broadened. "You know what that means, don't you, Smitty?"

"I think so. It's tornado, right?. Not sure though it's the best title for a wind generator."

"No, I meant what does it mean literally, character by character?"

Smitty laughed. "Okay, now I get it, a play on words of a sort, a revision of the past. *Lóng juǎn fēng*. Dragon, roll up, wind. Very clever."

Kat beamed at him. "A friend helped me with that. Say, do you still write haiku, Smitty?"

"Not so much these days. Movin' on into long-form literature."

"Don't tell me you're writing a novel."

"Nope, still poetry: distillin' down. Fact, I brought this for you two, but now I'm feelin' self-conscious." He held out a red, card-sized envelope to Kat.

She accepted it and extracted an art card with a black-and-white photograph on the outside, a shot from behind of a couple on a park bench, leaning into each other and looking out over a small pond rippled in overlapping circles.

She opened the card. The inside was inscribed in the careful calligraphic hand she recognized from Smitty's haiku. "Should I read it?"

"Maybe later. Maybe you won't like it."

Kat reached out and placed a hand on his arm. "And maybe I will. Would you mind terribly if I read it now—to Lenny?" Smitty shrugged, and Kat started reading. "It's called 'Halftone'."

It is a mystery written in India ink on black velvet;
A story whispered amidst a windstorm;

A play enacted by imposters with masks over their
disguises.
It is blinding high-beam headlights
approaching over the hill out of the setting sun,
Elongating dark lines on the road behind:
Within each beam, a searchlight,
Within each umbra, a shadow.
Beside the roadway, rows of windows close,
the curtains are drawn:
Behind each curtain a shade,
Behind each shade a blind.
Now blinded, we see nothing.
We watch in darkness and listen in silent assent,
Reading meaning into nothingness
And taking nothing away.
But we leave.
We feel our way through gray fog spreading
over what road remains,
Walking in half-light that is neither bright nor night
And within which the rich gradations of living are
illumined.
We abandon the alabaster
and leave the blackness behind.
We are left observing a halftone image:
An illusion in ink, dots and blobs,
out-of-focus grays,
But strangely beautiful, comforting.

Without a word, Kat took Smitty's hand in her left and Len's in her right and led them out onto the front porch to watch the approaching twilight.

Author's Afterword

True story: I was returning from delivering an invited keynote presentation at the Cyberworlds 2011 conference in Banff, Canada. My flight from Calgary to Denver was on one of those regional jets with one-and-two seating. Cozy. I started chatting with my seatmate who, it turns out, was returning from an energy-sector security conference. He was senior management in a natural gas company headquartered in the Southeast. I told him about my talk on cyberspace warfare with real-world physical targets, an extrapolation from the US-Israeli cyber-attack on Iran's uranium enrichment plant in Natanz. I also mentioned that I had written a thriller, *Web Games*, about a terrorist plot against electric generating plants and the US power grid.

He said that the vulnerability of the electric grid paled in comparison with that of the natural gas pipeline network. He then proceeded to outline for me a straightforward scheme for turning almost any section of gas transmission line into a gargantuan incendiary bomb. The technique was so simple that even I knew enough about industrial control systems and networks to be able to pull it off. With a little research.

On returning home, I told my wife about the encounter and said I thought the scenario would make for a great thriller novel. She counseled me not to publish: too dangerous, too easy to pull off. She did not want me to be giving potential terrorists fresh ideas, especially easy ideas that could set entire cities on fire.

The concept gathered cobwebs until we read an article reporting how Unit 61398 of the Chinese Army had been caught penetrating the computer systems of American natural gas transmission companies and stealing files. That's when we knew this story had to be written.

The threat is real. Many parts of our natural gas transmission pipeline system are controlled by networks that are wide open to intrusion and to sabotage by relatively simple methods. It would not be enormously difficult for state-sponsored terrorists or even enterprising independents or opportunists with an agenda to hack into or tap into these networks and turn some urban or suburban areas served by large gas pipelines into instant infernos. A concerted, simultaneous attack on multiple targets would be devastating.

Forewarned is forearmed—or at least that is what we are taught. Much could be done to enhance the security of our vast, varied, and widely dispersed natural gas transmission and distribution network, but little is likely to happen by voluntary action from the natural gas industry, and it is certain not to happen by continued inattention from the public and inaction by policymakers. Only enforced, industry-wide standards have much chance of substantially increasing the security of this vital part of our nation's infrastructure. Absolute security for our industrial control systems is impossible, but experts in the field already have advanced many partial solutions that would make our critical infrastructure far more secure than it is today.

I left that flight from Calgary ill at ease, not only because of what I had learned about the terrible vulnerability of our gas transmission network, but because an insider to the industry had been so ready to tell me, a complete stranger, about cavernous holes in our security. I hope I have demonstrated that his trust was not misplaced, first, by saying nothing, and finally, by telling this story. If we don't act in defense of our vital infrastructure, we invite others to take the offensive.

In addition to the anonymous gas industry executive who launched me on this adventure, I have a number of people to thank for their contributions to the story. I turned to industry insiders to help get the many technical details right. I want to thank industrial security experts Eric Byers, Charles Jeter, Tim Shaw, and Christopher Warner for taking the time to review the manuscript and for providing me with generous feedback, provocative comments, and useful suggestions. Technology journalist and screenwriter Steven Cherry talked me out of an earlier, flawed version of this story and then provided useful feedback on the final product. Fellow author Avi Azrieli once more gave me the benefit of his critical eye and broad life experience. Jim Hawkins, a veteran critic of my earlier novels, added his own good suggestions into the mix to make the story better. Finally, my faithful copy editor for nearly all my fiction, Janet Lemnah, once again worked hard to find and correct all my typos and to unwind my twisted syntax.

As always, I am deeply indebted to my brilliant and beautiful wife, Lucy, who helped shape the plot and define the characters even before I sat down at the keyboard and who then read through and commented on each of the successive drafts. She is my unfailing muse, my most insightful editor, and my very best friend.

www.ingramcontent.com/pod-product-compliance
Lightning Source LLC
Chambersburg PA
CBHW021330250626
47155CB00002B/675

* 9 7 8 0 9 8 8 5 2 7 5 5 3 *